W9-CFL-237

DUNCAN THORNTON

SHADOW-TOWN

annick press
toronto + new york + vancouver

Edited by Colin Thomas and Pam Robertson
Copy edited by Heather Sangster
Proofread by Kathy Evans
Cover illustration by Peter Ferguson
Cover and interior design by Black Eye Design

We acknowledge the support of the Canada Council for the Arts, the Ontario Arts Council, and the Government of Canada through the Book Publishing Industry Development Program (BPIDP) for our publishing activities.

 ONTARIO ARTS COUNCIL
CONSEIL DES ARTS DE L'ONTARIO

Cataloguing in Publication
Thornton, Duncan, 1962-
    Shadow-town / Duncan Thornton.

(The vastlands)
ISBN 978-1-55451-163-1 (bound). — ISBN 978-1-55451-162-4 (pbk.)

    I. Title. II. Series: Thornton, Duncan, 1962— Vastlands.
PS8589.H556S52 2008   jC813'.54   C2008-903383-3

Printed and bound in Canada

Published in the U.S.A. by
Annick Press (U.S.) Ltd.

Distributed in Canada by
Firefly Books Ltd.
66 Leek Crescent
Richmond Hill, ON
L4B 1H1

Distributed in the U.S.A. by
Firefly Books (U.S.) Inc.
P.O. Box 1338
Ellicott Station
Buffalo, NY 14205

Visit our website at **www.annickpress.com**

For my brothers:
fellow guests in the hills

I

IN THE HILLS

1

WHISPERS AT NIGHT

One warm night on their grandmother's farm in the sandy hills, Jack Tender found himself sleepless in the attic room he shared with his cousin Rose. He plucked at the bandage on his hand a moment, and then, because he didn't like to be awake alone, he whispered, "Tam and I went to Shadow-Town."

On the bunk just below him, Rose also lay awake, too warm even under only one sheet. *Shadow-Town*—her heart began to pound, but she kept silent, so Jack whispered again: "Tam and I went to Shadow-Town—"

"No you didn't," Rose hissed. "No one goes to Shadow-Town. Let me sleep. Shut up."

Jack waited until he thought Rose might be nearing sleep again, and then he said, "You can't go, because you're a baby."

Then Rose was glad of the dark because she felt herself flush. "I'm two months and a day older than you are. How am I the baby?" But she didn't dare speak loudly because of their grandmother, and Jack went on whispering as if he hadn't heard.

"Tam and me went to Shadow-Town together. He said he'd never take you, because you're such a baby. But that's why I was all scratched up, from the Tanglewood."

The Tanglewood, Rose thought. The Tanglewood! The dark forest that had grown up in the land between the shadow-march and farming country. In the Tanglewood, strange poplars grew sideways, and turned to grow straight up before they bent again. Poplars with branches like black veins among their dusky green leaves. The Tanglewood that belonged to the Whisperers at night, where farmers would find themselves become lost even in the day. The Tanglewood, where they weren't supposed to go.

Jack felt glad to have made Rose quiet, glad to have passed on some of the fear that Tam had given him. "It wasn't always Shadow-Town, you know," he added. "It was called Smithton when Tamlin's grandfather was Mayor, when Grandma was just a little girl. Before the sleeping sickness first came. Before the Whisperers scared all the farmers away. Now there's just old empty shops in Shadow-Town, and houses leaning against the wind, and there's none of them painted or still built snug; just old boards all peeled and splintery, and spotty glass, 'cause the Whisperers don't care about that."

"So it doesn't matter anyway. So shut up. Why are you telling me this? Shut up."

Then Jack had to wait a while before he could tell her the part that came next: "But people *do* still go there. Just only when the Whisperers catch them and make them stay. They *enthrall* them," he hissed. "They catch them in their whispered webs of sleep so they never wake, but have to do the creatures' work to the end of their days.

"And I saw them. Tamlin took me when I went to see a new hole he had dug by the Green Lake, off to the south of the long-road, and we went through the Tanglewood for hours to get to Shadow-Town and we saw them. *We saw them,*" he repeated, and now Rose thought that even Jack sounded a little scared.

Their attic bedroom was dark; very dark once Rose had put the candle out. But there was one small angled window that looked south, and when the moon was big and the sky was clear, a little moonlight still crept in.

Not enough light to see colors, Rose thought. Only enough light for the room and the wooden bed that closed her in to seem like a pencil drawing. Still, she could see how Jack's mattress was pressed against the bunk above her. He was crouched against the wall; he wasn't even trying to sleep.

Jack wasn't even trying to sleep, and he was glad Rose wasn't sleeping either. "*I saw old Farmer Mathom there!*" he whispered. "Old Farmer Mathom! The window of the Tall House was spotty and splashed with red like a chicken coop, but I still saw him. They thought he was dead from the sleeping sickness like Mother Greene and the Cutter children, but Tam told me the Whisperers only made Farmer Mathom look to be dead, and stole him from the train before his coffin was fired. Lots of people don't really die from the sleeping sickness. They become thralls and just work in their sleep for the Whisperers forever."

"First you said it was people caught by the Whisperers that got made thralls," Rose said. "Now you say it's people who died of the sleeping sickness. You're just making it up."

"*Thralls,*" Jack said again, with a kind of bitter satisfaction. "They *all* become thralls. And let me tell you what it is like for them. Mathom was climbing an Endless Stair, and wearing only rags, and his face was—" Jack paused, remembering, and he almost forgot to whisper the next words.

"His face was creased with pain," Jack said. "Like Grandma said about my dad. '*His face* was *creased with pain.*'"

"You shouldn't talk about it," Rose said, and she was hardly whispering either. "It's awful."

"At least my dad's really dead!" Jack hissed. "At least he wasn't taken to Shadow-Town like old Mathom, and just made to climb the Endless Stair in the Tall House with all the crows. Never really awake, but always climbing and climbing in his long dream, and in the dark the Whisperers would come and whip him and make their quiet laughs. At least my dad is really dead, not living like Farmer Mathom—"

"Shut up!" Rose said again, but Jack went on.

"At least my mom sent me here because she had to go to work in Longhill, not just because I'm a baby who couldn't help with real work, not just because no one wants me."

"My mom and dad have to work all summer to break land on our new farm," Rose said. "And they have a new baby."

"New farm," Jack said. "A good reason to send an extra baby away. What was wrong with the old farm except Rose was there?"

Rose's face burned. "There was nothing wrong with the old farm," she said. "It was close by the Inland Sea. We could see ships and gulls, and woke each morning to the rosy dawn across the water. Only, the land around us was sold to Speculators for ice-works and salting-houses, and then there was nothing but brine and fish-stink all around, and there was the new baby coming and we had to leave before our farm was worth nothing at all."

Jack stretched out and smiled up into the darkness. "And if you had been useful, they would have wanted you at the

new farm. But no one could break a new farm and take care
of two babies. No one wants you, here or there. That's why
they sent you away. That's why Grandma says I have to watch
after you."

"No she doesn't!"

"Yes she does, when you're not there. Because you're
a baby."

Rose kicked up at the frame of his bunk so hard that Jack's
head knocked against the wall, and kicked twice more, saying,
"Shut up! Shut up! Shut up!"

Jack held his head, but for a long moment he said nothing. In the big room below them, they heard their grandmother
shift in her sleep. She huffed and muttered something. Then,
when it had been just long enough, Jack murmured—very
quietly now, "Don't be mad, Baby Rosie. You're lucky: babies
will never go to see Shadow-Town. Babies can go on dreaming
happy baby dreams."

"All right," Rose said, despairing. "All right. Just let me
sleep. Shut up and let me sleep."

Then Rose saw Jack's face suddenly appear right before
her, hanging upside-down, large and strange. Still her cousin
Jack, but the Jack she hated, the Jack that would be there
all the long summer, the Jack she would never get away
from. Rose whipped the corner of her sheet at his face, but she
knew it wouldn't do any good.

Jack squeezed his eyes shut and whispered, "Don't worry,
baby. Baby Rosie will never go there because she doesn't even
know the Words to keep the Whisperers away. They'd just
steal little Rosie and lock her up in the attic of the Tall House
with the birds and with the bats, and make her spin yarn all
night while they laughed in their awful thin voices. They'd lick
at Baby Rosie's face with their whips, and in the day Tam and
I would climb up to look at her through the spotty windows,

and we'd laugh, but they wouldn't catch us, because we know the Words."

And it was more than a moment before Rose could bring herself to say, "What are the Words?"

He swung down closer, so that his looming face almost touched hers. "Terrible words," he said, very softly. "Tam said it would frighten you even to hear them. Terrible words that you couldn't bear to listen to, because you're a baby."

She shook her head. "I don't think you even went to Shadow-Town."

Still upside-down, Jack stared at her. Then he spoke in a strange, flat voice: *"We will come in the night for you, Baby Rose Tender."*

All at once Rose found herself crouched against the wall with her sheet pulled up before her. Jack watched her that way for a while, and then he swung himself back up and finally went quiet.

Just when Rose had nearly begun to fall asleep at last, Jack began to snore. Then for a long time she was the only person left awake on the Tender farm.

* * *

There had always been dark vapors in the hollows of the sandy hills and melancholy whispers in the deepest shadows of the Tanglewood. But not for long years had so many farmers gone to sleep not knowing if they would ever wake.

When Rose's parents and Jack's mother had sent them to stay with their grandmother, it hadn't been because any-one had thought they were due some sort of holiday. It hadn't been because their grandmother had wanted them to visit. But no one had thought that would be the summer the sleeping sickness returned.

So now Rose and Jack were bound in by the hills and the sleeping sickness and the Tanglewood. They could walk the dusty roads as far as the other farms where the plague hadn't yet come.

They could stay at their grandmother's and do her chores.

They could bicker and quarrel and wish the summer was already gone.

But they couldn't ever think they were safe at home.

* * *

Jack's snoring was loud and ugly and irregular. The longer it went on, the thicker and more unpleasant it sounded, like bone glue boiling in a pot. Rose knew she could kick the bottom of his bunk to make it stop, but that would probably wake him up too, and then it would all begin again.

Suddenly there was a queer closing noise from his throat — and then nothing.

Rose began counting to herself: *One, two, three. Four.* The house was quiet; the night was quiet. Somewhere far off a dog barked, and Rose wished she had a dog for company at least. *Nine, ten, eleven. Twelve.* Rose could hear night bugs flittering. She could hear her grandmother make thin, rattling breaths in her room below, but Jack stayed silent. *Twenty, twenty-one.* Rose realized she was holding her breath too.

In the silence, from far away, she heard the long whistle of the coffin-train, growing high, and beneath it maybe the murmur of the tracks, like the rumble of a living thing. Had more farms been visited by the sleeping sickness? And who were the dead — if they were really dead — the train carried that night? *Thirty-nine, forty.*

The whistle went low and disappeared into the wide night. Everything in the room was still quiet. *Sixty-one, sixty-two.*

She wouldn't be able to hold her breath much longer. Had the sleeping sickness suddenly taken Jack? Was she alive alone in this room?

There was a tremendous bubbling gasp from above and Rose finally took a long breath in.

As Jack returned to his simply ugly snoring, she realized that it didn't even matter if she hated him. Because they were cousins and would have to live together at their grandmother's for all the rest of the summer regardless.

Sometime much later, but before the dark began to fade, Rose became very sleepy again. *Vapors.* Were there unwholesome vapors in the night air? Would she sleep and never wake? No, no. This wasn't the sleeping sickness. Rose wasn't going to be afraid that it was the sleeping sickness.

In the last moment before Rose fell asleep, or in the first moment after, words came to her: *The train takes the coffins of the properly dead, and burns them for its fuel.* And through the rest of night, deep asleep or half awake, or in her dreams, the words kept coming back: The coffins of the properly dead. And burns them for its fuel. *Burns them for its fuel.*

✳ ✳ ✳

Jack woke, gasping, and lay still until he heard it again: *Tick.* And he didn't want to get up, but he heard it once more. *Tick.*

It was Tamlin's signal, and it was almost always less unpleasant if he did what Tam wanted from the beginning. So he slipped out of bed, crept downstairs, and went barefoot out into the warm moonlight.

Tamlin was smaller and older and meaner than Jack, but he only had his father, the Beadle Smith, to look after him, so once Jack's mother had made Tam a new oilskin jacket out of pity. And then Tam had told him: "Because your mother gave me this, now I'll show you about digging and fighting and worms and all the things you need to know, and now you have to do the things I say."

So Tam was Jack's friend, but sometimes Jack was scared of him. And sometimes most of all he wanted to impress Tam, and sometimes he only hated him.

Now Tam stood in the moonlight, grimy as ever from some hole or tunnel he had been digging. Tamlin Badger-Boy, the other farmers had named him, or his father the Beadle had, and as Tam held out an envelope, Jack thought there was something about the Badger-Boy's dirty face and white teeth that seemed nastier than ever. And some sickly fog seemed to cling around his ankles.

Tamlin made his worst smile yet. "I stole this from the post," he said. "Your grandma thinks she has the sleeping sickness. She means to send you away before she dies."

2

THE RED WINDOWS

———◆✦◆———

Jack never really slept again that night.

In the red-dawned morning, their grandmother huffed as she set down their breakfast—black coffee, cold cereal in buttermilk, thick slices of white bacon. Then she sat heavily on her own chair.

Rose gave Jack a wary look, and his heart was pounding, but he told her nothing. Rose said, "Did you have a pleasant night, Grandma?"

Their grandmother looked down at her plate and huffed again a few times. "I don't have good nights," she said. "I am old and my bones ache, and my one son is dead and my other son is trying to clear a farm in a faraway place, and when I sleep I dream of not breathing, of passing into a thin grey land, and my bones ache and I am old."

Jack saw her draw a letter out of her skirt, saw it was the same letter he had read last night, before Tam sealed it up again and returned it to the sack from the bicycle post. The letter from Grandma's sister Constance:

Hard news for you I suppose, sister, but then a great imposition on me as well, but if you're going to be dying better to send the children on now I suppose and save me all the bother of having to collect them later.

P.S. Please arrange for payment in advance to keep all accounts neat and tidy.

He looked at Rose, who still sat smiling and trying to be so nice, but he said nothing. Grandma smoothed the paper a few times, and he saw her lips move as she read it over to herself: *im-po-si-tion.*

But Grandma said nothing either; only she looked up at Jack when she was done and eyed him carefully — as if she were weighing him, he thought — and then she looked Rose over too. "Eat," she finally told them, her voice rough and tired. "It's washing weather, and you have special chores this morning. And tomorrow will be a long day."

* * *

An hour later when Rose and Jack were weeding the garden under the dark morning sky, they felt the air change.

Off on the road they could see dust devils pick up and whirl, and then there would be distant thunder, and a wind would blow over them — now dusty from the west, now damp from the south. And a few warm spots of water would fall, but there was no steady rain or wind.

Sweating already, Jack leaned on his long-handled hoe and looked at the trees around the farmyard, how they bent under the changing air. "Washing weather," he said. "This is twister weather."

"Grandma would have called us in," said Rose.

Jack shook his head. "She won't call us in until the shingles are blowing off. She is worse than ever. She is going to die."

Rose put down her hoe and looked up at the pressing clouds. "She's not going to die. And you always say it's twister weather—"

"I know the sandy hills better than you," Jack interrupted.

"—but there's never a twister. Only, heavy air always makes Grandma's bones ache, and that puts her in a bad temper."

"Stupid! She's always in a bad temper because there might be a twister. It's warm and damp and my neck itches. Tam says those are certain signs of some twister, or a lightning storm for sure."

"How would you know? How would you know any of it?"

"Tam says." Jack looked at her stolidly. "Tam says she's going to send us away and die."

Rose wiped her forehead. "'Tam says.' Don't be stupid. No one's going to die." The wind came up again and blew one drop against Rose's cheek and then moved on, scattering early fallen leaves around the farmyard. Off in the distance they heard the deep woof of a neighbor's dog. "'Tam says.' It's your turn to get the eggs," she added.

Although that was true, Jack shook his head. "It's your turn." Then, just as they heard a hoarse yell from their grandmother, a gust of wind pulled open the screen door at the back of the house and banged it against the wall. "See, she is calling us! It's time to hide in the root cellar!"

There was another rough shout. "No," said Rose miserably. "She's calling me to come help her in the kitchen."

* * *

Jack knew that Rose didn't like helping Grandma in the kitchen. "She's never happy, and she huffs all the time, and she always makes me do all the chicken's giblets, and she smells like an old lady," Rose had complained before heading inside. But Jack hated the chicken coop more—with its idiot pecking birds and terrible smell, its sharp bits of feather. Its hot and stuffy air. Its red-splashed windows. Hated how it was gloomy even in the bright sun of day—like Shadow-Town.

Jack had only gone to the very edge of Shadow-Town with Tamlin Badger-Boy, of course. They had left early in the morning and crept through the shadows and whispers of the Tanglewood for hours, and gone on hands and knees over the little railway bridge that crossed the river. But then Jack really had seen the sagging, peeling buildings, really had looked up at the Tall House. He had heard the wooden mill-wheel creaking, though the water was too low to turn it; had marked the strange signs painted on its walls, now pale and faded; had seen the red-splashed windows, all cracked and broken. And they slithered down the embankment and peered in to see the shadows that moved inside.

And he remembered how the midday sun had beat down on them. "That's old Farmer Mathom," Tam had whispered. "I told you. Can you hear him? The dead dun't groan."

"I only hear the mill-wheel and the other machines."

"That's why they groan. The water in't deep enough to move the wheel anymore. Mathom turns it by climbing the Endless Stair. And the stair twists a gear and the gear pulls a belt and the belt moves the whole engineery—"

"Why?" Jack whispered.

"Why? Dun't you understand the gears are just turning wheels? And turning wheels are one of the shadow-banes, which keep the Whisperers away—the quiet ones can't bear them, no more than they could bear iron or the shine of the sun. Why? So the Whisperers can make their thralls spin their cotton and weave their miserable clothes and grind their wild barley flour..."

Jack shuddered. "Why do they all look so ragged?"

"Because they labor all day and all night, Jack—and coffin-clothes ain't meant for working."

As they watched, the machinery slowly fell quiet and they began to hear the voices change. The thralls had turned towards the boys, and they were moaning now, pleading. Tam had squeezed his strange squinty eyes almost shut and started to mutter some terrible things. The Words, the shadow-Words, Jack knew. But he never knew what the Words might have done, because he had turned and fled, stumbling over the bridge to get away from the sight of the thralls reaching for them, because the two boys were still alive, properly alive—and Tam had followed him, mocking. For hours back through the Tanglewood while the sun yet shone.

* * *

They were still hurrying when they came out of the scrubby trees and saw a tended field behind a line of willows—and Tam's father, the Beadle Smith, working there.

As Beadle, Tamlin's father had some small authority in the sandy hills. The Beadle managed the bicycle post, for example. He settled disputes about property encroachments and trampling bulls.

Most important of all, each year the Beadle led the Beating of the Bounds—the march that went from the Fallen-Stone Man by the great river to the Last Broken Hill, and then back again to the dark Clay Pool. To teach children and mark once more for any who wanted to know where the Bound-lands began. The Bound-lands that lay between the hills that might be farmed and the shadow-march where the Whisperers had their proper home; the Bound-lands that had been decreed by the Accommodation made long ago, when Jack's grandmother was still a little girl.

Tam's father was not only the Beadle but also a big, cruel-looking man—dark but with great shocks of white among his black hair—so he would have frightened Jack at any time, even if he and Tam hadn't just trespassed the Bounds. So the boys had stopped hurrying as soon as they saw him, tried to stroll as if they had only been on some foolish boys' errand.

But the Beadle called them over and stared at them closely. "Have yous been someplace you shun't?" He cuffed Tam hard on the side of his head before the boy could reply. "Have you?"

Then the Beadle looked at Jack, but Tamlin said, "Don't hit Jack—he din't know about—about wherever we went. Just hit me again."

The Beadle hit his son on the other side of the head. "I'll kick you too, if you talk back again." Then he said, "Jack Tender."

Jack swallowed. "Yes, sir."

"I knew your father when he was a boy like you. And now he's dead."

"Yes, sir," Jack said more quietly.

"Did he drop while he was working?"

Jack shook his head and the Beadle looked away.

"He worked hard enough," said Tam. "But it was a fever in his heart."

The Beadle moved his hand as if he would strike his son by habit, but instead he asked Jack, "Did you keep coffin-watch for him?"

Jack nodded.

"What?"

"Yes, sir, of course," Jack whispered.

"First one?"

"Yes."

"How old are you then? As old as this one?" He tilted his head towards Tam.

"Thirteen. Thirteen, sir."

The Beadle scratched the back of his head. He looked at the sky for a long time, and then he pulled a big iron knife out from a wooden sheath he carried around his neck. "Hold out your hand," he said.

Jack looked at Tamlin.

Tam had turned white, but he said, "Dun't be a baby. Hold out your hand."

The Beadle took Jack tightly by the wrist. He used the point of the knife to cut a little x in the ball of Jack's hand. "Because you turned thirteen and your father wun't alive to do it," the Beadle said.

Then he slapped the hilt hard against Jack's bloody palm and Jack cried out at last. The Beadle closed Jack's fingers around it tight. "That's yours by blood now," he said. "Dun't lose it."

The Beadle let go and Jack stared down at the blade. "But that's your father's knife, Founder Smith's knife!" he said.

Tam gave him a shove. "My father the Beadle has just given you the shadow-bane of iron," he said. "Just speak what's proper."

"Thank you," Jack gasped. "Sir."

The Beadle hung his wooden sheath around Jack's neck and slid the knife into it for him. "And because your father in't alive, from now on I'll beat you too," the Beadle said.

"My dad wasn't like that," Jack said.

"No. He died of a weakness in the heart."

Jack looked down at his bloody cut, speechless, and began to tremble.

"Take him home before he cries," the Beadle told Tamlin.

Some way down the sandy road, when Jack knew he would be able to speak without crying, he said, "You're fourteen. Where's your knife?"

Tamlin pulled himself up straight and drew the small end of a broken harrow blade from his back pocket and waved it under Jack's nose. "My dad told me I wun't the sort to be *given* a tool for cutting. He said a boy like me should just steal something and sharpen it myself."

* * *

That had been a week or more before, and Jack's bandaged cut still itched, but he liked to feel the wooden sheath around his neck. It felt wet against his skin today; the storm still hadn't come, so the air had stayed damp and dusty together.

All that day Rose worked in the kitchen beside her nearly silent grandmother; and she wished the weather would break or their grandmother would speak at last.

All that day Jack labored in the garden or the barn; and really he wished the storm would never come and that their grandmother would always hold her peace.

And after supper, when their grandma retired to her room, it was only the evening breeze that came, bringing cool air at last, heavy with the scent of the fields, of the barn; and the whole house had the living smell of damp wood.

There is only working and waiting for us now, Rose thought. Working, and waiting with only a little time here and there to listen to a story, a few minutes now and then to draw, or walk somewhere near the farm, and then working and waiting again. And she and Jack were lucky. Somewhere, she knew, at the new farm along the river, her parents would soon stop building or cutting or plowing for the night, lie exhausted on some rough bed, hoping that her baby brother would sleep between them. Somewhere, Jack's mother was probably working in a small room in a big house, crocheting doilies by candle-light for some rich woman.

Suddenly Rose wanted to run. She would find somewhere, some place even outside the Dominion, where there would be no Jack, no waiting, no endless chores. Only there was no place like that. There is no place that isn't just work and wait-ing, Rose thought. There is no place to go.

I wish Tam had been lying, Jack thought. Now there is only waiting for the bad news to fall on us. He watched as Rose made some kind of decision and got out her pencils and pens. For a moment, just because she didn't believe in the bad news yet, he wanted to bump her arm so that the ink would spill across her paper.

Somewhere outside a nighthawk boomed, and Jack was startled—out of a dream, maybe.

"Grandma?" he heard Rose say, and when Jack looked up, he saw that their grandma was dressed in white taffeta and veiled in pink, and wearing ruby earrings.

"Grandma?" he said. They watched as she pulled the let-ter out again, smoothed it once more, and looked at it a while. Her lips moved silently.

She looked up at Jack and Rose. "Go to bed early tonight, because tomorrow you are going away to the other side of the valley where my sister Constance will watch you," their grandma said.

"Why?" said Jack.

"Because every night you keep me awake. Because every night I grow more tired and I fear that some vapor has entered the house. Because I remember when the sleeping sickness came long ago and whole farms were lost and there was no one left to even prepare the children for the coffin-train. Because when I do dream, I dream of passing into a thin grey land. Because I am old and tired and my bones ache."

"Grandma—," said Jack.

"If you stop getting my letters, don't come back," she said. "But tell Beadle Smith. I will sleep like this every night in my wedding dress to serve as coffin-clothes." The old lady pulled two pennies from her purse and put them on the mantel, under the glass brick she had brought from the home she had known as a little girl in Smithton. She made another huff. "And tell him there is money to pay my berth on the coffin-train here, under this remembrance of lost elegance."

3

THE SANDY ROAD

Rose and Jack woke early the next morning. When they were dressed and ready to go, they stood on the porch and waited a long while as Grandma looked them over. She nodded, and then she sat down on a stool and huffed, and made Jack and Rose each repeat the directions to Great-Aunt Constance's farm.

Then Grandma gave them strictures against deviating from the known and well-worn path down the long-road west, or going near any yard that flew the yellow banner of the plague.

"And don't dawdle," she added, "for it's a long way, and you must be at the edge of the valley by sunset. And remember to abide by all the terms of the Accommodation, and don't poke about in hidden places where you have no business being, and don't stray near the Clay Pool, which marks the Bound-lands around the shadow-march. And don't ever, ever think of going near Shadow-Town, to see or bother with those wicked creatures. Because after Shadow-Town there is only the train now—or the desert, which is worse.

"And don't," their grandmother added, "don't ever go near the Red Man's estate, or trouble him in any way—not if you want to come back children. Don't dare trouble with him who keeps the Bounds."

Which was a long speech for their grandmother, and then she gave them some chokecherry preserves as a gift to take to Constance, and told them what greetings to give her, and then Grandma only stood still for a moment. "You have been too much trouble, but at least you have done some of your work," she said.

She tied the strings of Rose's sun hat tight, and then as she fixed a little bag of rust around Rose's neck, she muttered an old rhyme:

> *Three shadow-boons to fright you —*
> *night and webs and whispered Words*
> *But sun and iron and wheels which turn*
> *are three shadow-banes to keep you.*

Rose had never worn the rust before, and she felt its soft weight while her grandmother looked at her closely. "You are like your mother, who took away my son," Grandma said, and huffed once more.

Then she fixed a bag of rust around Jack's neck. Jack touched his charm too, just to make sure of it, but this was not the first time he had traveled the sandy hills. He had worn the rust before.

Grandma straightened his cap roughly. "You look like my other son, who is dead," she told him.

She looked awhile at each of them. "And don't you go near the Clay Pool," she said again. "Or even think of troubling with the Red Man. But good-bye."

✳ ✳ ✳

In those midsummer weeks, the air always grew heavy with heat before the day was done, but Jack and Rose set out from the farmyard when the morning was still damp and cool. The path took them north until it met the long-road west. Years and years and years ago, when their grandmother was still a girl, the farmers had planted windbreaks of pine and willow alongside this road.

Now Rose and Jack walked between the trees, up and over hills, and for a long time Jack said nothing. Only he was flushed, and now and then he would kick small stones at Rose.

"It's just a precaution," Rose said. "I don't think Grandma really has the sleeping sickness. She's just feeling her years."

"That was the place our fathers were born, at least," Jack said bitterly. "But now either Grandma is going to die or she has turned us out after all. So shut up, Rose. Don't try to make it sound less miserable."

On that soft road, their footsteps were almost silent, but their talking let the creatures in the trees know they were there. Two white-tailed deer started and slid silently back among the willows. Rose looked up as a grey squirrel chittered loudly from high on a scraggly pine, but Jack paid it no attention.

Some time later, they had turned on to a stretch of road that cut through a tangle of aspen and scrub oak. It was a shadowed, whispery patch of bush and Rose wondered whether it had never been cleared or had just been abandoned so long ago it had returned to the wild.

But abandoned farms were such a melancholy subject to contemplate that Rose tried to make conversation again. "I have never met Great-Aunt Constance," she said.

Jack had been carrying a little switch of dry willow. Now he broke it against a tree trunk. "There were four sisters. Temperance was the oldest, who died of drink, and then Benevolence, who gambled her money away, and then Patience—who is Grandma—and then Constance, the youngest, who surprised everyone when she suddenly married an old River-man and moved to the edge of the valley."

"Is she like Grandma? What will it be like to stay there?"

Jack shrugged. "Great-Aunt Constance is more used to company so she talks more than Grandma. But she always wanted to have a boy of her own, so she'll treat me like her favorite."

Rose padded along quietly awhile. She began to feel the morning sun on her neck. "Don't be full of yourself. If she has never had any children, after all this time living on the edge of the valley with only an old River-man for company, I'll bet she yearns to have a girl around just as a change."

Jack shifted his pack and kicked some sand at her. "She has plenty of company. She has squirrels and robins, and she has a dozen fierce dogs and about three hundred cats, and I've seen deer eat from her fingers. But she told me once she used to wish my dad had been her son, not Grandma's—because she always wanted to have a boy of her own."

Rose brushed sand from her face. "Then she would have wished my dad had been her son too."

"Except that Aunt Constance always liked my dad better. Everyone did. Even Grandma. That's why she liked me better than you." Jack paused. "That's why she *likes* me better," he said.

"No she doesn't," Rose said, but she said it quietly, and Jack didn't seem to hear.

* * *

They had reached the bottom of a hill when Jack suddenly went stock-still and put out an arm to block Rose's way.

Up on the crest of the next hill some large dog-thing had stopped in the middle of crossing the road to stare back down at them. "Don't move!" Jack whispered. The next moment it had run off and was hidden in the bush behind a great rotting cottonwood.

A wolf. A wolf that would be hiding beside the road, waiting for them. Jack felt a mixture of terror and relief. He grabbed Rose's arm. "Now we have to go back to Grandma's whether she wants us or not."

Rose looked at him palely and shook off his hand. "Because of a dog?"

"*Dog?*" Jack hissed. He kept his eye on the spot where it had disappeared. "A dog? Haven't you ever seen a wolf before? That was a wolf who saw us and knew us for what we are—and now he's hiding in the bush beside the road, waiting for us."

In fact, Rose had never seen a wolf before, not a live one, but she looked at the bush and thought for a moment. She had heard and read stories about people who had been attacked by wolves—but it was always a pack of wolves, at night. Howling wolves. Not wolves slipping across the road in the middle of farmland. "A big dog," she said. "But not even big enough to be a wolf. Some farmer's dog. It might be one of the Beadle's dogs."

"You don't even know his dogs!" Jack shouted. He grabbed her arm again and began pulling her, struggling, back up the hill.

"You can't pull me the whole way back!"

"I'm the leader—," Jack began.

"No you're not!"

Rose thrashed wildly, but this time Jack didn't let go of her arm. "I'm the leader and my mother said I had to watch after you and Grandma said I had to watch after you, and I'm going back, so you have to come!" he finished. And with that, he saw that Rose was nearly in tears. But she spoke quickly and quietly.

"You're not the leader, and I'm not going to go back. We were told to go to Great-Aunt Constance's, and it can't be worse with her than it is stuck with just you at Grandma's. And if you go back without me, you'll look like a coward."

"If you go on, you'll get attacked by a wolf," Jack said.

They stayed like that, neither moving, until Rose said, "If you let me get attacked by a wolf when I'm alone, then what will Grandma think of you? —if she isn't really dying after all."

Jack only stared at her, until Rose grew ashamed at what she had said. "Come on then!" he shouted as he began pushing her the other way, up the hill to where the dog-thing had stood. "Come on, then, brave girl! Let's find some wolves; let's see all the brave things you're willing to do. Let's see how much you want to get eaten and killed!"

Rose found her heart beating wildly as they neared the crest and saw tracks in the sandy road. She might have been right— that it hadn't been a wolf—but it had been a large dog, at least, and she hadn't noticed a collar either. She tried to squirm closer to Jack as they came up to the cottonwood where it had disappeared, but he pushed her away and walked on, quickly, over the crest and down the other side.

"Wait for me," she called as she hurried to catch up.

But Jack didn't even look back as he went on down, shouting, "How's the wolf? Are you friends with it by now? Have you explained how you're not really frightened?"

Just as Rose was catching up, he stopped and turned back, looking past her to the top of the hill, and Rose felt her heart turn to ice. Jack put up his hand and shook his head. "Just listen!"

Slowly Rose turned too. From somewhere beyond the hill they had just come down, they heard an unexpected sound: the rustle of tack and the clop of hooves, and the squeaking of carriage-sprung wheels. Carriage-sprung wheels, but farmers never drove carriages unless they were traveling to a wedding or a funeral.

They waited as the squeaking came closer, and heard someone shouting curses in a high, town voice, the kind animals never listen to. Then they saw a broken-down pie-bald horse come over the rise pulling a black and dusty open carriage.

A man dressed in a shabby black frock coat sat in the front, attempting to drive the old horse. He snapped his whip against its flank with no instructions and to no effect, and he cursed and snapped his whip again. When he saw Jack and Rose, he turned and shouted to the man who sat behind him: "Right again, Master Whick! You did hear children! Some farmers' children!" Then he yelled, "Whoa!" to his nag, and "Whoa!" again, and snapped his whip against it three, four, five times. The horse looked up and began to slow, sliding a little as it came down the sandy slope. Finally the carriage came to a stop, more or less in front of the cousins.

The driver wiped his forehead with a gingham handkerchief and looked them over. He snapped his whip twice more against the horse. "Children," he said, and then as if he had just thought of it, he made a smile. The kind of smile that is all teeth, the kind that doesn't mean anything.

"Children," he repeated, and he turned around to the other man again.

"Perhaps ask them if they want a ride, Master Snap," the man in the back suggested. "They might be the sort of children it is useful to take for a ride."

Then the second man rose up a bit to look them over. He wore the same sort of coat as the driver, and he made the same sort of smile.

4

MSTRS WHICK AND SNAP

Rose and Jack looked at each other. They certainly didn't need one of Grandma's strictures to stop them from getting into the dusty black carriage.

"We don't want a ride," Jack said.

Master Snap looked down at them as if he hadn't heard.

"Thank you," Rose added. "We don't need a ride."

"They don't want a ride, Master Whick," Snap called back, as if Whick wouldn't have heard them himself.

"But they don't even know which way we're headed, Master Snap," Whick said.

"It doesn't matter which way you're headed, because we don't need a ride to get where we are going," Jack said.

Whick considered that for a moment. "Which way are we headed?" he asked Snap.

"That depends on where we are," Snap said.

"But, Master Snap, we don't *know* where we are," Whick said.

"So that's what you should ask these good farmers' children, Master Whick. *They* might not want a ride to where we are headed, but *we* certainly want to know which way that is."

"You're between the turn to the Tender farm and the lane to Beadle Smith's," Jack said.

Snap just stared at him.

"Beadle Smith, Master Snap," Whick repeated. "He is the Beadle of the farmers."

"Ah, yes," said Snap. "And the Tender farm." He frowned for a moment and then put on a patient voice. "We have been watching this part of the world for some time," he said. "Now we wanted to see it up close, to get a, a—"

"A *skunk's-eye* view, Master Snap?" Whick said.

Snap smiled thinly. "I meant to use some more poetic metaphor than that, Master Whick."

"A *snake's-eye?*" Whick tried. "Weasel's-eye? *Gopher's-eye?*"

"Let it go," Snap said. He turned back to the children. He smiled again.

Rose swallowed. "Back there is east. You're traveling west down the long-road. That way is north," she added, pointing.

Snap rubbed his chin with the butt end of his whip. He leaned forward and made his smile at Rose again. "Girl, I don't like you thinking I need you to tell me that."

Behind him Whick was bringing out a thick map that had been folded many times and marked over with many lines and measurements in pen and pencil. "But we do need her to tell us that, Master Snap," he said.

Snap turned and spoke with an excess of patience. "I said I didn't like her *thinking* that, Master Whick."

"No," said Whick. "You are right of course." Then he made

his own smile at Jack and Rose. "Children—," he began, as if he were about to make a speech. "Children, do you like us?"

Rose could feel her heart beating harder as Whick put more and more effort into looking patient. "No," Jack said at last.

Snap tapped the end of his whip against the horse's side. "Farmers' children, Master Whick," he said. "Stupid and rude."

"Perhaps they believe that honesty is the best policy," Whick said.

Snap made a kind of barking sound. "As I said, Master Whick, not just rude but stupid—stupid and rude."

Whick shook his head. "Stupid and Rude," he said to Jack and Rose, as if those were their actual names, "I am pleased to meet you. I am pleased to have met two honest farmers' children." He held out his map. "Now, honestly show us where we are."

Jack was red in the face. "That's not what we're called," he said.

Snap leaned over. "Did you know that Master Whick meant you just now?"

"Those aren't our names," Jack insisted.

Whick made a loud, dry laugh. "Those might not be your names, but if you knew who I meant, then you *are* called Stupid and Rude!"

"No use disputing with *you*, Master Whick!" Snap cried, and he laughed until he wheezed. "It must be this one who is Stupid. No use for you, Stupid, you lack the tools! Lack the tools of *cognition* and *disputation!*"

Jack stayed still and quiet as Whick laughed on, and Rose felt her face burning.

Then Whick leaned over to rustle the map at her. "*You* can read a map, though, can't you? You're not Stupid, only Rude."

"And ugly, of course," Snap added. "She is Rude and Ugly."

Rose looked at the paper Snap held, and the marks on it. They were marks like her father had made on the map of their old farm that they had had to sell, and on the map of the new farm where her parents were trying to break the land right now. Only this map was on a much greater scale, and there were many, many marks on it. She looked at Jack. He had known Whick and Snap were wicked in some fashion right away, just as she had, but did he understand this? "They are Speculators," she whispered.

"Whispering now," said Snap. "Speak so we all may hear, farmers' girl Rude."

"You are Speculators," Rose said. "Land thieves." And though she couldn't keep her voice steady, Rose said it again more loudly, "You are land thieves. Here to claim land by trickery, land that you never owned or worked. Then drive up prices for honest farmers."

"Yes, the other one must be Stupid," Master Snap said to his partner. "While this clever one is certainly Rude."

"Well, little Rude, we *are* Speculators," Whick told Rose.

"Speculators and *Projectors*," Snap put in. Then he worked a crank that slowly raised up a canvas awning over the carriage. "Observe and read, if you are lettered!"

The awning had been painted, and painted over again with large letters:

G. Whick *and* A. Snap, Esqs
◁ Only the Best ▷
~~Patent Medicines!~~
~~Lightning Proofing!~~
~~Automated Path Warding Whirligigs!~~
GENERAL PROJECTION AND SPECULATION
(also Property Agents and Notaries Public)

They gave the cousins a moment to admire the awning.

"'Automated Path Warding Whirligigs,'" Jack read out scornfully. "Tam told me about those last summer. When the wind blew they fell over, and when it didn't blow the whirligigs wouldn't turn, so they didn't serve as shadow-banes."

Whick gave him a hard look. "As you can see, Stupid, that particular Projection has been suspended—due to the difficulty of finding reliable manufacture. But as Speculators we continue to provide a valuable service to farmers. There is a plague in these hills—yes, a plague! Perhaps you have heard of it."

"And is one of your medicines a cure?" asked Jack.

Snap coughed.

"No," Whick said. "No, our Speculation is our service. Without our Speculations, prices would fall—fall even farther, I mean—and farmers could never obtain enough for their land to let them leave."

"Enough to leave!" Rose cried, bold in a way Jack had never seen. "While you buy good land for a pittance—that's not a service!"

"A matter of perspective, child," Snap said. "It certainly serves us." He pulled out a pocketwatch, as if doubting whether he had time to finish the conversation, then frowned. He held it to his ear and shook it.

"Speculators and their schemes drove us from our farm!" Rose said.

"Which ones, my dear?" Whick asked softly, pulling out a small book and a little silver pencil.

Rose stared at him for a moment. It wasn't a matter she liked to recall. "The firm's name was Crattle, Snope, and Windburn," she said.

Whick wrote something down. "Ah, yes," he mumbled. "C., S., & W. And their lovely Lakeland Development Enterprise. Dreadful sharp Speculators they are."

"C., S., & W.," Snap repeated. "Lakeland." He closed his eyes and smiled, showing his three silver teeth. "Still, they provided a service—a service in the *aggregate*. Granted, for some of the particulate—your family, perhaps—not so much a clear benefit as a, a—"

"As an injury?" Whick suggested.

Snap gave him a sharp glance. "As a new opportunity for finding some path towards comfort more suiting their particular *character* and *capabilities*, I was going to say," said Snap. "But overall, still—prosperity. Or at least some avoidance of risk, if not for any individual ant, then to the anthill *as a whole*."

"Or at least to the *species* of ants. Considered abstractly. A benefit to all antkind, if you will," said Whick.

Talking with the Speculators seemed to take all the air out of Rose. She took a deep breath. "But we're not ants."

"Perspective again, my dear," said Snap. "A difficult thing for one so young—"

"And ugly," put in Whick.

"—and ugly. A difficult thing for one so young and ugly to acquire."

"What if the farmers in the hills don't want to leave?" asked Jack.

Whick and Snap shared a smile. "Oh, they'll want to leave," Whick said. "Be sure of that. The plague isn't done here, not at all. But when it is done—well, then others will want to buy the land and..."

"Pick up the pieces?" Snap suggested.

"—and resume the endeavor with greater fortitude. Or, at least, with larger cash reserves."

"My dad told me all Speculators were conniving and wicked," Jack said.

"Yes, the boy certainly is the stupid one," Snap told Whick.

"Tell me then, little Stupid," Whick said, "has your farmer-father profited from his deep insight? Will he die rich and comfortable in his old age, do you think?"

"Will your father leave a great estate to you?" Snap added. "Or the map to a claim thick with gold or good soft soil? Will he—"

Jack was white and trembling now. Whick looked at him and considered before saying, "Master Snap—perhaps Stupid has no father."

"A *bastard*, Master Whick? Among these staid farmers."

Whick laughed. "No, no, Master Snap. Not a bastard, not a *lineal* bastard. I mean, an orphan."

"Yes, of course," Snap said. "The plague. Did your father die in his sleep, boy Stupid? Is that it? Was he a fine, hard-working man who passed quietly in the night?"

"Shut up," Rose said. "Leave my cousin alone. Don't talk about his father. Shut up."

Snap stared at her for a moment, and then he shook the reins until the old horse raised its head. "All good things must end, Master Whick," he said wearily. "As we petition each day. Stupid and Rude here have showed us the error of our way but declined to share our carriage. We are done with them, I think."

"Quite right," said Whick. "All prudent haste away!"

Snap made a clucking noise, pulled at the reins, and whipped the horse. He did those things a second time, and a third. At last the old beast began to back and turn in the sandy road, and slowly the black carriage began to rattle up the hill and away, leaving a cloud of fine brown sand behind.

Jack never moved, and Rose stood beside him until the carriage was out of sight and the dust it made had begun to settle.

"They're worse than Crattle, Snope, and Windburn," Rose whispered.

"My father was a fine, hard-working man," said Jack. His face was wet and he didn't look at Rose. "My father didn't slip away quietly. He died groaning, and his face was creased with pain."

Rose nodded silently.

"And you're not so clever," he whispered.

"I didn't say I was clever," Rose said quietly, but Jack felt a rage coming over him, and he went on.

"Speculators drove your family from your home, and you still didn't know better than to talk with them! You're not clever—you don't know anything!"

Rose started to say something, but Jack just shouted, "Just give me your rucksack!" She slid it off her shoulders uncertainly and held it out to him. Jack opened it, peered inside. "You think you're so brave and clever!" he said.

Rose shook her head. Whether she had spoken more or less than she should, these Speculators really had seemed worse than Crattle, Snope, and Windburn. It had been almost too much for her to bear. But to Jack she only said, "You're the one who keeps saying he's the leader."

Jack took the rucksack by its straps and swung it over his head, once, twice, three times, and then he let it go flying into the bush—jars, food, bits of clothing, all of Rose's little personal bundles scattering across the leaves and branches.

Then he turned and ran ahead without her. "Stupid Rose!" he shouted, not even looking back. "Standing and talking with Speculators when we have the whole way to the edge of the valley to go before night comes! Stupid baby!"

5

TAMLIN

------◆◆◆◆◆------

By the time Rose had found and packed away all the things Jack had scattered in the bush, the morning was well along and her hands and arms were scratched and bloody.

The damp heat of the day was already settling, and Rose took a moment to tie her jacket around her waist. At least the air wasn't hazy yet. When Rose climbed the next hill at last and turned to look back, she could see the marks of the Speculators' wheels for a long way and, farther off still, the little cloud of dust that followed their carriage.

She watched the dust for a while and then turned back west, where they were supposed to go. She didn't see Jack waiting for her at the bottom of the hill after all, as she had hoped—only the stolid, regular print of his boots. Somehow they annoyed her in the same way that Jack did, but she was still glad to have them for company. Down and up again, down and up—for miles over the soft and sandy hills.

She wasn't going to hurry after him. Jack was carrying the cider, but she was carrying most of the food, and he would have to wait for her along the road if he wanted to eat. There was a table in the crowding jack pines somewhere around the Green Lake. Probably that's where she would catch up to him, sitting there waiting, all cool and smiling and smug.

She walked alone, but she wouldn't hurry. By now even the Speculators' dust was gone. There were no bears in this country, not since the first Strangers had arrived long ago from far away across the ocean. The sleeping sickness didn't take you when you walked. And Jack couldn't really have seen a wolf—or if he did, they never really attacked people. Or almost never.

There were only the Whisperers, but daylight was the first shadow-bane, and she was following the road, and by the terms of the Accommodation the road and the day belonged only to the farmers, even in the Bound-lands.

Once, through the trees to the north, Rose saw the broken-down buildings of a ruined farm, and for a moment she thought she saw some flapping yellow cloth, but it was only a flash of the sun against a blaze of a dying poplar. Not the banner that farms flew when the plague had come.

Now Rose remembered she had seen this broken farm once before, when she had taken this road to be introduced to Tamlin's father, Beadle Smith. Those buildings had been broken and empty for a long time, probably almost as long ago as the Accommodation. So it was certainly not the plague. No one would have lived there for years and years. No gust of wind would carry vapors from the sleeping sickness.

So she was just alone, Rose thought; she was fine. She was only walking by herself, west down the quiet long-road, between overgrown dogwoods along the south and tall cedars along the north. Only a faint wind blew; bugs leapt and fizzed in the untended verge. And each step she took in the soft road made a little sound, and then there was a smaller sound following as the soft brown sand pittered back down behind her.

Rose had just gone over the top of a hill when something suddenly buzzed up from the grass to her right. It spat as it struck her face, and she shouted, whipped at it with her jacket—but it was already hidden in a little hump of dirt and tall weeds again, already sawing away like the other bugs. A grasshopper.

To the south, through the old dogwoods, Rose could see a rough field where three cows grazed in the morning sun. One made a strange long lowing. Near the ground, she heard a blackbird wheeze and flutter; some small hidden animal went scurrying off. Rose shifted her rucksack and looked up at the sky. Jack would be waiting for food, but she was already thirsty for the cider.

Rose had almost begun making a sort of dog-trot after all when a queer, thin laugh came from somewhere among the unkempt cedars. She decided it would be better not to move very much at all.

* * *

The noise had been strange enough that even Jack had been startled. From where Jack was hiding beside the long-road, farther down among the dogwoods, he saw Rose freeze in terror. Then slowly she made herself turn and look—first at the cedars, then back towards the other side. She hadn't seen him at least.

The noise again, and he saw her start once more. She might have thought it was a bird, he supposed, some kind of woodpecker drumming and laughing at the same time. It could have been. Rose looked back at the long-road, up towards the next hill, then down again. And then she had seen him.

It wasn't what he had meant to do, but Jack found himself making a wide wave, and he saw her shoulders loosen. He took a step in her direction, and Rose started towards him, running like a puppy, it seemed to Jack, in loose, happy steps. Suddenly there was a great rough scream and something erupted from beneath the verge, dirty arms clutching for her.

Tam.

* * *

As the three of them walked on down the sandy road, Tamlin went on laughing. "Hee-hee! That was a good trick." He poked Rose in the side until she looked at him. "A Whisperer wun't eat you anyway. Too bony."

Jack scratched under his cap. "Let it alone, Tam," he said. "A Whisperer wouldn't eat you either because you are too ugly."

Tamlin gave him a long, considering look, then he made an almost pleasant smile. "But at least I amn't as ugly as you."

"But I thought the Whisperers only ate flat barley cakes," Rose said. "I thought they only made you work their iron and turn their wheels."

"Maybe." Tam gave her a shove towards Jack's side of the road. "Or maybe they do worse things and you would only wish they had eaten you."

Rose stumbled, got her balance. "Shut up," she said.

Jack said, "All right, let's just go." To Tamlin he added, "She's my cousin. I get to push her and you don't."

"It's right that you look after her, Jack," Tamlin said. "That's fitting. You have to look after your baby cousin Rosie."

As if she were a pot that had just boiled over, the words spilled hot and quick from Rose: "I'm thirteen years old, just like Jack—I am two months and a day older than Jack—*why don't you call Jack a baby?*"

Now Jack shoved her so that she almost stumbled back into Tam. "Because you're such a good little girl. Because you'd never do anything brave like go to Shadow-Town. Because it's so easy to make you cry. Because you're crying now."

Rose just stood there, breathing heavily. Tears were running down her face. "Why is Tamlin coming along?" She wiped her nose.

"He's my friend," Jack said. "I said he could come."

Rose tried to move around him, but Tam jumped so he was in her way again. He stuck his tongue out. "Jack shun't have to go all the way to the edge of the valley with only his baby cousin," he said.

She looked at Jack. "When did you tell him about it?"

"Last night, at the well," Jack said. "In the dark."

"Did you tell him that you got scared of a little dog today?" Rose said. "Did you tell him you wanted to turn around and go right back to Grandma's?"

Tam looked at Jack and made his most unpleasant smirk. Then he turned and jumped down in front of Rose like a squatting toad. "I dun't need *Jack's* permission to walk this road," he said. "My dad is the Beadle. If I want to, I'll walk in front of you the whole way to the edge of the valley."

Rose tried to get by him again, but Tam caught the back of her rucksack and leaned around so his lips were by her ear and she shuddered. "*Baby,*" he whispered.

"All right," Jack said again as he tugged on Tam's sleeve. "Let's go."

"He won't want to come the whole way, not really," Rose said.

Tam sneered at her. "I can go to the edge of the valley. I can go anywhere you can and then make my way back, too."

Jack suddenly felt sick. The whole way. Of course, even if they went to Great-Aunt Constance's, Tam would come, to drive him. Rose glanced at him, but if there was a message in her eyes, Jack couldn't read it. Her face was set and pale, as though she had turned to stone.

"Actually, Grandma decided not to send us to Great-Aunt Constance after all," she said. "Because she's not sick of the vapors, she's just old and tired. So we're not going to follow the long-road west. We're going to go south, past the Green Lake. We're going to get something to make Grandma feel better. We're going to bring her something back from Shadow-Town."

Tam stared at her. "No you ain't. Jack wud've told me."

After a moment, without looking up, Jack said. "Yes we are."

"No, Jack. You wun't go there again without telling me. You wun't do that without asking me if it was allowed."

"I would too," Jack said, hoarsely. "She's not going to die. We're going to go to Shadow-Town, not just to the Tall House, but right into Shadow-Town, to get something to make her feel better. We're going to get her a, a *remembrance of lost elegance*—from when she was a girl, from before it was ever Shadow-Town."

"Like what?"

"Saskatoon Cordial," Jack said.

"Glass bricks," Rose said.

Tam smirked. "Glass bricks. *Saskatoon Cordial.*"

"Saskatoon Cordial," Jack repeated. He finally looked up into Tam's black eyes. "And I don't have to do what you tell me."

Tam laughed. "Yes you do."

Jack looked down at the ground as he said, "And I didn't want to tell you because I thought you'd be too scared to come."

For a moment Tam only stared at him. "You thought I'd be scared?" he said. "You thought I'd be scared?" All at once a wild, white rage overcame him. He made sounds deep in his

throat that reminded Jack of the Words, but they had no mean-
ing. Tam suddenly jumped, twisting and thrashing in the air,
and as he landed he held his old harrow blade in both hands,
his black eyes bulging.

"*You thought I'd be scared!*" he screamed.

He drove the blade deep into the soft road, and for a
moment he stayed like that, crouching over the broken iron,
trembling.

Rose took two quick steps back, but Jack put out his hand
to stop her. "Let him alone when he's like this," he whispered.

Now Tam looked up from under his wild bangs. Breathing
hard, but calm again—too calm, Rose thought. He made a
particular kind of Tam-smile, and that was when Jack's heart
began to hammer.

Tam looked Rose and Jack each in the eye, and then he
spat on the ground. The spittle made a dark bubbling spot on
the sand around the table. "I amn't the one who's scared," he
said quietly. "I'm the one who knows the Words, the secret
shadow-Words that will keep me safe. The Words," he added,
"that's too terrible to say."

Tam spat twice more. "I's Tamlin Badger-Boy," he said.
"I amn't just a farmer. I's Beadle Smith's son. I's the grandson
of Founder Smith, who was the Mayor of Smithton when it
was made, and when it was broken. Someday I'll be ruler of
Shadow-Town, by rights. Yes, rule it like a Mayor—see if I
wun't! With a fine golden cloak—and a dozen aldermen in
golden collars to discharge my rule!" Then he stopped and
seemed to look away into some far place or time to come.

And Rose found she couldn't keep from saying, very softly,
"But it's the Whisperers who own Shadow-Town now."

Tam's voice was low and terrible. "Still, someday I'll rule.
And I'll tell you when to be scared."

6

THE TANGLEWOOD

They didn't talk again for a while, but Tam and Jack led Rose
south off the long-road onto a narrow lane that took them to
the Green Lake.

Almost at once the hills were rougher and less tended.
Spruce had pushed their way back in among the pine, and
birch and poplar grew up near the water between open patches
of grass and fireweed. But there was a log table and bench that
looked south over the lake and the crowding bush beyond.
After a nervous glance at Tam, Rose said, "We have been walking all morning. We have to stop and drink."

Jack began pulling off his rucksack to get at the cider.
"Of course," he said. "We always stop here."

"Always," Tam said scornfully. "I only took you once."

The day was growing muggy already, but there was a

cool wind coming off the water. While Tam smirked and Rose looked away, Jack noticed something for the first time. "There is no creek here," he said.

"No one knows where the water comes from," Tam said.

Rose looked out at the water. She had grown up beside a big lake that fishers worked with boats and nets as though it were the ocean. "Can you even catch a fish here? Is it nice water? Do people swim or bathe here?"

"It's terrible water," Tam said. "There's only minnows and little crabs to catch. And there's long weeds that grab at your ankles, so you can't swim. And even if you just splash in it, you will get the Itch and big purple spots will grow on your skin."

"That's horrible," Rose said.

Tam smiled and drank some cider. "Very horrible," he said.

✳ ✳ ✳

Beyond the table the trail led wide around the lake, through a country of weeds and dry turf, spotted with tufts of long grass and thistle.

Here and there the side of a hill had slid away after a storm, and the bare sand beneath showed through, like flesh under a butcher's knife.

And by now the trail itself was only a pair of old wagon ruts among the weeds, a reminder of the time before the Accommodation when the path had been well used, when Smithton was the name of the town it reached at last.

But then the whispers had started, and at first, the farmers had thought they only heard the wind in the poplars. And then shadows had begun moving nearer each night, and the farmers told themselves they must be seeing wolves or wild cats prowling. And even when here and there farmers themselves had begun to go missing, to just leave and let their fields go to seed, the others had told one another that those must just have been the ones who had lacked fortitude, who couldn't bear the work or the weather.

But in time the farmers who were left came to understand that they were not the only ones who wanted the sandy hills; that the Whisperers had come there too.

Then there had been all kinds of trouble — trouble that no one in Jack and Rose's family would ever speak about — until the Accommodation had been made with the Whisperers, until Smithton had been abandoned and left to them, and until the Bound-lands to the shadow-march had been set.

Now willows planted long ago rose alongside the path, grown tall from the water that ran somewhere beneath the sandy soil, and then met and knotted their branches overhead. *A bosky track*, Rose remembered their grandma had called such a thing. She had said that willows reached out because like farmers they had husbands and wives, and so held one another close.

* * *

They had only just left the Green Lake behind them, but already the trail that would take them to the Bound-lands and the Tanglewood had passed beyond the high willows. Now they moved through shabby poplars in twisted, grasping shapes. Already the flies and grasshoppers seemed louder. Usually Jack didn't notice their sound, any more than he heard his own breathing, but now and then one buzz would stand out, grow higher and louder until it filled the open land, then higher again — until suddenly it turned to nothing.

Dry roots cracked under their feet, and in the trees above them the little leaves sighed, but Jack felt no wind. Everything just seemed still. Soon they would come to the Clay Pool, the first of the Bound-marks.

It wasn't long before Jack began to regret that Tam had ever learned about the expedition.

He had wanted to impress Tam, to scare Rose. But Rose and Tam hated each other, and she had become so stubborn, and Tam had grown a foul set to his mouth, like any boaster who'd been caught out. And somehow the result of it all was that the three of them were going to follow this dark path to Shadow-Town until one of them admitted they were scared.

Jack felt his heart beating faster as they made a last rise. Ahead of them he saw that the wagon ruts led into a little valley thickly grown with water-trees, with willow and birch and cottonwood. All of it gathering heat under the midday sun so that he smelled it in the air that rose up the hill to greet them: damp earth and rotting leaves; the warm smell of decay.

At their feet Jack saw some little broken wooden contraption. Tam gave it a kick, breaking it more. "Path-warding whirligig," he explained. "The shadow-banes that din't ever work."

"Why was it set here?" she asked.

Jack said, "Because just down this hill, in the hollow — that's where we'll find the Clay Pool."

"Is you ready to go?" Tam asked Rose. He smiled. "After the Clay Pool, we will be in Bound-lands. And after that there's only the shadow-march."

Rose's voice was tight. "It was my idea. Jack was —" Jack turned, but she only ended with: "Jack was ready to go, but it was my idea."

"It was her idea," said Jack, "but she doesn't really know how bad it will be."

Tam smiled. "Not like you," he said. He gave the remains of the whirligig another kick and led the way down the hill, through the clustered branches, and into the shadowed dell. The smell got thicker and damper as the light grew dimmer, until they reached the bottom, where a wide pool of water stood—black in the shadows; almost golden brown where the sun shone through.

* * *

By the water's edge, the air was warm and wet and almost stifling.

"Here all the farmers and their children come to beat the Bounds, on the last night of autumn," Tamlin told Rose. "For our own sake, and that of the Whisperers."

"This is the last part of *our* country, of the farmers' country," Jack added with as much pomp as he could. "We have come as far as we can—without crossing into the Bound-lands. And there we are only permitted while the sun still shines."

Now surely Rose would feel she had proved enough. Or Tam would realize he didn't want to go any farther, not really.

But Tam looked at him coolly, while Rose only stared down into the water. "Is this where they drown the children?" she whispered.

"Don't be stupid," Jack said at once. "The Beadle only throws one child in on the night of the Beating of the Bounds so that everyone will always remember that this is the first of the Bound-marks. Remember that the real country of farmers, of men and women, ends here."

"When I was three, I was the one my father threw in, and I din't drown," Tamlin said. He wiped at his grimy face. "We even come here by ourselves, sometimes, at the close of harvest, to wash the chaff from our necks in its warm water, when our parents is too tired to stop us. You dun't get the Itch from this water," he explained, "not like the Green Lake. And no one drowns. Almost no one ever drowns."

Rose hardly seemed to listen. As the boys watched, she knelt down in the rough grass by the edge and carefully put her hand in the water.

Tam edged close to Jack. "*Let's push her in!*" he whispered, and when Jack shook his head, he added, "Think of how she'll shriek!"

And the best reply Jack could think of was: "You just think that way she'll be too scared to want to go to Shadow-Town anymore."

Rose lifted her hand from the pool and got to her feet slowly. She looked at her palm and blinked, as if she had been dreaming. "Why do you bathe here? Why, when it's brown and warm and stifling?"

"The air is cool after harvest," Tam said slowly, "and we's even browner."

Now Jack knelt down amid the footprints on the muddy bank, amid the crowd of green-leaved suckers. He had never felt the water either. "We know what it's like after a harvest," he told Tam. "We work in the fields too."

At the edge of the pool the mud dropped away quickly and Jack rubbed his fingertips together in the warm water. It felt slick, somehow, not gritty. Then he felt the rest of his hand slide in, as though the pool were gently pulling. Up to the wrist, and there was still nothing beneath his fingers and Jack realized he was becoming dizzy.

He was just about to warn Rose that it would be easy to fall into the water when he felt some sudden force, and the pool reached up to embrace him. Jack couldn't see; he had a mouthful of water and he couldn't breathe. He couldn't find a footing and he couldn't swim. He spun under the water, no longer even knowing which way was up or down. He almost opened his mouth to scream, but he flailed wildly instead, until he heard his pulse hammering in his ears.

With the one small part of his mind that wasn't working to hold back his scream he heard again what his father had whispered in the spring, looking out over the flooded fields he would never work again: "*Too thick to swim, too wet to plow, too brown to drink.*" Jack had hardly been able to hear him, but then all at once his father had given Jack a sly smile and spoke quite easily. "*And you'll only breathe it once.*"

Black stars were bursting in Jack's head. *And you'll only breathe it once.*

Jack knew that to take a breath in the water would kill him, but he had to scream. And to scream he would have to take in that one last breath — but just then some other force moved him and his head came out of the Clay Pool and he breathed in air and didn't die.

It was someone else who screamed. Rose. Tam had pulled him up by the hair. Rose was dragging a long branch from the bush towards the water, screaming, "Help me! Help me get him out! Help me!"

She turned as she heard Jack begin to cough. "See," Tam said to her as Jack gasped. "Jack din't drown. Almost no one ever drowns."

Rose sank onto the ground, sobbing. For a long time, Jack lay on his side, wheezing in air, spitting up the thick water. A cloud had come over the clearing, and even through the bush he could feel a small breeze from the south. His clothes were soaked through and he felt suddenly cold.

"Well," Tam said gently enough. "Maybe yous want to go back to the long-road now."

Jack looked over at Rose. She was shaking more than he was, and her eyes were pleading.

He got up and hugged his knees to his chest. Tam was smiling down at him, magnanimous. The Beadle had thrown Tam in when he was three.

"Maybe —," Rose began.

Jack shook some water from his hair. How Tam must have wanted to shriek that night when he was so small, turning in the brown water, thinking he would drown.

Jack looked from Rose to Tam — Tam in the oilskin jacket Jack's mother had made him. And he remembered what Tam had said: "*Now I'll show you about digging and fighting and worms and all the things you need to know, and now you have to do the things I say.*" How Tam must have wanted to shriek that night his father had thrown him in the Clay Pool — and now he had just done the same to Jack. He ran his fingers through his wet hair. His cap was gone, he realized. For a moment he thought, *It has drowned in my place.* But he shook his head again.

Then he was surprised by his own words. "Why would we go back?" Jack said to Tam. "We're not scared."

With the breeze came a rustling of leaves and branches, and Rose was suddenly on her feet, stumbling back against Tam. "Is that them?"

Tam only looked up at the sky, then down at Rose, and finally at Jack. He was smiling and flushed, and his eyes were wild. "The morning's coming to an end," Tam announced. "Time to go to Shadow-Town."

Tam walked up to a pair of ash trees that met to form an arch at the southern end of the clearing. Beyond, the horizontal branches of the Tanglewood trees grew in confusion. Tam gave them a crooked smile — and turned and disappeared into the Bound-lands. Jack looked at Rose for a moment before he followed.

Then Rose was alone. She looked back at the Clay Pool.

She could just go back to the long-road by herself now. She could go on west to Great-Aunt Constance as Grandma had told them. Or she could just go back to the old Tender farm and hope Grandma was not going to become ill after all.

She could walk back along the path and down the miles of road alone. She couldn't decide, and couldn't move.

Then she heard a sudden burst of fluttering somewhere low in the trees behind her—and she knew it was probably a grouse puffing itself up, but she turned and pushed through the gap, into the Bound-lands.

"Wait!" she yelled. "Wait for me!"

7

THE BOUND-LANDS

As she struggled through the Tanglewood, Rose noticed footprints here and there in a spot of earth or mud. The prints of regular boots that had been walking towards the Clay Pool, and then prints of little pointy boots, as if children had somehow managed to walk there too.

Here in the Tanglewood, the poplars grew not just in their usual anyhow fashion, but in mad, half-sideways shapes. They stretched low like snakes over the ground before bending upward, and then turned sideways once more. Rose had to push and duck her way through tree after tree growing that way, the turned-up limbs of the living leaning on the fallen trunks of the dead.

Still ahead of her, the boys were walking as nearly beside each other as they could. Like they were just friends again.

Or like they were in a picture entitled *The Conquerors of the Clay Pool,* Rose thought scornfully. A picture she would never want to paint. "Wait," she called again. "Just wait for me!"

But she heard Tam laugh and begin to shout out a song: "Why there are crows, nobody knows — But the gnats are here to bite us."

That song, Rose thought. Even here. And Jack sang after Tam: "Or think of the flies, who trouble the wise — Like other things that spite us!"

Then they did wait for her, and just as Rose tripped over a low branch and fell at their feet, grabbing blindly, they were singing together: "And Roses are scorned, because they have thorns — So ugly that they fright us!"

Rose's hand was caught in some great cluster of silk. As Jack pulled her up, she found more of it clinging to her hair and skin, and she shouted as she brushed the thick webs from her hat and hair and pulled them from her face.

She could hear Tam laugh as he went on ahead, recited part of the same rhyme her grandmother sent her off with: "*Three shadow-boons to fright you — night and webs and whispered Words.*"

"What?" Rose said. "What is it?"

Jack poked her shoulder. "Look up," he said. "See where the sun catches the webs. See how many there are, stretching all along the path."

She brushed at her hat and her face again. "I'm not afraid of spiders."

Jack shook his head. He was still wet and streaked with the marks of the Clay Pool. He looked almost wild, like Tamlin. Or perhaps just wrung out, Rose thought. Perhaps they were all just wrung out already.

Jack gave her a little smile. "No, don't be afraid of spiders."

Rose did her best to keep up as Jack turned to follow Tam deeper into the Tanglewood. "But—but why do the trees grow so strangely?"

"No one knows." Then over his shoulder, Jack added, "Except maybe Tam's dad."

Tam himself had nearly disappeared already in the thick bush, but now they saw him climbing one of the Tanglewood trees as if it were a ladder. When he was near the top he stood swaying above the bush and looked down at them with a shout of triumph. What now? Jack thought. But he tried to stay near Rose as they made their way.

"Slowpokes!" Tam shouted. He tossed something that landed with a *plip* among the dry leaves at their feet. "Here's your dawdle-present!"

Jack had closed his eyes, remembering what Tam's dawdle-presents were like, but when there were two more small wet noises, Rose bent down. Nestling robins—the tiny severed heads of nestling robins. Jack saw another little head strike her cheek and mark it with a splat of blood, then another. When Rose shrieked, she looked so ugly that Jack almost felt she deserved it.

Tam scrambled back down with his bloody blade between his teeth. "*Snick-snick-snick,*" he said.

"Why did you do that?" Rose said, suddenly more frightened by Tam than she had ever been before. "Why would you do that!"

Tam scooped up three of the tiny heads. "I am Tamlin Smith-son, the Badger-Boy, the Beadle's child!" he cried as he juggled them in front of Rose. "I hold secrets! I crawl under! I climb up! I do what I want! Snick-snick, and off with their heads. *Snick-snick!*"

＊ ＊ ＊

After that, Jack stayed close to Rose while they pushed on, and she only looked down and kept silent—thinking about what she had started, wondering how she could get them all to turn back.

She looked down and saw more of the small, pointed boot prints. Not children's boots, and suddenly she understood what they were. She grabbed at Jack's arm. "They are the tracks of the Whisperers," she said—but he shook her off.

"Have you never seen the tracks of Whisperers before?" he said. "You can even see them in bushy hollows among the farms."

"But they're not supposed to go there!" Rose said. "And neither are we—because of the vapors!"

Jack laughed. "Tam has showed me many things we're not supposed to do."

"But—" Rose shook her head as she tried to take that in. Suddenly there were too many things that seemed wrong. The idea of Tam and Jack roaming about the vapor-ridden dells and hollows without fear of the sleeping sickness. That the Whisperers would visit the farmlands where the terms of the Accommodation had forbidden them to go. Too many things seemed wrong at once. So she only said, "But the prints of their boots are pointed at either end. Why are they pointed heel and toe?"

Jack shrugged. "Tam says that it's so you can't tell whether they were made coming or going."

"'*Tam says,*'" Rose repeated. "Oh, you know so much. 'Tam says—Tam's dad says—Tam knows, because his grandfather founded Smithton before it was ever Shadow-Town.' Does Tamlin say their feet are pointed too or just their boots?"

"Ask him yourself," Jack said.

But farther down the path, Tamlin was muttering something as he struggled through the Tanglewood. "What is he saying?" Rose asked.

Jack looked ahead and his face fell. "Be quiet!" he hissed. And after a moment he murmured, "Shadow-Words. They are hard to say and ugly to hear. He is saying a whisper-rhyme, to keep them away."

"But—" Rose began again. "But the Accommodation forbids the Whisperers from visiting the Bound-lands during the day."

Jack made a quiet laugh. "Well, Baby Rosie who always follows the rules, the Accommodation also forbids the farmers from visiting the Bound-lands at night. But Tam slips in sometimes. It forbids farmers from plowing up the copses or burning out the hidden hollows—or using them as muck-holes. And it forbids farmers most of all from visiting Shadow-Town, ever, and where are we going now? And whose idea was that?"

Rose was looking around desperately. "But how can they? Sunlight is the first of the shadow-banes."

"And are you in sunlight or in shadow?" Jack hissed. "Now be quiet!"

Rose tried to hold still, stock-still, and listen—Tamlin's murmuring. The whisper of the mad poplars. And another noise too. Not a rustle—shadow-Words.

She had never thought it would begin so soon, and then Rose saw the stricken look on Jack's face. She began to shake. "*Say them,*" she demanded. "You say the Words too, if you know them."

"Close your ears," Jack said. "They are awful."

He lifted his head to listen to Tamlin, and then Jack made the same terrible sounds: Words that formed far back in his throat to somehow end in whispers: "*Tharkle crith, ca-cawr rok,*" he began, and then he spoke things that were worse Words, and Rose did squeeze her hands over her ears.

Then she could see Jack's face turning white as he spoke, but she heard only her own sounds: the rasp of her breath, the surges of her heart—and over everything, the strange tide of silence.

What did the Words mean? she wondered. Were they a charm or a plea or a bargain?

Tam was pushing his way down the trail again, and Jack followed him, still reciting. Last of all went Rose, awkward as she tried to duck and twist her way through the clutching branches with her hands tight over her ears. She couldn't hear the Words, didn't really want to learn what they meant, but she could feel whispers heavy in the air.

Then, above them all, sharp enough she couldn't help but hear it, a louder rattling hiss. A horrible sound: a stream of Words from the Whisperers themselves. But through all the wind, and the yelling of the boys, and the noise of her own heart, there was one sound among the Words she could still make out—*Rose.*

She jumped and clutched after Jack, but he shook her off again to go on pushing through the bush after Tam.

The Whisperers knew her name. They had called her by name, mixed in with their awful whispered Words. And now that she had taken her hands from her ears, Rose heard the thin voices filling the Tanglewood. One voice, echoing, or a dozen voices, from all around them.

The boys shouted their Words back, but it was the whispers that filled the air. Horrible, ugly whispered Words that she wouldn't listen to. And her name mixed up in them.

"Jack!" Rose shouted. "Jack! Help me, they're calling my name! Jack! What do they want? Jack, help me!"

And then Jack grabbed her and pulled her down, and she tumbled into a small hollow full of leaf and rot and damp earth and lay at Tam's feet. And Jack was screaming at her: "*Shut up!* Shut up! They want to frighten us! Shut up! They want to frighten you so much you will do anything just to have it end! Shut up!"

"But it's the middle of the day!" she shouted. "They

shouldn't even be awake! They can't bear the day and the sun, everyone knows that. They shouldn't even be awake—"

Rose saw Jack's face fill with fear or rage, and she broke off. "They're calling my name!" she said again. Then Rose covered her ears and found that she was sobbing, sobbing until she couldn't breathe.

* * *

When Rose finally stopped and looked up, she saw Jack's white face and Tamlin's drawn mouth, and she took her hands from her ears and heard the Tanglewood quiet again.

Just in this last half-hour, Tam seemed to have become greyer, his face more pinched. "Have they stopped?" she asked. "Have they gone away?"

The boys said nothing, and then she heard it. —*Rose*, she heard. —*Rose Tender—come and work for us, little Rose Tender.*

Her name. How had they known to call her name, known any of their names? Tam suddenly took her hands and clapped them over her ears once more, and his face looked more ugly than ever. Jack had stopped, had sat down among the trees, and she saw that Tam was shouting at him. Then Jack was on his feet, and Tam was dragging her through the Tanglewood.

Tam pulled her, mindless of whipping branches and scratches and cuts, out of the hollow and up the path, and Rose saw he was yelling, and she knew it was something horrible, and she was glad she couldn't hear him—or the press of whispers that followed them. She couldn't really hear anything, except her own name now and then, but somehow she saw things in her mind: shackles and rags, and whips and dust.

Then the bush opened up and they stood on a narrow hillside lane. Farm wagons could never have used it. Horses or dog-carts, maybe. Or maybe it was just a road for Whisperers.

And now Tam and Jack had fallen quiet and Rose let her hands drop. The Words had stopped at last. Through the thickening sky a shaft of light shone down on the shaggy hills below them. Rose fell to her knees, gasping.

"Do you still think me scared?" Tamlin said.

Jack stood panting, and his face was streaked with grime and tears. "They want us to come and work for them," he said. "They will whisper Words until they make us sleep, or until we agree just so they will stop."

"But you knew they were here, even so close to the Bounds," Rose said. "Why would you come again?"

"They weren't like this before!" Jack shouted. "It must be you they want so much. They weren't like this!"

Rose shivered. The gap in the gathering cloud trembled and the shaft of sun moved on and another broke open right above them. In its light Rose saw a sharp gleam of gold somewhere on the edge of the bush they had just left. Gold in the Tanglewood. What did that mean?

Tamlin turned white. "Take out my father's knife," he said to Jack. Then he pulled the dirty harrow blade from his belt and put Rose's fingers around it. "Take this," he said. "The shadow-bane of iron."

Rose looked stupidly down at his iron blade. "But what will you use?"

Tam made a kind of smile that showed his crooked teeth. "Do you want to hear the Words I will speak?" Rose shook her head. "Then run!" he cried.

At first the cousins only stood and stared. Then as Tamlin began to call out awful Words — "*Tharkle, crith*" — he broke a branch from the bush and slashed it at Rose's face. "*Run!*" he shouted again, and then Jack took her hand and they fled down the sandy lane.

When Rose thought to look back, Tam was already gone.

8

AMONG THE BONES

———◆→◆◆←◆———

Some long time later, still on the lane, Jack slowed to a walk at last. "Tam!" Rose was shouting, but if Tamlin was near enough to hear, he didn't answer. "Tam!"

Grasshoppers buzzed around Jack, and above him heavy clouds hung bright in the midday sky. He began to catch his breath. Tam was gone. Now it was just him and little Rosie on the empty lane that ran along the ridge. She had stopped shouting at least.

"You're stupid!" he yelled. "Why did you ever tell Tam that story? Now we will never get to Great-Aunt Constance—" He stopped, because Constance and all her dogs and cats were no longer seeming real to him. Even Grandma's lonely farm, with the vapors rising in the shadows, and Grandma already in her wedding dress, as if she meant to go to the train like sleep's bride, hardly seemed real anymore. Where would he really want to go, if they ever got out of the Tanglewood? To Longhill, somehow—to his mother. And just for a moment, in Jack's mind it seemed as if they might even go back to their old farm, and his father would be there, alive, and everything would be as it was—but, no. No.

Jack stabbed the big knife into the ground and took Rose by the collar. "Now we will never learn if Grandma has really been taken ill. The Whisperers will find us and catch us, and we will sleep and work forever!"

Rose pulled herself free. "Why wouldn't you leave me alone? Why did you keep calling me a baby? Why wouldn't you ever stop? Now we are lost in the Bound-lands and shadow-things follow us—and it's your fault."

"It's your fault," Jack said, but now that the worst of his fright was over, his anger dropped away. Despair rose to take its place.

Rose looked up at him with red and hollow eyes. "At least if Tam were still here, he'd know something to do. At least Tam would actually understand the Words he said."

Jack took a slow breath. "I don't know where this lane goes," he said.

Rose said, "But *they* are in the bush, in the shadows." Jack nodded and she said, "So which way? Which way do we go?"

Jack wiped the sweat from his eyes. The lane ran along a curl of hills that opened to the south. Below them, and for as far as he could see, the hills were hidden beneath the Tanglewood: a sea of dull green seamed in black, rising and falling with the unmoving hills. Here and there a stand of spruce like crests on a wave, but otherwise all covered with the black poplars of the Tanglewood. All the same dusky leaves traced with red: all exactly the same.

In the bottom of the great hollow, miles away, he could see fingers of water gleaming—and south and west of the water, the hills climbed up again. This hadn't been the way Tam had taken him, but he knew that somewhere even beyond those hills was Shadow-Town.

Jack bent to pull his knife out of the ground and saw the marks on the dust. Little pointed boots had walked this way too, many of them, but he said nothing about them to Rose. He only put his back to the sun and pointed to the right. "That way. East for now."

Rose held herself tight to keep from trembling. "Why?"

Jack was silent for a moment. Very loud, from some branch above them that crossed the lane, a crow called. He felt a bead of sweat run down the back of his neck. "Because we can't just sit here. Because that's the way I said."

They walked that way for a long time, hurrying as they could. Once, they stopped and had the rest of the cider, ate the last of their eggs and buns and cheese, but even then they hardly spoke.

It wasn't until the afternoon was well grown that Rose said, "Where are we now?"

Jack stopped and blinked. It was as if their soft footfalls had lulled them to sleep even as they walked. He looked around. They weren't on the lane he remembered. This was some narrower track still. "I don't know."

"No," Rose said, sleepily. No. She tried to clear her head. She hadn't really been asleep, but she had been in a sort of dream. A dream of some dusty hall. And there she sat in gloom—or rattled some old loom—and would sit, always. Never to go home. Not to the old farm on the lake the Speculators had stolen, of course, but not even to the new farm by the river. Never to hear her baby brother again. Never to see her mom and dad. Not even Grandma, not even Jack. Alone.

Her skin crawled to remember it. Then she blinked again and looked up at Jack, at the thing in the trees behind him.

Everything seemed to have become very slow. Rose looked at Jack and the small crooked shadow in the trees behind him. She felt ready to faint. No. She touched the harrow blade she had thrust in her belt, put her hand to her heart, felt the bag of rust.

Jack didn't turn to look behind; he only saw Rose's face change. Saw her hair nearly standing on end. Then Rose fell forward, across the rough undergrowth, still clutching her chest, and Jack made a great shout of terror.

Rose closed her eyes and flicked rust from her fingertips, and from the shadows behind him there was a terrible thin scream.

That made Jack move. He pulled her up and they tried to run again, through the knotted bush, now filling once more with whispers and the echoes of whispers. Rose was whimpering, but Jack was too afraid to pay attention to her. The Whisperers stayed farther back now, and he couldn't hear the Words they hissed, but the echoes sounded across the slopes of the Tanglewood. They beat in on him, and now and then his vision would dim and the trees would seem to become the pillars in some great dusty hall of sleep. Some funeral chamber. And he lay dead within.

"Jack!" Rose yelled. They had been following an animal track, and now it came to an end in a jumble of branches wound about with thick webs. He stood for a moment, panting, trying to recover his senses, or remember some of the Words that Tam had taught him. Whispers still echoing from somewhere. And if he let them overwhelm him they would gather him as a thrall, and Rose too—*Doomed*, he thought. They were doomed.

"Jack!" Rose yelled again, more desperately, and this time it was she who pulled him through some low gap in the bush.

So they hurried, the Tanglewood tearing their clothes, scratching their flesh, shouting to drive off sleep, to wake each other.

Again and again their way was blocked by a knot of thick web and twisted branches and they would have to turn onto some less promising path as they ran from the moving shadows of the Whisperers—always just out of sight but never quiet. Rose was sobbing from fear and exhaustion now, Jack realized. So was he.

Only after some long nightmare-time did they find the narrowest of dry creek beds. It was deep with old leaves, and black branches stretched across it at every angle, but they had left the whispers behind at last.

Rose was just in front when they came to an especially thick overhang. As she ducked under it and went through a kind of curtain of old webs, Jack heard her gasp. An instant later he emerged to find her tottering on the lip of a steep gully, and he grabbed at her. For a moment they stood tottering together, holding tight.

They swayed, and Rose looked down and saw that a shaft of light had slipped out from among the heavy clouds and shone down on something white far below. Bones. The one calm corner of her mind understood that the Ealda had once used this slope as a buffle-kill. And in that long, awful instant, as she clutched Jack's hand and swept her left arm like a windmill to keep her balance, the same part of her mind flickered over all the things that might be done—only her stomach seemed to be falling already. Nothing. Nothing to do. Now they would just drop...

Only beside her, not thinking, Jack grabbed at the branches of a wolf willow and pulled them back. For a moment, they sat on the edge of rough ground before the drop, gasping.

"It doesn't make sense," Rose said. Her face was smeared

with dirt and blood and tears. Jack shook his head, not understanding, still trying to catch his breath.

"It doesn't make sense," she repeated. "They're not supposed to be out in daylight."

Jack made a small bitter laugh. They had just escaped
falling to their deaths, and now Rose was already complain-
ing about the Whisperers. "Baby Rosie isn't the only one who
wants to go where she shouldn't."

"Only because you went there first—you said!"

Jack felt a white Tam-like anger swelling in him—and then
drift away. He was too tired to be like Tam.

Too tired, there at the edge, but then just as he was starting to breath normally again, he heard something in the bush
behind them. He stood and pulled out his bag of rust.

Nervously, Rose got to her feet too, and she looked from
one side to another. There was the narrow creek bed they had
followed. There was the thick Tanglewood. There was the deep
gully behind them.

She looked back down into the gully. In the spring the
creek would have emptied into it. It would be full of water.
But it was dry now, deep and dry, and a great pile of bones
lay heaped at the bottom. Any other day and the bones would
have frightened her. But just now she was listening more than
she was looking, and she heard the faintest whisper and felt
the wash of weariness cast by those Words.

There was no way out. "We have been driven here," she
said softly. "Like the buffles who lie dead below."

"They're coming now," Jack said. His hands trembled as he
poured rust onto them and carefully painted it across her face.

The light rose up the hill and shone on them, and Rose saw
Jack's face: dirty and weary, with little lines she had never
known etched around the corners of his eyes. "You too," she
whispered. And just as Jack pulled the strings of the bag open

once more he heard a quick rattle of Words and saw a crooked face beneath a gleam of gold. He threw his bag of rust.

From the Tanglewood came a longer, more horrible shriek of pain, but neither Jack nor Rose saw how it was made. Without a word, with hardly a thought, they had grabbed each other's hands more tightly and took the last little step over the edge.

At first they managed to slide on the heels of their boots, tearing through weeds, sharp thin branches whipping at their faces. Then, hands still clasped, they could only slide on their seats, Rose's bare legs getting scratched and bloody as they went faster and faster down the slope.

Finally their grasp was torn apart as they began to tumble and roll, their rucksacks flying off as they went falling and bumping, head over heels, until they stopped with a smash at last, and lay among the broken bones and horned skulls of the great beasts who been driven over the edge to die there long ago.

Rose and Jack lay unmoving; not dead, nor unconscious, but hurt and stunned and surprised to be alive.

✳ ✳ ✳

When they moved on again, limping, leaning on each other, they only knew the evening light must come from the west; otherwise they were entirely lost. But they kept walking, following the gully north as it slowly rose from the floor of the Tanglewood, because they didn't know what else to do. By the time they were on a more open trail a breeze washed down from the hills above. Then the sun began to dim, and then the gnats arrived, hungry for their sweat and blood. Finally, it was night.

The moon hadn't risen yet, and few stars shone in the heavy sky. For a long while they only stumbled on through the crowded darkness. It wasn't until they felt a smooth road beneath their feet again at last that the full moon rose. Red and pearly, but in its light they saw careful lines of oak trees to either side.

Jack looked down, but there were none of the pointed prints of the Whisperers on this road. He looked at Rose's face, dark with dirt and rust. "This is not a shadow-road," he said. "We have escaped!"

As the sky broke into rain at last, Rose began to laugh. She took Jack's hand again and they ran that way, careless, through the quickly forming puddles, down the avenue of oaks, until the road came to an end at a tall hawthorn hedge. The hedge had a tall wooden door without latch or handle for a gate, and for a moment they only stood there under the black rain. Then there was a rustle among the trees behind them.

Jack reached by habit for his rust. Gone—and Jack remembered the beginning of the scream the Whisperer had made. Rose saw a red lantern appear from among the trees and slip away behind some shadows. She turned and pushed at the door.

The rain beat harder. Rose pushed at the door and it didn't move, and Jack pushed and it only creaked a little.

—*Rose Tender*, one voice called, and Rose went still.

"Close your ears," Jack gasped. "Don't listen!"

—*Jack Tender*, another called, and now Jack froze too. —*stop and rest—rest and sleep.*

Word, Words. Terrible Words, and maybe they used normal speech too, or maybe he simply had grown to understand them.

—*sleep and come and do our work.*

The rain filled their eyes and ears, swept down so hard it shook the door. "Please!" Rose shouted. "Please, the Whisperers have come for us. Please!"

Hopeless, and Jack could almost feel himself begin to slip into sleep again, the dream of not breathing, of a thin grey land rising over him. He struck the butt of the Beadle's knife against the rough door until it sounded like a great drum.

The red lanterns were coming closer, out of the trees. In their light, and under the rain, they saw the shapes of the Whisperers for the first time. Like enormous crooked dolls. Like small hunched men. A half-dozen, at least. In the flicker of lightning, for an instant, the creatures' eyes shone out: not round like a dog's or tall like a cat's. Sideways. Somehow that was what Rose noticed most of all: how the pupils stretched sideways in the eyes in those flat faces.

Now the thunder came, a long rumble, and as it faded, in the darkness, the Words began again. Horrible Words Tam had never spoken of to Jack. Rose was striking hopelessly at the gate with her little harrow blade, but he knew that wouldn't do anything. He felt his knees go weak.

—*klah, rashk.*

For a moment Jack thought that he might tear Rose's bag of rust away and pour it over his own face. He thought that he would do anything, really do anything at all not to go to Shadow-Town again, not to enter the dream of a thin grey land.

Then from beyond the gate he heard a chorus of howls break out. Great angry dog-voices, or wolf-voices, and he knew there was no hope beyond the gate either, and he only clutched at Rose's free hand.

The gate made an enormous creak and swung in, and the clamor of the wolfish voices was vast now, and the rain seemed to swell and roar with them.

Then Rose was pulling Jack to the side, and all at once a rush of immense dogs was howling past him, out of the gate and into the storm —five, six, a dozen dogs it seemed —charging at the shadows and the red lights already scattering once more among the oaks.

Only one tall man-shape was left to stand before them. Huge, dark, cloaked, and bearing some sharp light. It reached across Jack and pulled the little harrow blade from Rose's hand.

"Who uses rusty tools to scratch my gate?" a great rough voice demanded.

9

THE RED MAN

For a moment the cousins could only stare. The storm and the woods and the dogs and the Whisperers were somewhere behind, but before them a huge burly man filled the open gate in the hawthorn wall.

He had a wide hat and a heavy coat for the storm, and he held Rose's blade in one hand and a bright storm lantern in the other. He loomed over them like some dreadful fate, Rose thought, black against the darkness.

"Tell him who we are," Jack whispered.

The night clouds flared with lightning, but under his broad hat, the big man's features seemed dark and red. Only his hair seemed ghost white.

Thunder came and the clouds flashed again. "Tell him," Jack repeated.

"*Rose-and-Jack*," Rose whispered. Then, more loudly, "We are Rose and Jack. He's Jack. I'm Rose."

"Rose-and-Jack," the man said, and his voice rumbled with the thunder. "Farmers' children from the sandy hills."

"Yes," said Jack. "And you are the Red Man who keeps the Bounds."

The Red Man. Rose felt her heart drop. Their grandma had forbidden them to cross into the Bounds. And she had warned them against troubling the Red Man. "We should never have left the long-road," Rose murmured.

"Shut up," Jack said.

"Farmers' children out at night when they should stay in," the Red Man called. "Farmers' children who have wandered into the Bounds, where they shouldn't be, who scratch my gate with rusty tools."

He stuck Rose's harrow blade into his own belt. "Do you want to stay here, in the shelter of my thorns? Or go and join the Whisperers in the wood-shadows?"

The Red Man, Rose thought. The Red Man. And her thinking didn't go much further than that.

But as the lightning flashed again, Jack swept the wet hair out of his eyes and looked up at the big man. "I know about you. You are not a shadow-friend. You only watch the Bounds."

The sky rumbled as the Red Man stepped aside so that Rose and Jack could enter. "The Bounds, where you shouldn't be," he said. He made a sharp whistle.

Almost at once the dogs were back, snarling and shoving ahead of Rose and Jack to get inside the gate. Huge dogs but not howling at least. Three of them. Had there really been more, Rose wondered, or were these three so big and loud she had only imagined they were a dozen?

In front of the cousins, the dogs were leaping and pushing at one another to get through the gate and into the open wood beyond. Somewhere in the night and the storm behind them Whisperers would be gathering again. Rose stepped in through the gate. The moment Jack followed, the door swung closed behind him, and a small log fell to latch it shut.

The Red Man picked up a gnarled stick that leaned against the hedge. "Follow us, then," he called over his shoulder. He walked with a heavy limp, and now the dogs bolted ahead.

"Don't be afraid, not tonight, not in my House of Woven Trees," the Red Man said. "You will hear the train, but don't mind the whistle. The train won't be coming for you. Not for your bodies. Not for your souls."

When the clouds lit up again, Rose saw a great iron-toothed trap set just beside her feet. She shrieked. "Don't step off the trail," the Red Man called. "Don't fall behind!"

The thunder came and the cousins began to hurry. When the lightning flashed next, Jack jumped, and then there was another flash, and Rose saw that he was right beside a tree with a knot grown into the shape of a quarrelsome face, wide-eyed and staring.

There were more flashes, and more faces, and the wind blew. Jack and Rose stayed together and followed the Red Man and his dogs as closely as they dared.

As they emerged from among the trees, the dogs began to bark and leap once more. Jack watched them closely, his hand at his chest, where the Beadle's knife hung, but Rose only stared at the house. The Red Man's house really was made of trees.

Not built up carefully from notched logs like their grandmother's house, but made of trees that had been taught to grow and weave themselves together. Different trees, Rose saw as they came closer: maple and ash and birch and oak, joined more closely than any carpenter's work, so there were no gaps for the wind or the storming rain to find—and from its top emerged the trunk of a great cedar, rising until it disappeared in the night sky, its branches spread out to shelter the house below.

As the Red Man and his dogs pushed their way inside, Rose paused at the threshold, remembering their grandma's words. She put her hand on Jack's shoulder. "*Not if you want to come back children,*" she whispered.

Jack looked at her, at the storm, and the rain behind them. Then he shrugged her hand off. "I haven't been a child for a long time," he said and stepped inside. After a moment, Rose followed him.

In the House of Woven Trees on that warm wet night, a small fire still burned in a great stone hearth, and the dogs' nails clicked loudly on the wood-tiled floor as they sniffed over the house. Odd shadows jumped against the intricate, tree-patterned walls.

The biggest dog jumped up and put its huge paws on Rose's shoulders. As she staggered under its weight, the dog opened its jaws and made a wolfish noise deep in its throat. "*Jack!*" she whimpered, but the dog had already moved to do the same to him, and Jack had to turn away from its orange eyes.

Rose looked to the Red Man, but he busied himself with the kettle and paid no attention as the other dogs looked them over too. The dogs moved on to sniffing Rose and Jack's boots, and then they sniffed one another and made small yaps and growls until the Red Man knocked his staff against the floor. Then they arranged themselves on a rug before the hearth.

"They smell to see if they like you, and if you are people or the other things that walk on two feet," the Red Man said. He showed them the wooden chairs where they should sit.

"What if they didn't like us?" Rose asked.

"They would like us; we are people," Jack said.

"Some people are faithless and some people are just," said the Red Man. "Some generous, some cruel."

"Which kind are you?" Jack said.

"*Jack —,*" Rose whispered in fright.

But the Red Man looked down at them, his eyes lake green and calm. "I am none of your kind at all," he said. Inside, the kettle whistled; outside, thunder rolled.

The Red Man gave them biscuits to go with their tea, and then he sat heavily in a wide armchair. For a long time he only stared into the flames, as if Rose and Jack weren't there at all. The biggest dog moved to his master's feet, and Rose saw that the other two only seemed to be resting by the hearth. Really, they were watching the cousins, and she hardly wanted to move. "Drink your tea," the Red Man said at last, without taking his eyes from the fire. "There is nothing else for you tonight, but I will give you work in the morning."

As her eyes met Jack's, Rose felt as though the chair and the floor had begun to sink, and all the weariness of the long day rose up and closed over her.

"But you are not a farmer," she said. "Is there much work to do here?"

The Red Man looked up from the fire and stared at her as if he were a long way off. "I have my own little farm," he said. "My goats and cows and berries. That is a little work. And I keep the Bounds. That is much more work. And since I came down from the east, I have tended the whole of the sandy hills. That is some work, much more work. Harder work."

"Did you come from the east to settle here like the farmers?" Jack asked.

"Before the farmers," the Red Man said. "I began this work before the Whisperers. Before the Ealda ever hunted or the buffle ran." He leaned back, and stretched and snapped his suspenders, and made a noise: *hrmph.* "Some work," he said again, and he nodded and made a long yawn. "Here and the whole of the sandy hills. I'll find you some work to do."

Then they just sat, listening to the ticking of the big wooden clock while Rose watched the dogs. At first she thought of how she might paint them — *The Dogs Gathered at the Fire.* But then she noticed that one always looked at Jack, and one always looked at her. Each time she took a bit of biscuit she saw its eyes flicker. Each time she sipped at her tea. Just as Rose began to feel it was hardly safe to move at all, Jack whispered, "Maybe you should try patting him."

The Red Man startled them with a loud laugh. "Yes," he said, and the fire suddenly rose and his skin glowed like an ember beneath his ash-white hair. "Yes. Good doggy. I'll pat you, good doggy!"

There was a wooden rattle and whirl, and the clock opened to show a ring of little carved dogs. One rolled forward and raised its head to make a small chiming howl and then another; twelve of them, and then they all howled together. Rose had never seen anything like it, but she thought, *Midnight — only midnight!* Jack stared at the clock too, thinking of all that had happened since they had woken that morning. They had crossed the Bounds. They had stepped over the Red Man's threshold.

The Red Man laughed again. "Boys and girls and good doggies should sleep now," he said, and he stood by the great trunk and reached for a door in the ceiling that let a narrow ladder down. "Two beds up there," he said. "One little window. Just right."

Rose was looking at him fearfully, but Jack looked the Red Man in the eye and nodded.

"Just right," he said. "Thank you."

But as he followed Rose up the steps, it seemed to Jack that the night before, when they had gone up the stairs at Grandma's house, had been a long time ago.

At the top of the ladder, he looked down to see the shining eyes of the watching dogs. The Red Man was looking up too.

"Don't be afraid, not tonight," he rumbled. "You will hear the train, but don't mind the whistle. It won't be coming for you. Not for your bodies. Not for your souls. Not tonight."

Then he raised the ladder, and Jack and Rose were shut up in an attic room once more.

Beds to either side of the great cedar pillar here, with mattresses made of knotted rope, and over them the arms of other trees met to form the rafters. The polished wood shone dimly in the candlelight. "He says we'll be safe tonight," Rose whispered. "But what will happen tomorrow?"

The shadows made her face seem strangely gaunt and old, and Jack turned away and looked into the corner of the eaves. "What will happen tomorrow? Tomorrow we won't wake up in Shadow-Town at least. And tomorrow Grandma won't make us fetch eggs or clean the silo. But otherwise it will just be the same. If we hadn't turned off the road, if we had got to Great-Aunt Constance, maybe tomorrow would have been different. But tomorrow it will only be the Red Man who makes us work instead of Grandma. And we will have to do whatever tedious or terrible task he says."

"For how long?"

For a moment Jack couldn't speak. He grabbed the heavy bedpost and squeezed until he saw stars. Finally he made a vicious whisper: *"How long do you think?"* He pulled at the post until it began to squeak. *"Why should I know? How long do you think?"* He fell back and lay until he could breathe normally again.

Then there were only the sounds of the passing storm, and the squirming the children made as they tried to find a comfortable way to lie, despite their aches and scratches and bites.

Faraway thunder. The house, built around a living tree, swaying in the last of the wind. Rain washing out of the wooden spouts, rain still falling on the roof above their heads, shaken out of the sodden branches above. Dripping and dripping.

Jack felt sure at least that this was a safe house in the storm, but he doubted he would ever sleep.

After a while he thought he heard Rose softly weeping, and this time Jack found himself saying, "We will be here until I think of how to escape. I'm the brave one. I'll think of how to escape." He didn't know if Rose heard him over the sound of the water, but slowly she seemed to become quiet.

Jack had just begun to find his way into sleep after all when they heard the long whistle of the coffin-train. Closer here than at Grandma's, but still far away, echoing through some unknown hills. The whistle blew and blew again, and its note grew higher and higher.

It was the train that had taken his father's coffin away, Jack knew, but he didn't know its route, didn't know where it stopped at last. The whistle blew again, far and wide, a sound from some unknown place, and Jack heard the far-off rattle of its tracks. The note began to slide lower and softer. Then a long time passed before it sounded again, smaller and lower yet, like a message from some farther place, some lost and lonely world.

"Not for us, not tonight," he said, and this time he knew Rose heard him.

After a time the curtains of sleep began to open once more, but this time it was Rose who broke the spell.

"But where is Tamlin?" she whispered.

Tam.

Jack found himself hissing desperately. "*Shut up!* Why are you bothering me? Shut up!"

II

—•‧••‧•—

THE COFFIN-HALL

10

NIGHT TERRORS

———◆━◆◆━◆———

Where is Tam? Jack and Rose had wondered as they fell asleep at last, and as they slept in that dark attic and heard thunder rumbling they shared the same dreams. *Where is Tam?*

In their dreams Tam was crawling through some tunnel in the sandy soil, dirty and alone but for the ants and the prairie dogs and the pale grasping roots. In their dreams Tam was a thrall in Shadow-Town; or Tam had been thrown in the warm pool and was drowned and alive at once; or Tam gestured about and the Whisperers bowed to a king on a broken throne, and were quiet even beyond their whispering.

And the Whisperers who bent to the king smiled, as much as they could with their flat faces. He was the king that all the thralls must serve, yet he had to serve the Whisperers' bidding. He was their king, but he belonged to *them*. His face was hidden by the shadow of his crown, but he was the king of silence and shadows, of the dead and the drowned forever and ever.

But then the king grasped his own crown as if he meant to take it off, and Tam looked out of the dream and into their eyes.

Here is the throne, here is the crown made of bone and iron. See the majesty that rules the drowned and the dead and the quiet. How I would rather be out of this thin grey dream and crawling in the dirt to trouble Baby Rosie.

Then it was as if Jack and Tam were the same—or as if it was just Jack who sat in Shadow-Town while Tam slept in Jack's bunk in Grandma's attic. And the Whisperers bent their knees to the king, and made some long hiss, and in that dream Jack or Tam would never hear a warm voice again, not from Rose, not from the Beadle, not from Jack's mother, not even from Grandma.

* * *

Sometime after the storm had passed, but still in the dead of night, Jack woke with a gasp. All awake, all at once. His heart racing.

At first he only lay there, still, watching the deep shadows gently swaying, remembering he was in the House of Woven Trees. He could hear the movement of the house. He could hear Rose breathing evenly, asleep in the other bed. And the Red Man snored in the floor below them; and somewhere in the ground below him, Jack knew, crawled wormy things that neither actually woke nor slept, blind and silent among the deep roots.

But no, it was nothing about the house that had woken him. It had been the dream. The dream of the king of silence and shadow. The king who was ruler of the thralls but servant of the Whisperers.

In the House of Woven Trees that night, the attic was warm, and the creaking walls began to seem too close, as though they would sway in and smother him.

The Red Man had helped them escape the Whisperers, but who would help them escape the Red Man? *"Don't be afraid of the train,"* he had said, *"not tonight."* Not tonight, because the Red Man had been there almost forever, but still there was work enough for them to do; there would be work until it was their night to ride the train — body and soul.

Who would help them? Who would ever be cunning and daring and mad enough to find a way into the Red Man's estate? *"Where is Tamlin?"* Rose had said before sleep had taken her. And he remembered again his dream of the king in the crown of bone and iron, and Jack thought of Tam, wicked and mean and brave. Tam was the only one who would ever come, but in his dream Tam had entered the long grey doom of the king.

Not just a dream, Jack thought. A real dream. A dream that came because even across the hills he had felt the weight of the doom settling over Tam. Or because asleep he had understood what he hadn't wanted to know while he was still awake: what had happened to Tamlin Badger-Boy, who hated Rose but had given her his own iron blade even as he was about to be taken by the Whisperers, even as he shouted Words.

Who would ever help Tam? Who would ever want to see Tam again?

All at once, Jack found he had slipped off his bunk and was crouching in his stocking feet beside Rose. For a moment she seemed so pale and still that he wondered if she had breathed some sickly fog in the Tanglewood and passed in her sleep, but then she threw one arm over her forehead.

No. He would come back for her if he could, but Rose would never come with him willingly, not for this. He checked that he still had the big knife in its wooden sheath, and then, very gently, he reached out and took the bag of rust from Rose's neck.

Jack tied his boots so they hung over his shoulders, and quietly as he could, he lowered the steps. There was a wooden creak that startled him, and he heard one of the dogs stir, and it took him a while before he worked up his nerve again. Then he crept backward down the ladder.

In the hall, the fire still burned in red coals and ashes, and Jack stopped dead when he saw the Red Man still seated before it, leaning back in his chair. In light of the dying fire, he seemed as odd and sinister as in the moment he had first appeared through the gate. His skin was flushed; his hair seemed bone white. But the Red Man's eyes were closed, and he nodded slowly in time with his breathing, and his dogs lay still too, stretched out before him.

From the door, Jack looked back just as the clock struck. Two of the little wooden dogs howled, and he slipped out onto the damp stone step and around the corner of the house, and into the wide night.

* * *

Jack pulled on his boots and tried to catch his breath. The stars were out at last and he saw their shapes: the Great Bear and the Loon. And in the southeast, high above the tree-roughened line of the hills, the hazy moon, with the bright Wizard Star swinging below. A strange moon, a red moon, and somehow it drew him.

Because he hardly knew where he was, after so many hours in the mazy Tanglewood. But if he followed the moon he must go southeast and then he would leave the Red Man's estate by a way other than the thorn-gate. And then, still following the moon as it wheeled across the night, in time he would cross some branch of the great river to the south.

He laced his boots again, more tightly. The blood-red moon would take him to the river, which marked the end of the Bound-lands, and somewhere across the river was Shadow-Town. And somewhere in Shadow-Town he would find the king with the crown of bone and iron. Tam. Tamlin Badger-Boy, mean and wild and dirty.

Yes, he would follow his dream and this blood-red moon, through the whisper-haunted Tanglewood, even to forbidden Shadow-Town, to find Tam. Because no one else ever would.

So Jack headed southeast through the Red Man's estate, over boards laid down through rows of raspberry bushes, over vegetable plots, past flower gardens. Then across some wide pasture under the strange moonlight, and finally to another gate that opened into the pressing Tanglewood.

He stood for a moment, wondering what was beyond it. Then from back in the House of Woven Trees, one of the dogs began to howl. Jack slipped out and the gate swung shut behind him. He was in dark bush now, and strands of web lay across his face. He was alone in the Tanglewood in the black night and the dog howled on, and all at once Jack's fever to escape had broken.

He tried the gate from the outside, but it was locked against him now, of course. He was alone in the Tanglewood, foot-sore and weary before he even started.

What a very stupid thing he had done.

✳ ✳ ✳

For an hour or so, Jack pushed through the night wood, still trying to follow the moon, but of course he could only manage whatever way was easiest.

Sometimes he saw the branches and leaves become reaching arms and faces and eyes in the blackness; sometimes he thought he heard rustling beyond the sound of his own footsteps.

He could only manage the easiest way, he thought, but of course it was the easiest way for the Whisperers too. If there had been more than moonlight, he knew he would have seen a hundred sets of boot prints on the path beneath him, prints that were pointed heel and toe. He had not been brave. Some madness cast by his dream, by this red moon and the Wizard Star that swung beneath it, had come over him. Soon the whispers would gather, and this time he would not have the strength to say the Words.

This time the Whisperers would catch him in their webs of sleep, just as they had caught Tam, and take him away to some endless labor, while Rose would stay on alone with the Red Man. None of them would ever find their way home.

Jack felt as though some black water were rising over him. Foul, bitter like everything since his father's death; drowning deep, and he was swallowed within it.

In the distance, Jack heard the rattle of the train, heard a long, low whistle; low but rising higher. *But not tonight*, he remembered. It hadn't come for him tonight.

The rustlings he might have been dreaming became more articulate: —*Jack Tender—Jack.*

But Jack was already running again, heedless of twigs and thorns and scratches, not listening.

—*Jack Tender has come back.*

The train. The Whisperers were coming for him tonight, not the coffin-train. But the train ran on iron rails, and iron was a shadow-bane.

He would go to it.

11

THE TANGLEWOOD
AT NIGHT

Just before the whispers grew too loud to bear, Jack saw some long gleam in the dark. Rails, right before him. The railway at last.

For a moment he let himself rest between the tracks, cosseted by the iron. Then he got up again and ran, stumbling over the ties, gasping in the smell of the ash and the creosote. He ran, and the whistle of the coffin-train grew closer and higher. How close? The length of a few fields? It wasn't about to devour him, not yet—but already it was loud enough to drown out the whispers that moved beside him in the Tanglewood. Then the bush opened and suddenly Jack was running across a narrow bridge towards the sound of the train. A bridge over a strange dark creek that wound through the Bound-lands and disappeared without ever going anywhere, a long bridge—but he could still cross it in time, Jack thought. Far below him, water shivered under the blood-red moon—but Jack hardly looked down because he could hear the coffin-train coming closer, and if he met it on the bridge he would die.

Coming closer, and still he ran towards it. He couldn't see it yet, hidden behind some turning of the hills, but the train whistle echoed, wide and piercing, off the water below. Perhaps only a field's length beyond the bridge. Jack ran, gasping, haltingly, over the open ties. Now he heard not just the train whistle but the huffing of the fire-engine, the rattle of the cars. He stumbled but didn't fall, and some corner of his mind was happy he had left Rose behind—*little Rosie*—because she would have been too scared. Jack felt his heart ready to burst, but still he wasn't over the bridge. Was the train too close after all? He looked down and wondered whether there could be enough water in the blackness below to preserve him if he fell.

Then a sudden, terrible noise. The worst thing Jack had ever heard, worse even than the curses of the Whisperers. Iron wheels scraping across steel track: a high, rough, awful sound, louder every second—and finally through the trees ahead, just around a little bend, Jack could see the headlight of the train, growing brighter. But Jack was over the bridge now and the train had not caught him, and he was not dead.

Not dead yet, but running too hard to stop all at once, and then the toe of his boot caught on a tie. Jack fell, measuring his length along the track. He lay with his face in the gravel and waited for the coffin-train to crush his skull.

The squeal came to an end.

He hadn't died, but for a moment Jack could only lie there still, trying to understand. The train had come close, but it had stopped, and he hadn't died.

* * *

Jack got up and stumbled stupidly down the track. Just around a little bend the coffin-train waited. Jack stopped and stared. He hadn't died, and now the whole world seemed somehow newly made—even this thing on the tracks that had nearly killed him, this long black thing, the fire-engine at its head making long, low hisses. He might never have seen a fire-engine, might never have helped carry his father's coffin into a train.

The engine gleamed blackly in the light of a bright globe lantern. It had a sharp beak: a prow, a cowcatcher, on its front. And windows like eyes, with a dim shadow moving back and forth behind them. Jack noticed the station house as if he had never seen one before either: the narrow peaked roof, a wide door with flags hung over it—stars and snow for the Dominion, a cogged gear for the Clatterfolk who ran the trains.

And the smells seemed as though they could have been carried from some unknown country too: the greasy smoke from the fire-box; the hot steel; the cinders and gravel of the rail bed; the oily black of the squared-off timbers—all cutting through the night damp of the enclosing forest. He heard sounds so familiar he had almost forgotten them: the panting boiler, the ticking of the metal cooling in the idle train. The flutter of the flags above the station door. And the wind in the leaves of the Tanglewood. The Tanglewood, in the Boundlands, and then all the things in his mind reformed and became whole and simple again.

He had thought he was going to die, but instead he was at a station house in the Tanglewood, staring at the train he had hoped never to see again in life. But even if the iron shriek of the train had driven them back, the Whisperers must still wait for him in the wood beyond.

Jack took the steps up the platform two at a time. He stood with his hand on the door, caught for a moment between his fears. The station house, the whispers that still echoed in his ears, the machine that stood trembling on the tracks. Then the fire-engine made a great sudden hiss of steam, and Jack found himself inside the station house.

And he was there alone, except for the bugs flittering around the lamps on the oak desk. An empty chair; a tall shelf of pigeon-holes. But it had no mourners' benches after all. No coffin-hall. Jack breathed more easily. Of course, this little station would only handle the mail. It might even be here just for the Red Man's sake. There would be no need for a funeral station, not this far into the forest.

Jack stepped back out onto the platform and looked at the fire-engine, the tender-car behind it, stacked with coffins. A half-dozen more cars. A caboose. And beyond the circle of lantern light, the crowding blackness of the Tanglewood closed in on every side.

"Hello!" Jack yelled over the noise of the engine. The Engineer looked down at him from the side of the cab, but the Clatterfolk rarely spoke, in spells or words or even their own clatter-talk. And none of the Clatterfolk were as big as a grown man—or as big as Jack either, but to him they were more frightening than any giant. The Engineer was all black. Night black, Jack thought. Soot black—and beyond the Engineer the door to the fire-box was open, and what was inside burned red, and brighter than red.

The Engineer patted the levers to the engine. The coal-black hand moved slowly, as if there were all the time in the world. It scratched carefully among the knobs and dials.

"Can you help me?" Jack called. The Engineer shrugged and turned back to the levers and gauges. The engine's smoke-stack was blowing dark clouds now, obscuring the stars, and Jack shivered as though he felt snow on the back of his neck. He turned, but there was nothing to see. Only the train and the station house.

The fire-engine made a sound and a little lurch, as if it were about to wake, and Jack saw a man—a living man, bigger than the Engineer so that he had to stoop as he worked, bare-chested and grimy. He pulled a black coffin from the tender by himself and slid it all the way forward into the flames and slammed the door of the fire-box shut. The coffin-train. He was the fire-man for the coffin-train. He looked out at Jack.

"Tell me if I am safe here, at least!" Jack begged. The Engineer looked at him, then at the fire-man, and seemed to speak, but it was clatter-talk, and Jack heard nothing in it but hisses and rattles.

The fire-man wiped his sweaty face and nodded at Jack. He called out hoarsely, "Anyone can come to a station house. Does that make you safe or sorry? Anyone. Even you. Even them."

The Engineer struck a bell, pulled a chain, and made the whistle blow, almost too loud for Jack to bear. A black hand pushed on a great lever and the fire-engine shook and rattled on the steel rails. From the far end of the train, Jack heard another clattering voice and then the fire-man looked at him again and yelled, "*All aboard!* All aboard for Shadow-Town!"

Shadow-Town. Of course, even Shadow-Town would receive the train, would have a station left from when it was only Smithton, long ago. The whole train shuddered, and Jack heard the squeak as the wheels began to turn. It was leaving him behind for Shadow-Town. He looked into the trees. The Whisperers or the train.

"Can I come with you?" Jack called desperately.

The Engineer looked at him without answering.

"*Can I*—," Jack began again, but the Engineer turned away.

The fire-man looked Jack over and mopped his forehead with a checkered handkerchief. "This is the coffin-train. It carries the dead; it carries the mail."

Jack looked down the line at the coffin-tender and then the half-dozen other cars that followed the engine. The first car was just edging into the light of the station lantern. It carried the dead; it carried the mail. No living passengers. For once he wished Rose were with him because she would have had an idea, even a stupid idea, even if it was just some notion of how she might paint the black train and the smoke against the night sky.

In the gap between two cars, Jack saw a shadow move in the forest. The train was still moving only very slowly but smoothly now, deliberately. Slow, but slowly getting faster.

But as the second car passed, Jack pulled out the Beadle's big knife and cut his finger and then wrote in blood across his other arm, wrote the only address he could think of: *Tam, Shadow-Town.* As he wrote, the third car passed, then the fourth and fifth.

And there were still iron wheels turning on the rails and the chuffing fire-engine to hold the Whisperers away, but now there was only the caboose left, and when that had passed, he would be left to wait alone in the station house to greet the quiet ones who would be calling.

Jack held up a penny.

A white hand reached out and pulled him onto the step behind the caboose. And all at once the train was no longer leaving; for Jack, it was the big station lantern that was disappearing into the darkness.

He had gotten away. He had written in blood to mail himself to Shadow-Town of his own free will, and now he traveled there with the dead.

Jack turned to look at the pale figure who had pulled him aboard.

12

THE COFFIN-TRAIN

At his father's funeral, Jack had been one of the pallbearers, so that night he had sat with the others at the funeral station and kept the coffin-watch.

Rose's father had been there, come to help his brother pass, and two uncles from his mother's side, and two other farmers who had liked to work with his father. Jack had known all those men well enough, but now he hardly remembered who they had been. He only remembered waiting in the dark station house with grown men sitting in their best clothes. Now and then one of them might have given him a nod, but it was quiet except for the small noise of the lantern and the bugs that circled it. Now and then Jack would realize he had been thinking about something else, and his head would snap up and he would see his father's coffin and remember.

But he must have nodded off, because he woke up when Rose's father put a hand on his shoulder and said, "It's coming." There was a loud, long whistle, and the sound of braking wheels, and then they had lifted the coffin again. Six pallbearers, but even so Jack would always remember his surprise at how easy the work was. *It should weigh more,* he had thought. *He was a strong man once. It shouldn't be so easy to carry your father's coffin.*

He didn't want to think about their burden, about the work of keeping it level, about the shifting weight inside. And he didn't want to see the train either, not really. So he had looked down the whole time and only seen the fire-engine out of the corner of his eye: a black iron thing that sputtered steam and flame.

Then came a queer, rattling sound. *"The little Conductor wants his two pennies,"* Rose's father told him, and Jack had pulled out the leather bag and held it up for his uncle.

"You do it, please," he whispered.

"A good berth," his uncle told the small pale figure. *"And keep the fire-box burning hot. Let his ashes rise."*

"Burn it hot," the other men had repeated, and then Jack after them, *"and let his ashes rise."*

Then the Conductor's queer voice again, like a jet of steam and the rattle of gears, and after a few minutes the train had whistled and started up. The pallbearers stayed and watched it leave, and then the men had snapped at their suspenders, and shifted their caps, and turned back from the platform.

Even on the long walk home, Jack hardly looked up, so he didn't know which of his father's friends had spoken to him: *"It's not so bad, son. The Clatterfolk are little fellows, you know, not as big as you. The one who works the engine is soot black and the one who works the post and the funeral trade is ash white that's all. And they'll take care of your father now. They'll help him pass into the sky."*

"They'll help us all pass someday," one of his uncles had said. *"Straight from the flames to the wind and let that be that."*

"*I don't want my body to burn*," Jack had said. "*I don't want to rise into the sky. We shouldn't have to die and have our bodies burned.*"

His father's friend had said, "*We all die. Didn't your dad teach you better? Aren't you a farmer's son?*"

Jack's tears had started at last. "*Take your time, son,*" Rose's father had said. "*Let's walk on,*" he told the others.

So Jack had sat by himself in the dirt and for a long time he could only weep. As if he had been a baby.

✳ ✳ ✳

Now Jack looked at the pale figure who had pulled him aboard, who was pocketing his penny. The Conductor was ash white, dead white, Jack thought, and he found himself asking, "Are you the same one?"

For an answer the Conductor made some sound like a falling piston and gestured for Jack to come farther in. The caboose was low, built for the small Clatterfolk, like the rest of the train, and it was hardly high enough for Jack to stand. It had a small desk fitted out with pigeon-holes like at the station house. But these weren't empty; they were nearly filled with letters and small parcels tied to labels with the obscure marks of the Clatterfolk.

The Conductor scratched a line with a few careful shapes on a label and tied it around one of Jack's buttons, then opened the door onto the platform between the cars and gestured for Jack to go through.

Jack hesitated. The door let in the dark and the rattle of the train in the night, and the doorstep to the next car swayed back and forth. Then the Conductor made a sharper kind of clatter, and Jack jumped across and pulled the door open.

But this car held no desk, no mail. He saw black silk

gleaming in the light of a few small candle-lanterns set in a narrow aisle between rows of coffins. A coffin-car—Jack turned and tried to push his way back out and at once found himself swinging out over the hinge between the cars, clutching desperately to the door.

"Only postage!" Jack yelled towards the closed caboose. "Only to Shadow-Town! Don't give me a coffin berth! I am to be shipped to Tam in Shadow-Town! Don't burn me in the fire-box with these!"

As he swung between the cars, just for an instant Jack thought of letting go. He might land in the reaching Tanglewood with nothing more than scratches and bruises to show for it. But as the train swayed, he felt how easy it would be to miss his footing, to fall or be dragged off, to let his feet slip under the hinged platform. How quickly the train would crush him under its wheels at last.

Then came hoarse words from inside the coffin-car, and Jack nearly jumped anyway: *"Better here with the properly dead than working in Shadow-Town."*

But they were the words of a living man, of the fire-man coming down the car to help him.

* * *

All the rest of the night, the coffin-train wound its way through the sandy hills, and the crowding bush was full of sharp and wicked shadows, and the gleaming eyes of animals that stopped to watch the iron beast.

Every now and then the Engineer let the whistle out, and Jack heard it differently now; neither fading nor rising but one long clear note that echoed back from the slopes of the Tanglewood.

The railway followed an easy, winding course. It curled

around the tallest hills; it stepped along narrow bridges over creeks and gullies; it rose slowly up the northern slopes. But Jack saw almost none of this; he only sat crouched in an empty berth while the fire-man shared out food and drink and spoke about the long life he'd lived on the coffin-train.

"I'd had a dread of it since I was your age," the fire-man said in his smoke-scorched voice. "To be burned up in that little fire-box, even when I was good and dead already. *'Burn it hot and let the ashes rise,'* they say when a coffin ships aboard, but that was horrible to me.

"And my father said, 'Do you want to live by the sea, then, where they'll dump you in the ocean deep, and see how long that will take before you find your way beyond the cracks of the world?'

"And my mother said, 'Do you want to live among the Ealda, then, and get buried in the earth and wait till the world is refashioned before you find your way into the heavens?'

"And I said, 'I don't want any of those things. I want to rise up without never having been moldered in the ground, or dissolved in the salt sea, or most of all without never having been all burned up in the fire-box, like I was no more than some trash in a barrel, just to drive the train.'

"Then my parents wept, and they said no one but the Clatterfolk could promise me that, and I would have to talk with them, thinking I was too afraid of the burning to ever go that near the engines.

"But I had it in my head that nothing would be so bad as to wait for the train to come for me. So that night I walked alone to the station and I waited there until I heard the whistle of the train. And the train that came was called the *Iron Stellification.* The *Iron Stellification,*" he repeated, as though he still couldn't believe the glory of it. "Or the *Stellify,* for short. If you want to be short about a thing of such significance.

"And I tried to ask the Engineer, but it only shook its soot-black head and clattered, and I tried to ask the Conductor, and it only shook its ash-white head and hissed. But finally I said, 'I will do anything, only I don't want to rise to the heavens in burned-up ashes,' and then they gave me my reward for being afraid.

"'Come aboard,' the Engineer said, and he spoke in people-talk at last, 'and be my fire-man, work your way over the Blue Mountains instead, when you will find your end at last.' And he gave me leather gloves and a poker and a shovel and began to teach me the trade. And that was this very train," he said at last, proudly. "That was the *Stellify*—that was the *Iron Stellification*, which we now travel."

The first fingers of dawn were showing through the open door at the back of the car by the time the fire-man finished his story. Jack studied the man's face, seamed with dirt. "Now you will ride the train and feed other coffins into the fire-box forever," Jack said.

The seams in the fire-man's face seemed to make a smile. "Not forever," he said. "Year by year they build the lines farther west. It's funny, after so long handling coffins, it doesn't frighten you anymore, but then it's too late, and you only want to help the work. Year by year, west and west towards the Blue Mountains and higher and higher until they cross the peak. Then they'll cry, 'All off for west of west, and the heavens above!' and we'll step out easy and free and pass beyond the cracks of the world at last."

"How long has it been?" asked Jack. "How long will it be?"

The fire-man shrugged. "On the train we see the world go by, and night and day, but the time doesn't really belong to us anymore. Only the Conductors keep the clocks."

"You didn't live your proper life," Jack said. "And you'll have to wait so long before the next one."

The fire-man shook his head. "I wouldn't recommend it. But there's more like me on the trains with the same story. On the *Great Eastern*—on the *Western*, the *Northern*. On the *Flammifer*. A long, lonely time we have, except when we meet now and then to have a whoop-up in some roundhouse under-hill, but we help others pass another way. Up over the mountains," he added.

Dawn was coming, and Jack could see the sky had nearly cleared. The whistle blew sharp and long.

There was a shudder and a horrible iron squeal and Jack could feel the train begin to slow. Just for a moment, through the door in the front, he saw a burning sliver of dawn reflected somehow, and then it was gone, and he felt the train shaking as it began to cross a rickety bridge. Below them old houses and sheds and broken-down warehouses were scattered on low ground by the great river which marked the end of the Bound-lands and the beginning of the shadow-march. Jack felt his heart begin to race.

Ahead he saw they were coming to a big station at last. A funeral station, built up on the embankment south of the river. And just beyond the station rose a high and imposing old building. The Tall House.

The Tall House.

The little Conductor opened the door at the back of their car, carrying a bell in one pale hand and ringing it nearly loud enough to wake the dead. The Conductor spoke in words Jack could understand at last, and the clattering voice sounded quiet now, even sad.

"Shadow-Town. All off for Shadow-Town."

The fire-man stood up and put on his cap. "Stand there by the wide door and when we stop you'll be able to step right off into the coffin-hall—into Shadow-Town, on your own two feet."

He gave Jack a nod. "Good luck, boy."

13

SHADOW-TOWN

———◆◆◆◆◆———

In the dim light of early morning, before Rose had even woken to find him gone, the train shuddered and squealed, and Jack watched the grey buildings above the embankment come closer.

The slowing train ran above a long main street fronted by abandoned shops with shattered windows. Dim avenues stretched out beyond them, the houses broken and leaning against the wind. But no people — only two bony dogs running alongside the train. And then they were coming into the station.

A fine old building — as these things were judged in that part of the Dominion, where nothing yet was so old it needed brick or stone to still be standing — with a gabled turret and many-windowed bays. But the windows were all cracked and splintered now, and the turret flew no flag.

The fire-engine and the cars groaned as the train crept the last few yards, and they passed the sign on the side of the station. A proper big brass sign, and it would have said Smithton when it was built, in the long-ago time even before his grandma was born. But the letters had been chiseled off and replaced with a smear of charcoal—which stood for Shadow-Town, Jack knew.

The fire-man had been exactly right; when the *Stellify* finally shuddered to a stop, Jack was looking right into the open doors of the old coffin-hall. Inside, two men stood before a wooden writing desk, dressed in city clothes, with green visors to preserve their eyes and brass arm bands to keep their sleeves from the ink. One of the men was looking at a watch on a silver chain.

"Right on time, Master Snap," he said.

"*Barely* right on time, Master Whick," said Snap, and he looked up just as Jack realized who they were.

"But 'right on time' is an absolute statement by itself, Master Snap—"

Without taking his eyes from Jack, Snap interrupted, "*Master Whick*—"

"—so 'barely' doesn't enter into it," Whick continued, "no more than you could be *extra perfect* or *somewhat unique*."

"Master Whick!" This time Whick looked up and saw Jack's eyes too.

The Speculators were silent for a moment. "Well, here's an odd thing, Master Snap," Whick said. "Come from the coffin-train with no coffin! And these aren't coffin-clothes. An odd thing!"

"You, thing! Boy!" Snap called. "Come down and account for yourself!"

Jack was too surprised to know what to say. "See how stupid he is, Master Whick," Snap said. "And half asleep, of course."

Whick came over to take Jack's arm and pull him down into the coffin-hall. "Coffin, boy—coffin! Coffin!"

Then very slowly, "*Where—is—your—coffin?*"

"I don't have a coffin," said Jack. He looked back and forth between the Speculators. Neither of them seemed to recognize him. But then, he must look very different from the clean Jack they had seen the morning before, just after he had set out from his grandma's farm.

Snap raised his cane and poked it into the hollow of Jack's throat so that he wanted to choke. Pushing a little harder with each word, Snap spoke to him as if he were an idiot: "Then—why—are—you—on—the—coffin—train?"

Jack was sure he shouldn't let Whick and Snap know he had boarded the train on purpose. "I was running away," he gasped. "From—all the farmwork. And then I was running from the Whisperers—and I was on the tracks—I heard the whistle—and I thought the train would, would—"

"*Smoosh* you," said Whick with some odd sort of satisfaction.

"Smoosh me," Jack repeated. "Yes, I thought it would smoosh me. I heard the whistle blowing. And—"

"*And?*" said Snap and Whick together.

"And...that's all I remember," Jack said. "Until the door opened and I woke up, just now."

"Look at the scratches and bruises on him, Master Snap," Whick said. "He must have died—nearly died—when the train hit him, not nearly died because of the sleeping sickness."

"I *thought* I was going to die," Jack said helpfully.

"Close enough," said Snap. "Close enough for our purposes."

Whick adjusted his visor and peered at Jack more closely. "But why would the Clatterfolk have carried him? Who would have paid his way?"

"I was holding a penny for the post," Jack said.

Snap poked his throat again. "What post?"

Jack blinked and tried to keep himself from checking to make sure his sleeve covered the address he had written on his arm. "It was . . . a letter—about running away."

"Ha-hah! I see it all now," Whick said. "Stupid here was nearly smooshed by the train, and when the Clatterfolk found his body they took the one penny as payment—enough for some budget, no-coffin rate perhaps."

Snap nodded. "Or perhaps when they understood he was only *nearly* dead, that was sufficient at least to deliver him to us, as by our arrangement, since we became postmasters for Shadow-Town."

"Because they don't carry passengers," said Whick. "Not living passengers."

"As I say, Master Whick, as by our arrangement. Only—" Snap poked Jack's throat harder again. "Only, where is this letter?"

"I . . . I don't know," Jack said.

"Of course *you* don't know," Snap said.

"Blew away when he was knocked down by the train," said Whick. "Stands to reason."

"That's it. *Stands—to—reason.*"

"So, no coffin, but a fine new thrall, with no wasting from disease. Just walking along and—" Whick snapped his arm band. "And, *knock!*, he's very nearly dead. Would you say that was a bit of luck, Master Snap?"

"I certainly would, Master Whick."

Whick adjusted his visor; he checked his pocketwatch. He waited another moment. "Master Snap?" he finally said.

Snap furrowed his brow and looked from Whick to Jack to the papers on their writing desk and back to Whick again. He snapped his fingers. "Ah, I perceive! Yes, Master Whick, *I do say that was a bit of luck.*"

Jack could no longer restrain himself. "*Luck?*"

"*Luck*," Whick repeated with satisfaction. "Well put. Here we have a fine new stupid thrall *willingly* come, as if he *wanted* to help with our work."

"Willingly!" Jack exclaimed, but the Speculators regarded each other fondly.

"Yes," Snap said. "A new, *strong* thrall. Now, any other business with this train, Master Whick? Any post to send out? Any complaints for the Clatterfolk about service?"

"No complaints." Whick smiled. "The higher quality of this cargo inclines me to allow that this train, that the, the—" he held up his hand as he thought. "That the, the *Iron Stagnification* was right on time."

"*Stellification*," said Jack, somehow concerned for the dignity of the train. "Her name is the *Iron Stellification*."

Snap nodded. "The *Stupefy*, for short, I think."

"The *Stellify*," said Jack.

Whick looked up at the rack of empty pigeon-holes. "And no post for the *Stagnify*."

"Conductor!" Snap shouted. "Back there, Conductor! Any post on the noble—*Iron Jellification*—for us?"

Suddenly the pale Conductor stood at the coffin-gate. He passed a fat envelope marked with stars and snow to Snap without a word.

"No other post?" said Whick. "No other shipments for Shadow-Town? No other thralls-to-be? Or, I should say, no *coffins that cough?*"

Snap issued a loud, barking laugh, but the Conductor only made a few quiet rattles and shook his head.

"Clatterfolk never catch my little jokes," said Whick.

"No sense of humor," said Snap. "Nothing but *clatter-rattle-snargeler-glerg-glergy-rattle-rattle-clang* for them."

Jack noticed that at front of the *Stellify* the fire-man was letting up the pipe from the water tower. The Engineer made a long bright whistle. The Conductor rang his heavy bell. Then the fire-man leaned out from around the coffin-tender and caught Jack's eye before shouting roughly, "*All aboard!* All aboard for the end of the line, and west of west. All aboard for leaving Shadow-Town!"

The fire-man turned away, as expressionless as one of the Clatterfolk now. The Conductor made some last rattling sounds. This was Jack's moment, if he were only brave enough to do as the fire-man had done. Leap aboard and escape from Whick and Snap, from the Whisperers and the sleeping sickness, from Shadow-Town. Escape from the coffin-fire. Just leap aboard and let it all fall behind—Rose and Grandma and Tam. Only—

But now the door was closed, and Jack watched the train pull out—slowly first, then faster. The rails rattled as the train went puffing faster, faster and faster, into the west. Just before it rounded a wooded bend, there was one more whistle from the *Stellify*. Even as the train disappeared from sight, the whistle rolled on over the station house, long and wide and sliding lower and lower.

Morning had come to Shadow-Town. And Jack was alone in the coffin-hall with the Speculators.

Snap smiled at him. "Knocked down and nearly smooshed but brought here instead. Do you call that good luck or bad?"

Jack couldn't speak. But Whick answered for him. "Good luck, Master Snap. Good luck for us!"

Snap laughed. He unfolded the letter the Conductor had given him. "From the Regent's Office," he said, happy. "A preliminary statement of our claim! We only have to finish the survey now."

Whick signed in satisfaction. "Then we can claim the empty lands."

Jack blinked. "You *want* there to be a plague! To drive away the farmers. To claim their land."

"Not a *real* plague," Whick said. "No pustules or effusions of bodily fluids or, or—" He made a dignified shudder.

"—or *spots*," Snap said.

"Thank you, Master Snap. Nor spots." Whick smiled. "You might name it an *affliction*, but even the afflicted don't die, not of the disease at least—"

"—usually," Snap put in.

"Not usually. The Whisperers are sadly limited in conversation, but they are skilled mechanists of sleep. Able first to encourage a wider distribution of less pernicious vapors, and then to almost wake the only nearly dead—to rise to work as thralls."

"Work as *somnambulists*," Snap said with a sigh. "Why, the Whisperers might almost make Projectors themselves— if only they were larger, or could speak properly, or move in daylight—"

"Or withstand the touch of iron," said Whick. "Or use turning wheels."

"But why so many?" Jack asked. "All the Whisperers need is some miserable weaving for their clothes and some barley ground for their bread. What work is there for so many thralls?"

Snap came out of a reverie to cuff Jack hard across the ear. "Don't be smart," he said. "Your king will tell you all you need to know."

Jack put a hand to his ear. "King?" he shouted. "King? There hasn't been a proper king since long ago, the King Across the Ocean. You mean the *thrall-king?*"

The Speculators looked at each other. Snap sighed. "This thrall isn't right, Master Whick. He's almost not nearly dead."

"That will be the king's business now," Whick said. "He will teach him how to be dead."

"A quaint thought, Master Whick. Learning to be dead."

Snap shrugged and grabbed Jack's collar and tugged him after them, through the broken station, down many steps, and out onto the dim street.

They turned right. The sun had risen behind them now, and their shadows stretched far down the road. Almost to the Tall House that waited at the end. Here and there along the road, clay smudge pots burned, obscuring the morning with smoke.

As they walked, Snap struck Jack hard on the head with his cane. "*Don't* be smart," he said as Jack put his hand to the spot. "*Don't* speak unless you're spoken to. *Don't* eat, drink, or relieve yourself in any way without permission. Don't think, don't hope, don't disobey your king. Don't..." he paused, trying to remember the other things thralls shouldn't do.

"*Don't* draw blood," Whick put in. "The Whisperers are most particular about that. *Don't* draw blood, *don't* bleed, and *don't* allow the bleeding to live and walk. *Don't*—"

When Jack took his hand away to see if he was bleeding now, Snap used his cane to knock him on the same spot. Not as hard, but it hurt more the second time.

"Don't bleed," Snap repeated. He paused and made a few quiet whispers as if he was trying to remember a conversation. "Yes, yes, that's the important one. The Whisperers will burn you all alive if they find bleeding is allowed."

"But, what, why—?"

"Just don't do anything," Whick finished. "That's all the stupid have to recall. Don't do anything, except as you are told."

14

THE KING OF SILENCE
AND SHADOW

The Tall House. With the strange and faded patterns on its high
walls: suns and moons and other shapes Jack didn't understand, and its big wheel, unmoving now, while the water in the
low creek bubbled around it. The noise of wooden gears and
brass chains, and old men coughing.

As the Speculators dragged Jack closer, he looked away
from the Tall House, remembering what he had seen with Tam.
Remembering the moving shadows of the thralls. Remembering
the creaks, the hopeless moans.

Now he thought even Tam was caught there, and he had
come to Shadow-Town thinking he would somehow rescue
him—but instead he was just being escorted to the same fate
by Whick and Snap. Jack could already see rag-clad figures
stepping out the side door. Human things, moving slowly about,

as if they still slept. People he had known once; people he had seen lying in their coffins. Here was Farmer Mathom as he had seen him laboring in the Tall House already. Here was Mother Greene too, now wearing some rough cloth instead of her coffin-dress. Sour-faced Mother Greene, but she had passed him a kind word once. Miser Cooper in his coffin-suit, torn and ragged. Farmer Sawyer. Plump Mother Vining. And two children — the Cutter boy and girl, who had been left to die alone and then laid to rest in flour sacks. Sacks that were just rags and tatters now.

All the thralls shuffled slowly out of the workshop, each hobbled around the ankles and attached to one long chain. And bearing glass bricks — Smithton bricks like the one his grandma treasured. After the thralls carefully set down their bricks, they stood and saw Jack, and reached to him in supplication. Mathom even moved his mouth as if to speak but made no sound. And Tam was not among them. Had Jack been wrong after all?

Jack felt his knees go weak. He had been wrong at least to ever be afraid of anything else. No chores on the farm, no imprisonment at the Red Man's estate, no Whispers or death or endless service on the coffin-train could be worse than this.

The Speculators dragged him closer. "No!" Jack shouted, madly trying to twist free. "Let go!"

Whick kicked Jack's feet out from under him. As Jack's head struck the hard dirt road, Snap pressed the end of his cane down onto Jack's throat again so that he lay pinned like a butterfly.

"On the whole, I think I prefer the sleepers the plague provides to these happen-chance cases," Snap observed.

"Perhaps we should summon the king and get on with our business," said Whick.

"Your majesty!" Snap called, but he said it without any

reverence. He called the same way a farmer might yell for an unloved dog. "Your majesty!"

Jack tried to squirm away one last time, but Snap pushed down harder on his cane. Whick shook his head. "Thralls who pay their own way. Someday the world will end because of all these novelties."

Jack was beginning to choke. "An odd sentiment from a Speculator who is also a Projector, Master Whick," Snap said.

"I utter no judgment," Whick said. "I am indifferent as to the world's ending—as long as there would be sufficient profit in the matter."

Jack couldn't breathe at all now; his world began to turn grey. After all this, and now he would never even know what had become of Tam. But at least he would die before he suffered like the thralls. Then he saw the silhouette of a crowned figure bending over him.

"He'll do," the king said quietly, and the cane came off Jack's throat, and someone else was clapping brass fetters around his ankles. Jack turned onto his hands and knees and coughed up a little of the food he had eaten on the train.

"Y-e-s," Snap said with some distaste. "Master Whick, I think I shall go and count the bricks now!"

Jack looked up at the king left to stand over him. Tamlin Smith-son, Badger-Boy. Tamlin was the king, and he wore a crown of bone and iron.

Tam's eyes were hollow, and he did everything slowly, as if he bore the weight of more than his crown. For a long moment he only stared at Jack with unseeing eyes, and then he scratched the side of his head, just below the iron rim.

When he spoke, it was in a hoarse and weary voice. "Why'd you come?"

Jack shook his head first and then said, "To find you."

Tam made something like a laugh. "Ain't you stupid."

Jack said nothing. Ever since they had turned off the long-road west, he had been falling farther away from a world he understood. He had thought he would somehow rescue Tam but had only been chained with the thralls himself, and Tam his jailer. He was in a nightmare and he would never wake.

"Seven hundred and eighty-three more bricks for the tower, Master Whick!" he heard Snap call.

"Seven hundred and eighty-three!" Whick bent close to Tam with an ingratiating smile and presented him with a small cloth purse. "That's five gold pieces for your master!"

Tam took a willow switch and slashed hard at Jack's legs. "I am the king. I have no master."

Snap laughed brightly. "Twenty-six and a half stories high, already, Master Whick," he said. "So, counting ten feet a story, and sixty feet across to start..." Then he seemed to lose his place in the calculation.

Whick spoke with an excess of patience: "That's right, Master Snap, this load will take us to nearly twenty-six stories, six feet, and—"

"And nine inches!" Snap said, guessing wildly.

Whick smiled. "So congratulations to us, I think."

"Yes," said Snap. "And to you and me as well!"

They looked at Jack again, and at the ragged thralls standing about them stupidly, like so many stooks of wheat.

"Your majesty," Master Snap said to Tamlin. "We *humbly* beg you to encourage your subjects to make more bricks."

Tam had no more hope in his face than the thralls. But as Jack met his eyes, he understood there was one thing left that gave Tam some dignity.

"Your hands ain't blistered yet," Tam told him coldly. "Your hair ain't singed."

Jack felt a drag on the chain pull him towards the wide

wagon door of the Tall House. Tam slashed hard at the back of his legs. "To work!" he cried in a thin, hoarse voice.

As Jack shuffled inside after the others, Whick observed, "It's this reluctance to do even the simplest honest work that makes them seem so miserable."

"Ingratitude—for a second chance to be useful," said Snap. "Waste no pity on them!" Then the wide door closed behind Jack, and Tam threw the bolts shut, and he heard them no more.

Then they were all locked inside the Tall House together, Jack and the other thralls, and Tamlin, their king.

15

THE WORKSHOP

The Tall House must have been a kind of granary elevator once, Jack knew. The smell of it, of the grain dust, would never leave. Its highest levels were lost in shadow, and lower down, the light of the new day came only through cracked and red-splashed windows. Then it spread—thin and rusty—across the machinery-crowded floor.

Tam nodded at Mathom, and the old farmer took out a key. One by one, he released all the thralls from the long chain, gathering it as he went. Jack was last of all, and after he was freed, Mathom laid the great bundle of brass links at Tam's feet.

Mathom looked at Jack and again seemed about to speak, but Tam raised his switch and twisted his face cruelly. So Mathom only turned his grey face towards the light a moment. Then, with a wheeze, he began climbing a set of wooden stairs mounted on a kind of large barrel. The long chain was gone, but like the others, Mathom was still hobbled by a set of links between his fetters. He couldn't take more than one small step at a time—but still he climbed. The wood was unfinished, but worn smooth and slick now, as if it had borne thousands of steps: tens and tens of thousands of steps. Mathom wheezed again and his chains rustled and the barrel creaked, and its axle turned a rope fitted with empty buckets that stretched up through a long square chute. And, slowly, from somewhere hidden in the attic above, Jack heard that the rope began to turn some much greater wheel.

And the other thralls each had some similar awful task. They worked stone wheels that slowly ground sand and rock. They pumped water into tubs and stirred rubble. They fed coal into the oven. They hauled at levers that swung hammers to beat at something gold.

The Cutter children, chained to each other, had crept up a stair to a ledge where the girl began to spin some glittering yarn and the boy began to rattle a loom.

Except the mill-wheel that ground wild barley, Jack didn't understand what any of the jobs were for. None of them seemed to have a purpose, or an end.

He looked at Tamlin, standing beside a tall chair of bare wood set in the middle of the workshop floor—the empty throne Jack had dreamed of in the Red Man's house. At last he found his voice. "When did you become king of silence and shadow? When were you crowned with bone and iron?"

Tam's eyes narrowed. "How'd you know my titles?" he hissed. "What do you know about the crown?"

"I saw it in a dream," Jack said slowly, remembering. "A dream I had about you."

Jack had seen Tamlin make many horrible faces. Some on purpose, to frighten Rose; worse ones when he couldn't get his way; and more frightening than those when he lost his temper and turned red and blind with anger. But now his face was something of all of those—there was terror in it too.

Tam slashed at Jack's face so hard his willow switch broke, and slashed at him again with the broken end. Jack covered his eyes and felt the sting of it on his palm. Then Tam fell on him, knocking Jack's head onto the hard dirt floor with one hand, tearing at his hair with the other.

"It's mine!" he screamed. "My crown! You can only be a thrall and not the king!" Tamlin knocked Jack's head against the floor again and again. "Dun't speak of the crown! Dun't dream of the crown! It's mine!"

Jack twisted desperately out from Tam's hands and the two boys rolled and tangled as they fought on the floor. "Stop it!" he shouted. "What are you doing?"

Tam wasn't as big as Jack, but he was older and stronger and meaner. And he was more than mean now: in a moment, he had Jack pinned to the floor, an arm across his throat. "Help me!" Jack gasped. "Someone help me!"

The thralls only made a kind of moan, and the noise of the Endless Stair and the creaking wheels and the grinding stones came louder and faster. With his free hand Tam reached for Jack's face.

Jack only saved his eyes by knotting his fingers up with Tam's. "Will you kill me?" he croaked. "If you hurt me more, you have to kill me, or I will use your father's knife!"

That made Tam pause. "My father's knife!" he exclaimed. A smile spread over his ugly face. He leaned back so that Jack could breathe again, and shook his fingers loose. "My father's knife!" Very quickly, Tam drew the big knife from the wooden sheath around Jack's neck. Tam held the knife up and looked at it. He smiled again in a way that gave Jack no comfort.

Jack no longer even heard the laboring thralls around them, but he felt his own heart hammering wildly. "He gave it to me," Jack gasped. "Your father gave it to me. Remember?"

Tam ran his thumb very lightly over the edge of the blade. He took a few breaths and looked at Jack again. "Your gift of iron," he said at last. "Like my father never gave me."

Jack opened his mouth, but no words came out. Tam bent down once more to hold the knife close to Jack's face. He whispered, "Dun't dream of my crown. It is all that keeps me from being a thrall like these."

Tam's arm wasn't on his throat anymore, but Jack still felt the pain of it as he swallowed. "Get off," he said. "I don't want your stupid crown."

"No," Tam said. "You dun't." Tam sounded more normal again at last, but for a long moment Jack waited, trembling, unable to take his eyes from the big knife. Then Tam leaned forward and slid the knife smoothly into the sheath around Jack's neck.

He rolled off, and Jack scrabbled to his feet too, ankles still hobbled together.

Tam passed his hand over his eyes. "Why's you the one who wanted to come?" he asked.

Jack looked around the workshop, at the empty throne; at all the thralls, unmoving now. Why had he thought it was his job to come for Tam? As he waited for an answer to come to him, Jack looked up at Tam and saw that his crown had been set on crooked. But when he reached to straighten it, Tam pulled away with flashing eyes.

"It's just—" Jack found a way to put it in words for the first time. "It's just there was no one else who could help."

Now Tamlin had lost all color, looked utterly forlorn. "You's a fool. No one can help me now."

* * *

The workshop was quiet. Somewhere up high in the darkness, Jack heard a sudden flutter of wings.

There was a kind of groan. All around them the sound of the thralls shuffling closer. Tam looked at Jack, then he touched his own face. "Am I bleeding? Jack, tell me if I's bleeding!"

Bleeding again. The Speculators had told him blood was forbidden, but he hadn't expected Tamlin himself to seem so afraid. In the rusty light, it took Jack a moment to be sure. "No blood," he said. "But what's happening?"

Tam shook his head. "I dun't know."

The thralls were moaning something. As if they could only speak in a kind of echo, Jack heard them repeat Tam's words: "*Help! No one can help us now! Help!*"

In a low, urgent voice Tam said, "Quick, Jack. There's still time for you, just you—unless you want to stay and rattle my looms! Get out and tell my dad I remembered the Words anyway. Tell him I din't run away, and I din't forget the Words!"

Then only old Farmer Mathom found some new thing to say. "*Flee,*" he said, vaguely, still in the dream of the thralls. "*Leave. Flee, and help us leave.*"

The other thralls took it up: "*Flee and help us leave,*" they repeated after him. Mathom squinted and for a moment his vision seemed to clear and his face changed. "Jack," the old farmer said, as if he had just remembered his name. "Jack Tender—*Jack Tender, help us leave.*"

Jack shuddered. To Tam, he said, "I heard you say awful Words: '*Tharkle crith*—'"

"Never say them!" Tam cried. "They mean 'Let me pass—'" Then he chanted:

I'll come back later to make amends.
Let me pass in shadows; I am a friend.

"Never say them!" Tam repeated. "Not here, not anymore."

"But—"

"Friend! Jack!" called the thralls. "Help us leave!"

Jack stepped back and they reached for him as the drowning try to grab those still above the water, but they would only pull him down into their thralls' dream, their thin grey world.

Jack pressed himself back against Tam. "Tam, help me," he said.

Now Tam took his switch and his face went white as he slashed at the thralls again and again. "Work on! There's no help for you, no escape!"

"*Help us, Jack!*" the thralls called again.

Then as Tam went on slashing, he began to shriek shadow-Words Jack hadn't heard before: "*Schlach-thim, rheem!* I's your king, not Jack Tender! *I—is—your—king!* Work on!"

The thralls stopped with a long, hopeless noise that was harder to bear than any Words. Slowly they shuffled back to their stations; slowly the ugly noises of the machinery began again: chatters and creaks and groans.

Panting, Tam wiped his brow at last and looked at Jack once more. "I thought that rhyme'd always work," he said. "I thought 'later' never came. But the day we went by the Clay Pool with Rose, the Whisperers answered me back: '*Now we will give you a crown and set you above the other thralls.*'"

"But you are a shadow-friend," Jack said.

Tam went on as if he hadn't spoken. "And they laughed like dry leaves rustling and said, '*Now is later, redeem your pledge. Or be only a thrall to turn our wheels, to rattle our looms.*'" He smiled. "So I got the honor."

The honor. Just for a moment, Jack put his hands to where he remembered the crown of his dreams. "But why wasn't it 'later' anymore?"

Tamlin laughed bitterly. "Din't you see the tracks by the pool? You wun't the first to go into the water that day. That old king had been there before. That's where kings go to die."

Jack shuddered, remembering how the warm water had seemed to reach for him. "But why did they want you?"

Tam spoke so quietly Jack could hardly hear him over the engines of the workshop: "That's where kings go to die, and that's where new kings is born. Because before my father ever named me a shadow-friend, he threw me in the dark water of the Clay Pool and drew me out again alive. Only those is fit to wear the crown."

Tam paused, then spoke more loudly: "But better to be drawn from the pool and made king than to labor like these."

16

THE PHILOSOPHER-KING

Jack looked at his friend, and then at the thralls, the marks of Tam's switch fresh across their faces.

"We should burn Shadow-Town," he said. "We should kill them all."

Tam said, "Like before the Accommodation—"

"Yes!"

"—before the Accommodation when our grandfathers burnt them like logs and struck them down in the day, and the Whisperers filled the woods with webs and caught farmers' babies at night, and made the wells run salt..."

"But they are doing these things again!" Jack cried. "They walk the Bound-lands in the day. They have made a plague and sent the living into coffins to rise and labor here!"

Now Tamlin's eyes seemed hollow again, and Jack realized how nearly Tam now lived in the shadows himself.

"What they do is horrible to us," Tam said. "And what we do is horrible to them. But they want the hills, and we want the hills—and if the Ealda still bothered to want the hills the farmers and Whisperers would both quarrel with them too."

"So you and your father serve them."

Tam raised his head so his face came out of the shadow of the crown. "My father and I treat with the Whisperers because we ain't fools. I'd kill them all if I could. But not because they's bad and farmers is good. We's just enemies. And now they caught me and I made a bargain to drive their thralls until I escape or die—only those is the same for me now."

"Why?" said Jack. "You drive the thralls, but who drives you?"

"At night, or in the shadows, the Whisperers. In the day, the crown holds me."

"Then take it off!" Jack pleaded. "Cast aside the crown and escape with me!"

Just for a moment, the white rage came over Tam's face again, and then he put his hand to the crown, closed his eyes, and smiled as if he was remembering something especially horrible. "It's iron, you know, bone and iron. So they cudn't even bear to touch it, but made me crown myself—if I din't want to be a thrall like these.

"And I knew better, but last night after they left me I tried to pull it off anyway. But I cudn't. 'Cause the crown has thorns of iron that grow in my flesh, Jack. Into my skull. And I thought I'd try to escape, to dig some hole the Whisperers or Speculators wudn't ever see—but the more I dug, the deeper the thorns dug too.

"So I willn't ever really leave, Jack. They'd only grow deeper until I screamed, or went mad, or died."

At different times Jack had tried to follow Tamlin, had hated him, had wanted to be like him. But he would never have thought Tam had the strength to face this doom.

The Badger-Boy has become a philosopher, he thought. He really is braver than I could be.

"It is like you are caught in the never-ending task in some fairy tale," Jack said, whispering in horror. "You will labor here forever. And at night or in the shadows, they will mill around and you will have to suffer them."

Tam took his seat on the bare throne. For a moment Tam only felt his crown and looked over the thralls laboring at the spinning wheels, the looms for shadow-rags, the glowing furnace, the molten glass.

When he finally looked down at Jack, Tam seemed almost careless. "Not forever. Until a new king comes, or until I can bear it no more and return to the Clay Pool and slip again into its warm embrace."

Jack shook his head. "I escaped from the Red Man to help you," he said. "Rose is still there, but his estate is a paradise next to this. Tell me what to do—"

Tamlin held up his hand and Jack fell silent, as though his friend really were a king.

"Stay and work and suffer until we die. It's the fate of everyone born in this world."

"Work and suffer until you die!" Jack almost screamed. "But what for?"

Tam slowly made his sideways smile. "Why, what's anything for, Jack? What's you for?"

Jack looked around the workshop, at Farmer Mathom on the Endless Stair, at the Cutter children working the wheel and the loom, at all their dull pained faces. "What is all the labor for? Why so many, when all they need are some shadow-rags run off on a loom? Why all the bricks, why the gold?"

"Perhaps if you went to some high place you'd see it all and understand. Some Tower of Glass. Some vantage in the sky."

Jack turned around, watching the motes rise from the creaking machines, old grain dust that showed orange in the light that came through the red-splashed windows. High windows he would never reach. The bolted door. He felt his heart hammering. "How would I escape and rise so high?"

"I's king now Jack, not your friend."

No, Jack thought. Not really, he wasn't. He shook his head. "No."

"And if it is my crown, I can't let you out the door."

Jack swallowed. "But I will tell your father you kept your bargain. That you remembered the Words."

"Is you willing to labor like a thrall?"

"Anything."

Tam led him to a thick loop of rope in the middle of the floor. He heaved up on it to open a square of gloom: a door down into some pit thick with decay.

He gave Jack an old sack. "Climb down," he said. "Labor like a thrall. Gather the food the thralls eat, the fruit of the dead." Jack looked at him in confusion. "The yellow mushrooms," Tam said. "Not the red."

Jack looked down, saw only shadow.

"This is the way you can escape," Tam repeated. "But I speak as the king, not as your friend."

Jack swallowed. "I know."

Tamlin put out his hand, and Jack reached for it—they had rarely shaken hands, but it seemed the right thing to do now, when they might never see each other alive again. But instead of taking Jack's hand, Tam stuck out a foot and gave him a shove. Jack tumbled down into the darkness until his head struck dirt. He was just dimly aware of the thump of the door closing above him, and then there was nothing.

* * *

A long time later, some cold thing ran across Jack's face. A bad dream—but no, not a dream; he was just alone in the blackness, the vegetable silence.

As if he were already dead—and the only place that could be worse than a berth on the coffin-train was the dirt beneath him, and the endless time to wait in the ground until the world was remade—

Jack shouted in fear, sat up in the darkness, shouted again, and then he remembered properly. He had come to Shadow-Town to find Tam. And then Tamlin had cast him into the darkness even below Shadow-Town, to gather the fruit of the dead. Tamlin had. Not his friend Tam—Tamlin-king.

And he was blind now, or in a place that was black as death; pitch-black, rot black. Only—a red glow here and there. His eyes were already used to the dark, but still it took a while for him to understand what he could just barely see.

A faint, faint glow. Like little hooded figures. Like bells. Like—mushrooms. Jack-o'-lantern mushrooms. Hundreds of them, lambent with poison.

Jack scrambled back almost overcome by revulsion, smelling foul waste and corruption everywhere, tumbling over uneven ground, places where the jumbled earth rose high. He felt mushrooms there too—not glowing red, but large and damp. Tribute mushrooms, Grandma called them, he knew, because they were a food that could only be harvested from among the bushes, not planted or tended. Rot-hoods. The mushrooms that grew where the earth had closed over a body. *"Gather the fruit of the dead,"* Tamlin had said, and as Jack understood, the horror of it all became too much for him. The yellow mushrooms the thralls ate had themselves fed already on the bodies of the thralls, the ones who'd died at last, or been killed perhaps. He tried to scrabble to his feet but fell in the darkness and would have begun shouting in horror—except he heard the door somewhere above him creak open. No light, but a rush of damp air poured down.

The machines in the workshop were louder now, but there was another sound too: Tam's voice, thinly. "I have these sleeping thralls who labor," Tam was explaining to someone. Something. "I have the things I cast down here among the mold."

And a Whisperer's reply: —*kli-octh, t-nak.* No spell of sleep, just shadow-Words it spoke to Tam. —*Jack Tender, the waking thrall.* Then there was a noise like dry leaves crackling, the laughter of a Whisperer, and Jack pressed his face into the mushrooms, breathed in their warm scent of decay.

He hugged the damp mound beneath him, and for a moment he thought, *If only I were already dead like these.*

✳ ✳ ✳

Jack didn't know how long he had lain in the blackness, his face pressed into the earth, after the hisses of the Whisperer had ceased at last, but he must have slept.

Now he opened his eyes and saw the mushrooms around him rising like a forest from the dark earth. It was hunger that had woken him, he realized, and the smell of mushrooms. The glowing jack-o'-lanterns, the dim rot-hoods that had cushioned his head. Rot-hoods, he thought. Pale yellow mushrooms Grandma served as if they were a delicacy. But he couldn't eat something that fed on the thralls that lay in the earth beneath him. Or the shining jack-o'-lanterns that were poison either.

Jack had some matches in his pocket and now he lit one with his thumbnail the way Tam had taught him. The red glow disappeared even in the weak light of the match flame, but he could see the jumbled earth, the legions of yellow rot-hoods. The old sack Tam had given him. Just as Jack noticed some moving thing in the earth closet, the match went out.

Quick as he could, he took out another match, dropped it, took out a third, lit it. And saw nothing. Just earthen graves, the rot-hoods, the jack-o'-lanterns. And no steps, no ladder. Just the vague outline of the door in the ceiling, too high to reach.

What would he do? His match went out. What would he do? Jack felt himself begin to shake. No — what would Tam do? Tam would shriek and rage.

What would his father do? What would Rose do? He smiled. Rose. Rose would be too scared to come in the first place. But then he thought of how she had acted when he had left her alone on the long-road. Rose would never have come, but if she had found herself here she would get all slow. She would act very carefully.

Jack squeezed himself hard, trying to stop shaking. Then he felt carefully in his pocket. There were only four matches left. He had four matches, and he was imprisoned in the dark with the dead.

* * *

Without lighting a match, Jack opened the burlap sack and felt inside. No clothes, no water, no food. No tools. I have his father's knife still, he thought. But there was something else — some glass thing.

Jack lit a fourth match. A candle-lantern, bound in brass. Tam had given him a sack with a candle-lantern. He put the candle-lantern between his legs just as this match went out. Jack took a deep breath. He had three matches left.

He had three matches left, and he took one of them out and flicked it with his thumb. It didn't light. Flicked again, and again, until the head was worn off. He had two matches left.

Two matches and Jack waited before trying another one, but it lit, and with shaking hands he put it to the candle. The wick flared, the flame rose—and went out just as the match burned down to Jack's thumb.

It was a long time before he could bring himself to try his last match. There alone in the earth closet with the dead.

17

CHILD OF THE WIND AND
THE MORNING SUN

That morning Rose had woken alone in the attic of the House
of Woven Trees.

"Jack —," she said. Downstairs she said it again. "Jack?"
But there was no Jack, and no Red Man either, only the big
dog that watched her. And on the table a note written in a big
old-fashioned hand, like the letters in her grandma's closet:

Jack is busy today.

*So you must do the work for both of you, and have it done before
I come back at noon. Pick two buckets of raspberries, and boil
them into jam, and seal them with wax...*

The Red Man's letter went on that way—as if she didn't know how to make jam perfectly well. As if the Red Man thought she was useless too.

Rose looked down at the big dog watching her and felt a flutter of fear. But the Red Man had left her a place at the table. "I will have some coffee and toast before I do any of that for you," she told the dog, just as if it could understand, and it did seem content to watch her and wait. Any other time and she would have enjoyed that breakfast, the fine morning. But as Rose was finishing her coffee, the dog made a sudden bark that startled her into spilling what was left.

And it barked again, and she took a bucket and hurried out the door, and followed the dog down a path to rows of raspberries.

* * *

By lunchtime, when she sat down to rest, Rose could look at a half-dozen jars of jam cooling on the counter and the syrup dripping through a cheesecloth bag to make jelly.

The wooden clock made a whir and a little door in it opened. A bird came out now and whistled twelve times, and Rose jumped as just then the screen door banged open. The other two big dogs pushed into the kitchen, followed by the Red Man.

He took off his hat, wiped his forehead with a cloth, laid his staff against the wall, and turned a chair to sit on it backward. He looked around at the work she had done and lifted down one of the steaming jars with his bare hand. Then he pulled a spoon out of his back pocket and put a big scoop of jam into his mouth. The jar was too hot for Rose to hold, but the Red Man didn't seem to notice.

"Where is Jack?" she asked.

The Red Man took another spoonful and smiled at Rose.

"I thought he was with you," she said, more anxiously. "Why wasn't he here to help me with my labors? Where is Jack?"

The Red Man pulled the spoon out of his mouth. "I have not seen Jack since he walked out the door to follow the whistle of the train last night," he said. "By dawn it would have taken him to Shadow-Town. Unless he chose to stay on the train."

Rose sank down on her chair. Jack gone to Shadow-Town after all. On the coffin-train. She put her hands on the table and took a deep breath. She stared at the Red Man, suddenly faint. Jack had gone on the coffin-train.

She opened her mouth, closed it again. Then tears were rolling down her face. "Stupid Jack," she whispered.

The Red Man looked away for a moment. "Yes, farmers' children are very stupid," he said. He licked his spoon and stuck it back in his pocket. "So I wanted to ask you why Stupid Jack left."

She had stopped crying now, and the Red Man pulled out a calico handkerchief and passed it to her. While Rose blew her nose on a corner of the cloth, he opened his pocketknife and began to cut and core an apple in his other hand. Rose wiped at her eyes. As he worked, he only watched her, Rose saw, as if he knew he would never cut himself. She folded up the handkerchief as neatly as she could and passed it back to him.

Then he smiled in a way that gave her no comfort and popped a quarter of the apple into his mouth. "Why *did* Stupid Jack leave?" he asked again. "And why did he leave you alone, and why did he go to Shadow-Town if farmers are so afraid of the Whisperers?"

"We're afraid of you, too," Rose said quickly, and then she went on as she remembered their last, whispered conversation. "And Jack—thinks—he is braver than I am. So he would have thought he needed to leave without me. But if he has gone to

Shadow-Town, then maybe he means to help his friend Tam first, if he is held there working as a thrall."

"In Shadow-Town," the Red Man said. "Yes, Jack is brave or scared or foolish if he went to help this friend in Shadow-Town. Those fetters are worse than any I have here in my seat in the hills."

"But I know that's what he means to do," Rose said. "And then he'll come back. So don't think you can beat me or lock me up or make me go on doing work forever. Jack knows I am captive here, and he will tell our grandmother, and —"

"Yes," the Red Man said. "I am very afraid of sickly Grandma Tender. That will keep you safe in my house. That is a good threat to make. That is a good way to scare me now." He put the rest of the apple in his mouth and stared at her as he chewed. "Now — when Jack Tender has gone to Shadow-Town."

Rose felt what little courage she had gathered drain away. She tried to think of anything she could say to impress the Red Man, but there was nothing. It was all she could do to just look him in the face. "But what will happen to him?" she said. "And when will you let me go? What will I do?"

The Red Man stared at her, unmoved. "You should recover yourself," he said. "Without waiting on happy endings to stories I cannot tell. Recover yourself and do more work, unless you want to sit and weep forever."

"More work," Rose said, tears starting once more. "After all the long day in the Tanglewood, and all this morning picking berries and boiling jam like your scullery maid. More work! Will I just work for you here alone forever then, with no hope or reward?"

The Red Man shrugged. "You can choose to have hope, if it will comfort you." He handed her a jar of jam, still hot, and a spoon. "And keep this for later."

As Rose began to recover herself, the Red Man led her out

to a shed where two cows had come to be milked. He showed her the stool she was to use.

Rose wiped her nose on her sleeve. "What are their names?" she asked, but the Red Man laughed at her.

"I call this one 'Cow,'" he said. "And I call the other one 'Cow.' And if I need to call them both, I say, 'Cows!' They don't want people names, they want to be cows."

She looked at the dog that watched her, and the other two that had followed the Red Man. "Is it the same for your dogs?" she asked.

The Red Man put a pail down beside the stool. "The day is for working, not for talking."

"Will you talk to me later? Will you answer my questions when I am done milking?"

"Then there will be other work to do," he said. "But maybe there will be time for children-talk in the evening."

"'Children-talk,'" said Rose. "I'm not a baby. Why do you call it *children-talk?*"

The Red Man sighed and leaned on his staff for a moment. "Cows have cow-talk. Farmers have farmer-talk. Whisperers in the Tanglewood have shadow-talk. Children have children-talk."

Rose stared at him. "What about you?" Rose asked. "What is your talk? You don't have friends, you don't have a family. You just have your dogs and your animals and people like me and Jack that you keep to do your chores."

He nodded, made his noise: *hrmph*. After a long moment he said, "Ruminate. That's what you would call it. Like cows chew their cud. I have what I know and what I've thought before for company. I don't need any kind of talk."

"But what are you?" Rose persisted. "You're not a farmer, not a Whisperer, not a River-man. Not even one of the Clatterfolk. You speak as though you have always been here, so you're not one of the Strangers. Are you something from a fairy tale like an ogre or from one of the old stories like a troll or—"

"Farmer girls shouldn't speak of those things!" the Red Man rumbled, and he seemed like a wild thing again, just as he had in the night at the thorn-gate. Rose was frightened then, not just because she was captive in the House of Woven Trees, kept under the eye of the big watching dogs, but frightened of the Red Man himself: of whatever he was.

His face seemed to be burning as he pushed himself up on his staff. "Don't speak about things that you don't want to see! Even the Ealda and the River-folk know better. I'm not some thing you know but aren't to name—I'm not anything Strangers understand."

Rose began to step back, but he pointed the head of his staff at her and said very sharply, "Girl, stand still!"

Whether Rose was held by fear or because he commanded her limbs, she didn't know. The world might have stopped, except that she could hear the cows. And she knew that she breathed in the smell of them, and of the dogs, and of the warm straw.

When he spoke again, the Red Man's words were slow, as if he was remembering a dream. "A long time ago when the wind met the morning sun, I woke. And I have been waiting here, in the middle of this place—not north or south or east or west—for a long time since. A long time, and I will be here a long time to come."

"The child of the wind," Rose said, and because it was stranger than anything she had imagined about the hills, stranger than the trains of the Clatterfolk that ran through it, stranger than anything about Shadow-Town, she said it again. "The child of the wind and the morning sun. You are the Red Man of the East."

"Who told you that?" the Red Man said, sharp again. "That's not in any Stranger's book."

"Grandma told us once," Rose said. "She said Aunt Constance's husband the River-man told her one night when the moon was high."

"A River-man." The Red Man nodded. "Yes, a River-man would know—or one of the Ealda, though they would tell the story differently."

"But this is not the east," Rose said. "Why are you here?"

"Of the east, not in the east," the Red Man said. "The child of the wind and the morning sun. And there are three more like me, if you want to know what I am, but we have no talk. We can never meet. And you will never meet them either."

"The White Bear of the North," Rose said, "the Yellow Woman of the West, the Black Bird of the South."

"Yes," the Red Man said, almost to himself. "That is who we are, the children of the wind and the sun and the moon, or so I think I knew a long, long time ago. You were told well, or you remember well."

"It's easy to remember colors," Rose said. "But why is there no one who is blue? If there is yellow and red, there should be blue, and then you could paint the whole world, paint anything."

"Blue, blue. The whole of the sky is blue. The King of the Winds is bright blue. The Queen of the Hall of the Stars is night blue. That's blue enough."

"'*The Red Man's province is the earth,*'" Rose went on, still remembering. "'*And he brings fear.*'"

"I help things begin," the Red Man said. "It is the same thing."

"You help things begin to grow in the earth, maybe," said Rose. "But I think this is the end of my story. I will never leave. You hold me like the Whisperers would."

As the Red Man took a great breath in, Rose thought she heard the windows rattle. As he let it out, the air seemed to roar through his throat. She was still trembling when he said, quite quietly, "Like the Whisperers? Have you been their guest?"

Rose felt very small now. Like a mouse talking to some huge cat. "They are honest, at least," she said. "They would say, 'You are our thralls now, and will stay forever.' But you say nothing."

The Red Man grounded his staff. "The day is for working, not talking," he said again. Then he left Rose alone in the shed, except for the shuffling cows and the big dog that watched her every move.

* * *

Rose had milked cows more times than she could count, so when she saw the Red Man's cats come crowding around, she squirted milk for them to catch from the air. All this her minder watched carefully, and when Rose shifted her stool and bucket to begin milking the second cow, she began to speak to him to calm her nerves.

"He says you have no people-name, or people-talk," Rose said. "But I think dogs are born to like people. And you watch us carefully. So I will call you a name. I will call you 'Raff.' You could be a frightening dog and be called Raff, but a good dog, a nice dog, could be Raff too."

She worked for a while, and just for something to say, she went on: "It's warm and damp and my neck itches. Tamlin says those are sure signs of some storm or twister coming."

Raff looked at her closely. He got to his feet. The cats screeched and bolted for the door. The cow shied, nearly overturning the pail. "Good doggy!" Rose said quickly. "Good Raff, good doggy, be good! Rose likes you, good doggy."

But it wasn't just Raff; all about the farm, she suddenly heard the wind begin to blow, and somewhere outside stone chimes began to sound. The cows began to low uneasily. Somewhere cats screeched again. Raff paced restlessly for a moment, then went to the door and began to whine; the first noise he had made just for her.

Rose went and took him by the collar and saw the farmyard alive with the damp and rising wind. A warm wind—a storm wind, she thought. It blew grit in her eyes, tossed her hair, nearly lifted from her head the tattered hat she still wore. Then Raff began to run for the path through the woods, pulling her along after him.

"Raff!" she called. "Stay! Down! No, stop, please!" She might have let go, except that being left behind seemed worse than anything the dog might drag her to. So she ran after him into the woods, down some path through the beeches, towards the sound of the stone chimes.

Raff stopped in a little clearing among the biggest of the trees. The stone chimes sounded louder here, not so much chiming as cracking into one another like rocks.

Rose looked up. On every side, hung high up in the trees, were twisted stone figures. Horrible shapes surrounded her, all swinging, hung by the neck. Whisperers. She was too scared to move, or shriek. Her blood might have been frozen. Whisperers. Still, stone, and dead—but no longer quiet. In the wind of the coming storm they swung and knocked against one another, louder and louder, like the laughter of boulders.

Raff began to howl, and then Rose could fall to her knees at least. She couldn't bear to look at the stiff and awful shapes. She buried her face in his fur. But the stone things went on cracking like thunder above her. On and on, until a louder sound made Rose shake.

"Dance, stones!" a great voice shouted, and Raff howled louder and longer and Rose peeked under her arm to see the Red Man standing over her. He must have sent the other dogs away because he was alone for this, and his arms were out-stretched and his face shone with passion.

"They thought to come quietly into my estate!" he called. "Now see how these trespassers entertain us. Dance!" he roared again, and there was a huge gust.

The trees shook and the stones knocked harder and harder. Rose put her hands over her ears, but the enormous discord went on. Raff howled, and the Red Man laughed in some awful delight.

Rose could take no more. The ice in her veins melted. She yelled, "Stop it!" She got up and kicked the Red Man on the shin. "Make it stop!"

She kicked him again, as hard as she could. He looked down at her, and raised the head of his staff.

Only then did she think about what she had done.

Now I will become stone like these, Rose thought. *And Jack will never find me*.

18

THE STORM

The Red Man swept his staff to one side and the banging ceased. Raff stopped howling. In the farmyard back beyond the trees the other animals became quiet, but the wind blew on, bending the beeches so they creaked, tossing Rose's hair.

He swept his staff a second time and then the wind itself paused. Only the ropes high in the trees squeaked as they slowly twisted. Two of the stony figures knocked together, more quietly, and then they were still.

The Red Man looked down at Rose, panting with his efforts. She stepped back and clutched at Raff. "So I keep the Bounds," the Red Man said, still harsh but quiet. "So I skin and stone the Whisperers and so their hollow bodies dance and warn the other quiet ones away."

"It's horrible," Rose said. "Is this how you labor each day?"

The Red Man grounded his staff and began to breathe more gently. "Don't think the Whisperers deal more softly with those who trespass on their grounds."

"Even to do to them, it's horrible."

He looked down at her for a long time. "Then I won't make you help with that part of my work," he said, and the hair on the back of Rose's neck began to quiver as the wind slowly rose again.

"I wish Jack were here," Rose said. "I wish he would come back and take me away, or that he would come back and you would make him help me with your work at least."

"You say 'stupid Jack,' you say Jack should rescue you, you say Jack should come and share this work."

"I hate Jack," Rose said quietly, "but I am scared to be alone without him."

The lower branches waved again in the wind. The Red Man's cloak tossed, and his white hair flew about his glowing face. Rose tightened her hand on Raff's collar. "Don't expect Jack to help you now," he said. "Jack is beyond my estate, and he will be hard-pressed to save himself, let alone your friend the Badger-Boy."

Rose gave the Red Man a shrewd look. "How did you know Tam was called the Badger-Boy? Is he with Jack now? Do you know what has happened to them?"

The Red Man laughed. "Tamlin Badger-Boy, Smith's son, has roamed the hills, has dug holes everywhere. He is ugly like a goblin. Once I caught him on my estate and almost skinned and stoned him like these. I caught him again and thrashed him like a stubborn bull. I caught him a third time and had him make me tea. Now he comes and goes and tells me tales of what he sees."

Rose shivered. "Is Tam good or bad? Tell me. I hate him, but he is Jack's friend."

The Red Man laughed again. "You hate Jack too. And do you call me good or bad? I only keep the Bounds. Sometimes the Badger-Boy is good, sometimes bad. Sometime he will have to decide."

"But you let him go."

"I can't keep him out. I can't keep him in."

"Will you let us go too? Will you let me go if Jack never comes back?"

"Go? You don't know how to go home. You don't know where home is—and the Whisperers have heard and smelled you now, and they will wait in every ditch and hollow and shadow in the sandy hills to catch you."

Rose shuddered. "You could take us," she said.

"Yes," said the Red Man. "That is my job. I nurse-maid foundling farmers' babies and then I put them in a little carriage and I push them home."

Rose raised her head. "Your job. Red Man of the East," she said bitterly. "What is your job, except to catch those who trespass on your estate and torment them?"

"I keep the Bounds. I tend the hills. I work my farm."

She shook her head. "But you know what happened to Jack, don't you? Tell me!" She was weeping, but she beat her hat against his leg. "Tell me where he is!"

Suddenly Rose thought of what she was doing. She saw how the Red Man loomed over her and she began to tremble.

But the Red Man only said, "He is in Shadow-Town with Tamlin. They are laboring to build a Tower of Glass in the desert."

"The desert." Rose felt faint. "What is the Tower of Glass?"

"You can come and see it if you really want to know my work," the Red Man said. "If you want to see the measure of a child of the wind."

Without any more words, the Red Man began to lead Rose and Raff along the hedge. It ran north and west some way yet, and then they slipped out another gate to see a wide valley opening before them. The wind was blowing higher, and shafts of light pierced the deep clouds to run across the thick woods in the valley's heart.

After all this time shut in by the Red Man, by the Tanglewood, the open view made Rose smile. A countryside she would want to paint. "That's not the Tanglewood below," Rose said. "Are we still in the Bound-lands?"

The Red Man looked into the wind and shrugged. "You walk with me. I make the gates of gloom that keep the Bounds, but I am not kept by them," he said.

"But—," Rose asked. Before she could finish, the Red Man was already taking long steps up the ridge that wound along the south face of the enclosing hills and she had to hurry to keep up. Climbing on and up, and up higher still, to the greatest height Rose had known in the sandy hills.

She looked down and saw how high the sheltered trees, how thickly the wildflowers grew on the slopes that faced the sun, how lush the grasses.

Just before the top they came to three great cedars, and then they were on the lip of a hill where the north wind broke. A kind of throne made of boulders knotted up with the roots of stunted oaks looked south down over the valley they had climbed. Behind the throne, a heath stretched back some long way north, the dry grasses rolling in vast waves under the wind.

The wind flattened Raff's ears and he barked expectantly at the coming storm. The Red Man slowly climbed up to stand on the seat of stone, and Rose turned back to look out over the south.

Heavy clouds had put most of the hills in shadow, but far away Rose saw bright cracks under the sun; and beneath them, across the valley and beyond the Tanglewood, far, far away, she saw pale hills shining: the desert, she knew.

The desert, beyond the land of shadows, more horrible still, where even the scraggly spruce and poplars came to an end and the sandy hills became only hills of sand at last. The desert that no one would ever try to farm.

The wind rose at her back, and the cracks in the clouds opened a little more. "There!" the Red Man said, pointing with his staff. "The Tower of Glass. Isn't it admirable?"

Rose stared, seeing only a splinter of light among the pale hills—and then the sun caught it properly, and even from this far away, she understood it really could only be a tower of glass, burning so brightly that her eyes watered and she turned away, shaking her head. A Tower of Glass standing in the desert— where no one went at all. "Who made such a thing?"

He shrugged. "Creatures that walk my hills."

"What is it for?"

"For weeding, I think."

"I don't understand," Rose said.

"No. There is much about my work you don't understand." The Red Man laughed and stretched out his arms and Raff began to bark, not glad or angry or frightened; only as though he knew something was going to happen.

"My work!" the Red Man cried. "See how I tend the garden of my hills! See how I cultivate the desert!"

He raised his staff high in the air. "Gather lightning!" he called, and his voice echoed through the storm, and lightning did flare and strike, from the east and west and south of the land they overlooked. "Rattle hail!" he cried, and the lightning struck nearer yet, and first cold rain and then pellets of ice swept down and stung Rose, as though she had suddenly been caught up in some winter tempest.

But the Red Man only roared on, loud enough that she

could hear him even through the thunder: "Clouds pour down water! Gales roll back the sand!"

The north wind blew harder, staggering Rose as a torrent of cold rain rushed down across the hill. It tore Rose's hat from her head and sent it sailing off over the edge and down into the sheltered valley below. Even there, trees shivered and bowed to give the storm its due.

"Rain!" bellowed the Red Man, and the skies opened further to obey him. "Blast!" he shouted, and wind blew harder at his command. He raised his crooked staff. *"Storm!"* he called, the word falling like thunder, and now Raff yelped in fright, and the dog pressed himself against the boulders beneath the Red Man, his coat quivering. Raff looked up at Rose and she heard his whine beneath the roaring storm.

Rose noticed that her skin had begun to itch. Then there was a great flash, like all the light in the world.

19

THE STROKE OF LIGHT

A great flash, and Rose heard no sound but only felt a tremendous blow come down on the crown of her head.

A stroke from the sky that shook her bones, her guts, her brain, and cast her flat. As though she were less than a girl, a mouse, a scrap of autumn leaf —

For a long time Rose lay face down, unmoving, her eyes closed tight but still seeing the flash, her ears filled only with silence, and she didn't know herself if she was alive or dead. Except that the force of the blow still ran through her. Every nerve and sinew quivered, and she shook against the wet ground.

Only when her body was quiet did Rose feel the rain once more. She still heard nothing, but she opened her eyes. Raff was gone, but from where she lay she could see the great cedars just below her. One of them had been split in half, and the bare wood of its heart sparked and sizzled in the rain.

The Red Man lay slumped against the part of the tree that yet stood. His white hair smoked like cinders, and he was still as the wind played over his figure, tossed his cloak and hair and hat.

The storm pushed on, silently to Rose, south and west, and still she only lay there as she watched the wind and the shadow move across the valley and onto the hills beyond.

Her parents had sent her away; her grandma had sent her away. Jack had left her. Even Tam. And now Raff. Now the Red Man.

Now everything has fallen away from me. Now everyone has gone, Rose thought. *And I will be utterly alone, forever.*

Then thinly, from somewhere far away, she heard Raff barking, and she pushed herself up to kneel on the wet earth.

She had heard him from far away, but really Raff was right beside her. The big dog licked her face, and without even thinking she scratched behind his ears. The world was not utterly empty; there was the storm, and Raff, and Rose herself, and for a long while that was enough.

For a long while, and then she thought, *What will happen now?*

Somewhere to the south, lightning flickered and Rose heard no thunder. But when Raff barked again, it seemed a little louder now.

Then the Red Man opened one tired eye. Not dead. He looked for her, and said something her thunder-filled ears couldn't hear. She couldn't hear him — but the Red Man was not dead, and Rose scrabbled and slid down the wet slope and as she crawled to him every feeling she had ever known rushed over her. The world seemed to begin again.

As he began to sit up, he spoke again. "*Jam,*" he whispered, or it sounded like a whisper to Rose. His head began to loll backward, and his eyes rolled until his pupils almost disappeared and he stared up at the raining clouds without sight.

"Jam," Rose repeated, and though she felt the word come through her throat and her bones, she didn't really hear it. Then she understood and began fiddling with the jar he had given her, the lid slipping in her grasp.

The Red Man's green eyes rolled around until they saw her properly. "Now I am weary," he said. "Feed me some jam."

He was too weak, she thought. He would faint again, or perish.

Rose wiped the lid with her skirt, tried to turn it again. Too wet or too tight. She pulled out the spoon and jabbed the end under the lid again and again until it caught. Then she pried at it, and it slipped and she pried again, pushing so hard the spoon began to bend. But the seal broke and the air rushed in. Then Rose opened the jar and began feeding the Red Man as if he were a baby.

After a few swallows, the Red Man reached for the spoon himself, and held it in his fist, and ate more and more until the jar was empty. He smiled and his mouth moved, and then he pointed with the spoon at the dark clouds rolling south. He seemed to shout, but his voice was just loud enough for Rose to hear.

"So I cultivate the hills!" he cried. "So the winds slowly roll south the sands. So with each storm I claim another inch; each year another foot, for the grassy meadows, for the Tanglewood even, for all these sprucewood hills."

Rose stared as the Red Man brushed some cinders from his hair. "Storms are like cats!" he called. "They might suffer you to call them, but they are not tame."

Just then there was another *crack!* —loud enough for Rose to hear. As Raff jumped back, the trunk of the cedar split wider.

In its heart there was a lump of dark wood, and the Red Man got up and dug at it with his knife until he pulled out a ball the size of Rose's fist.

"So the storm-eagles lay their eggs," he said.

"The storm-eagles," she said.

"The storm-eagles serve the King of the Winds," said the Red Man. "They tell him what they see; they carry his tidings."

"Which story are they from?"

"Stranger-girl," he laughed. "From all the stories of the Vastlands. From my story. From your story." The ball sizzled in his grasp, but he held it out for her.

The egg, if it was an egg, was still smoking, and it smelled like hot cedar, but it wasn't too hot to hold. Rose looked down at it uncertainly. "A kind of eagle's egg?" she said.

"A kind of storm's egg," he rumbled. "This tree grew for a hundred years to be tall enough to catch the lightning and give you this egg. Take it as your reward from this wild storm."

"Will it hatch?" she said.

"If it is ever broken," the Red Man said. "Think of what a gift you have earned—to carry a storm! Thank the tree, and thank me." And when she did, he got back to his feet and added, "Now I will lean on you and you will help me walk back down to my House of Woven Trees."

So Rose led him stumbling back down the path with Raff at their heels. Through the hills and onto the grounds of his estate, and back into his parlor at last.

The Red Man cast down his staff and sank deeply into his chair. He mopped his face with a handkerchief. "Sit now," he told Rose. "Sleep now. Only rouse me if someone comes."

Around suppertime, Rose put the kettle on to boil and began to cut ham and slice bread. When the coffee was ready, the Red Man stretched and opened his eyes, looked at the table, and made his *hrmph*, as if she had only done what she ought.

Only when he had eaten a dinner's worth, and asked for more, and eaten that, did Rose speak to him.

"Jack and I could have left whenever we wanted, couldn't we?"

He leaned back and looked at her for a moment. He snapped his suspenders, though Rose heard no sound. Then he barked a laugh. "Yes," he said. "Run out into the woods and through the shadows where I couldn't help you. Go home. Or get caught by the Whisperers. It wouldn't matter to me."

"Yes it would," said Rose. "You are really kind."

The Red Man laughed longer. "I tend the Bounds," he said. "Is a farmer kind to the corn and the apple trees?"

"Farmers are kind to their animals."

"Until they eat them," the Red Man said.

Rose shook her head. "We scratched your gate and you took us in. When the Whisperers trespass, you turn them to stone chimes and hang them in your trees."

"Farmers shoot wolves but keep dogs," the Red Man said. "Wolves aren't bad, but dogs are tame."

"The Whisperers are bad. You know that," Rose said.

He shrugged. "It's not my business. But the Whisperers don't listen when I talk. Farmers and their children sometimes do. The Whisperers won't help make jam or watch me after I have summoned a storm, that's all. Since before the Accommodation, since before the Whisperers or the farmers, I have tended the Bound-lands and all the sandy hills. Tending farmers' children is not my work."

"I don't believe you. I think you like me. I think you even like Jack. Even Tamlin Badger-Boy."

The Red Man passed his handkerchief without a word. "If I like you, it doesn't matter. My place isn't here so that I can help little lost Strangers."

"You let us in your gate," Rose said.

"Yes. And you helped me after the storm. So we are done."

Rose wiped her face and sat for a moment. "Now what happens?" she asked. "Where is Jack? And what will we do here?"

"What happens?" the Red Man said. "On this midsummer night, in the after-blow of the storm? Anything might happen. Anything at all, here or in the hills of sand, where the tower stands."

20

THE SHADOW-FRIEND

To Rose, the Red Man's ruddy face and cinder-white hair made him seem a furnace himself. But after she finished washing the supper things, he had her build up the fire, and he sat heavily in his armchair and was still for a long time.

The wooden clock ticked on, slowly. Through the windows, Rose could see the sky deepen, hear all the big animals grow quiet, the little bugs begin to whine. Somewhere a nighthawk purred; in the field the goats made their gathering noises.

After a while the Red Man roused himself to give her a hard look. Rose realized she had been kicking the leg of her chair.

"Bored girl," he said.

"Yes," said Rose, bolder than she could remember feeling. "Aren't you going to call up a storm again, or set the dogs dancing or stone some Whisperers or something?"

"You could go out and play catch with your ball," the Red Man said, and Rose reached into her pocket without thinking. The smooth wood had cooled, but it still held the memory of the lightning's heat. She snatched her hand back and looked at the Red Man. His eyes were still closed, but he was almost smiling. He had been making sport with her.

The clock ticked, and Rose looked around at the tree-patterned walls, at the shapes inlaid in the wooden floor, and then back at the Red Man as he rested. He was really a painter too, she thought. He had painted this house of trees. He used the winds and the rain to paint the whole of the sandy hills on top of the desert.

Could she stay here? Her parents still had all the work of breaking a farm. Her grandmother had sent her away. Jack had run off. And she had never met Great-Aunt Constance. But the Red Man had taken her in.

She could stay, and Raff and the Red Man could look after her. He wasn't really a man; he was some other terrible kind of thing—he could stone Whisperers and call down lightning; he was the child of the wind and the morning sun. Terrible, but somehow even now the air in his estate held the freshness of dawn, and there was no taint of vapor.

Rose stood. "Evening is coming," she said. "What chores should I do?"

The Red Man didn't open his eyes. "Put out food for the dogs. Put out milk for the cats. Bring in the goats. Lay out straw for the cows."

She went to the door. "Dogs and cats, goats, cows," she repeated.

He shifted to rest his head, as if he was just about to sleep. "And lock the thorn-gate," he added.

✳ ✳ ✳

In the farmyard that evening, the leaves were still soft and wet, but there were no puddles, not here in the hills where the water flowed into the sand below almost as quickly as it could rain down.

Rose found she liked doing the chores with Raff for company. She fed the dogs and the cats. Brought in the goats. She took her time with the cows because after that there would still be the walk through the trees with the staring faces to lock the thorn-gate.

When she was done in the barn at last, she stepped out, closed the wide door, and turned around to find a big man with black-and-white hair standing before her. "Rose Tender," he said.

The Beadle Smith. Tam's father. And he cradled a musket in his left arm. Raff began to bark, and when the Beadle kicked him hard in the side the big dog leapt up snarling. "Don't shoot him!" Rose shouted, and the Beadle roared:

"Down then, dog, or I shoot! Down!"

Raff bent low, but the Beadle kept his musket pointed at him, and the dog went on snarling. From inside the House of Woven Trees, Rose heard Jack's minder and the other big dog begin to bark.

Tam's father smiled. He looked like he had been in the woods a long time that day. He looked like one of the faces in the trees. "Tell your dog to shut up," he said, "and take me inside. I have a letter to present from your grandma."

Rose stared for a moment. "It is not my home. It is the Red Man's—"

"You know my son?" the Beadle interrupted. Rose nodded. "Then you know I dun't mind correcting children."

She looked at the big farmer's hands. "Is that why Tam is mean? Because you beat him?" The Beadle said nothing, and Rose went on. "The Red Man is—is indisposed. And I won't bring you in just because you hit me."

"Take me in because I have some post to deliver. That's reason enough." The Beadle cocked his musket. "Take me in or I'll shoot your dog," he added.

* * *

Inside the House of Woven Trees, Rose read aloud from her grandma's letter. "The Beadle tells me you have not done what I asked," it began:

and I am an old woman, and my bones ache and I am tired. And my sister Constance on the edge of the valley will not have your help with her many cats and dogs and dishes and beets. And her husband the River-man meant to teach Jack to manage horses and boats —

Rose broke off. "That isn't fair! Why would Jack get to work with horses and learn the river when I would only pickle beets and tend cats?"

"Cats dun't take much tending," the Beadle said, and the Red Man remained quiet. The letter went on:

so if you are with the Red Man, which I told you to avoid, in the Bounds, which I told you to avoid, stay there while he will have you, and don't go traipsing through the Tanglewood again, which I told you to avoid, where the Whisperers must be waiting.

Stay until the end of the summer and see if you like his work better, and then maybe if I have not been given a berth on the train, you can come back to help bring in the harvest, and then even return to your parents if they will still want you.

But do not under any circumstances go to Shadow-Town, or trouble with the coffin-train, or ever dream of going to the desert. For I am too tired to find you or help you and my bones ache, and I am tired.

Rose looked up at the Red Man, eyes sharp, but unmoving still after his work in the storm, and at the big Beadle, who sat across from them with his musket on his lap.

"Is it a nice letter?" the Beadle asked.

Rose stared at him. "How could it be?" she said bitterly. "Now, after we have done everything she forbade."

Tam's father smiled as if he remembered some private joke. "I went to some trouble to deliver this letter," he said. "You should be glad to have it to read at all."

"How is she, really?" Rose asked. "Do you think the sleeping sickness could be coming over her at last?"

The Beadle shrugged. "She was muttering to herself, but that might not be from the fever. She might just be old. The next two days will tell the tale."

"What will happen?"

"If she is sick, she will rave and babble and finally only whisper. I'll look in to see if we need to bring a funeral wagon." Rose stared at him and bit her finger. He shook his head. "That's part of my duty, as Beadle," he said. "You dun't need to thank me."

The Red Man shifted a little. "I let you in because you carried the post," he rumbled. "Now your job is done. Go now, Beadle. Night comes."

The Beadle nodded. He looked from one door to another, up at the attic ladder on the ceiling. He said, "Wood-worker, where is my son?"

"You ask, who taught him the way? You a shadow-friend, come to hide from the darkness in my house?"

The Beadle shook his head. "Tamlin knew Words to keep him safe from the shadows."

The Red Man made the thin, rough sounds of shadow-talk: "*Tharkle crith, ca-cawr rok,*" and the Words sounded flat and hollow in those tree-patterned walls. "'Let me pass, I will return.' Did you think that was a pledge he would never need to honor?"

The Beadle ran a hand through his black-and-white hair. "If his Words wun't protect him, he wud've run here, where you taught him to break his word. He's run here to get away from me, and been beaten for it—and then run here again. He'd run here from the Whisperers too."

The Red Man sighed and sat up straight in his chair. Rose quickly got his staff from the door and gave it to him. He said, "I caught Tamlin once and nearly stoned him and hung him like a bell; only he was almost worth the trouble of talking to. But all he promised me was to run away if he could—and so he did. He dug his way under my fences and gates, and later he came back the same way; over and over, until I stopped bothering to trap him. He kept his word only too well, just as his father taught him."

"Old nook-haunter, shut up," the big farmer said.

"Jack is gone too," Rose said. "Maybe they are lost together."

Tam's father swore and cursed again and again. To her own surprise, Rose said very softly, "Be quiet."

Softly, but the Beadle turned. "And is you Tamlin's little girlfriend? Is that how you came to travel the same path?"

"Tamlin's girlfriend?" Rose stared. "I hate him!"

The Beadle laughed. "So Tamlin's mother hated me, but we married." He stood, and his face took on the same wild look Tam sometimes got. He cocked his musket and swung it towards the Red Man.

The dogs began to bark loudly, and as Rose cried, "No!" the Beadle shouted, "Grizzle-pate! Where is my son?"

The Red Man spoke gently. "*Bang,*" he said.

Rose heard a *crack!* and saw the musket kick in the Beadle's arms. A splintering hole appeared in the tree that stood at the heart of the house and gunsmoke began to fill the room.

The Red Man thumped his staff on the floor and got to his feet. "Now you sit!" he said, and struck the floor again so that the whole house shook. "Both sit!"

Rose sat at once, just on the floor where she had been standing. But somehow the Beadle still stood. He sneered down at his musket and said, "My son. I willn't sit because you tell me, dawn-man. Unless you mean to ride the winds and fetch him in my place, while I only stay and nest in yours."

21

TAMLIN'S LITTLE FRIEND

———◆◆◇◆◆———

"Your son is not in my estate," the Red Man told the Beadle. "He is beyond the Bounds I watch."

"You wun't take him in, so he was driven away, just as Jack Tender was."

"That's not true!" Rose said. "Tam disappeared hours and hours before we came here. And Jack left himself in the night."

"To go where?"

"He rode the coffin-train to Shadow-Town, after your son," the Red Man said.

The Beadle nodded slowly, and the deep seams in his face made him seem very old. "The children of the winds is removed from mortal lives," he said, "but still what wicked things they do. You tend these hills but just sit and watch farmers and Whisperers fight."

"You're the Beadle," Rose said. "You're a shadow-friend. You're the son of Founder Smith. Can't you go to Shadow-Town and ask for Tam?"

The Beadle only shook his head. "My son has been your guest, but you willn't help him," he said to the Red Man.

"I roll back the desert, but what takes root beyond my little estate is not for me to say. And of the farmers, Ealda, River-folk, Tinkers, Clatterfolk, Whisperers, goblins, wolves and wild-cats, which are weeds and which are flowers is not my concern."

"But you have your favorites," Rose said. "You like farmers better than Whisperers. You like boys and girls better than wolves."

The Red Man looked at her a moment. "So if I do? I must still do my work. Only all reasonable things like company."

"A bit," said Tam's father. "Sometimes."

The Red Man smiled at the Beadle for the first time. "A bit. A reasonable amount. If my company is reasonable, and good, I like them a little better. And if they are stupid and bad I like them a little worse."

"Yes," the Beadle said. "So you try to keep visitors out so you dun't have to worry about good or bad."

The Red Man rumbled. "Shadow-friend, tell us what the Whisperers say about good and bad."

The Beadle waved his hand through the smoky air. "If they's concerned, they keep their thoughts to themselves," he said, "and only speak in whispers."

"I won't go beyond the Bounds I keep," the Red Man told him. "And if Tamlin Badger-Boy has helped me while away the winter nights hunting and catching him and watching him escape so I could hunt and catch him again, still he has not been my guest. And you are not my guest—even though you have come here with your musket and kicked my dogs and asked so politely."

Tam's father's eyes darted from Rose to the Red Man, and then to the dogs. He turned to look at the door and out the window into the night.

From far, far off, from what might have been the edge of the world, Rose heard the faint rumble of the coffin-train. She had never wanted to imagine it before, but now for the first time she thought of it as a picture: the iron engine, the bodies in their berths, the coffins waiting to be thrust into the fire-box. From far, far off, the whistle blew, low and very quiet, and then lower and quieter still.

"Please," the Beadle said. "If Tam in't here, he's held by them. He is in the Tall House working."

"So you taught him to promise," the Red Man said.

Rose thought of Tam, wicked and laughing and mean. But she remembered her dream. If Tam was in the Tall House, he wouldn't be laughing. He would never trouble her again, not while she was awake. He would labor there in her nightmares, labor forever in the quiet, and no one would help him.

"Please," the Beadle said again, and his face twisted. "I dun't often say that. Please. Or my son will suffer and bear the crown forever."

"The crown of bone and iron?" Rose said. "Tamlin himself wears the crown?"

The Beadle laughed mirthlessly. "An honor," he said. "One that only those swallowed into the Clay Pool and then drawn out again alive is fit to bear."

Rose said nothing, but at those words she felt herself begin to shake. The Beadle turned to the Red Man and said, "Child of the wind, if you don't want to help me, maybe you should help this girl. Her cousin and her little friend both in Shadow-Town and her all alone."

"Please," Rose added. "If the Beadle can bring them back, please help him."

The Red Man stood higher, so that to Rose on the floor he seemed to fill the House of Woven Trees. "Would you have me break the Law that holds us all? Would you see the children of the wind not only tend but play with the world, for good and bad?"

He didn't shout, but his voice shook the walls. "Would you see me bared of my robes of flesh and blood, clad only in my changing power?"

Not even the worst shadow-Words in the Tanglewood had been so ominous. Not even the thunder above the valley had seemed so terrible. Rose hid her face as his voice rolled over them.

At least this would be the end of it. Now at last even the Beadle would fall quiet, then flee back into the Tanglewood.

And when the Beadle spoke back nonetheless, Rose was sure he would die for it. "Tamlin is my son. You have twisted the trails in the Tanglewood once more. At least unmaze your gates of gloom so I can find the way."

Rose peeked out from between her hands. For an instant she thought the Red Man actually shone white with wrath and power, and then he bowed his head and his color seemed to fade. Just dull and grey, and then just the familiar red glow again. The Red Man passed his staff in the air. Then he said, "Now you have only to get to Shadow-Town. Only to find your son. Only to find Jack Tender. Only to get the Whisperers to change their Law. Only to find your way home."

The Beadle gave a small nod. For a moment he looked at Rose and then he shook his head. "She wun't help. She is just a girl. Little Rosie Tender."

Rose whispered, "I'm thirteen years old. I'm older than Jack. I'm two months and a day older than Jack."

But the Red Man rumbled over her. "No. She does what she says, but she still pretends animals have names and thinks they are her friends."

As the Beadle went to the door, Rose asked loudly enough for him to hear: "What will you do when you find him?"

The Beadle turned so that she could see him smile. "I will beat him. And then I will tell him that his girlfriend will be safe as long as she dun't want to leave the estate of the child of the wind and the morning sun."

"I'm not Tamlin's girlfriend," Rose said. "I don't even like him. I don't even like Jack."

"Probably no one likes you either," the Beadle said, and then he went out into the night.

✳ ✳ ✳

Inside the House of Woven Trees, everything seemed different to Rose.

The wooden clock still ticked, and the Red Man—almost himself again, almost only a man—sat deep in his chair and made his noise: *hrmph*. Not impatient this time but only weary, Rose realized.

The wooden clock still ticked, and all the while the fate she had dreamed of was drawing Jack and Tam closer. And the Red Man wouldn't help, but even if he did, in his flesh and blood he was tired and old. And the Beadle in the Tanglewood seemed old and weary too.

An awful fate for Jack and Tam. Because just once, she had tried to show that she was brave too.

Just once, and she had led them into the Bound-lands, to the Red Man, to Shadow-Town. To her nightmare. No matter whether thrall or king, each alone in that thin grey world. Because she had pretended to be brave. And now only the

Beadle was left to help them, and he already seemed old and weary.

Rose looked up to see the Red Man was not looking into the fire anymore. He had been watching her face as these thoughts worked through her. Now she stood, her heart racing, and stared at him.

He was the keeper of the Bounds. He was the child of the wind and the morning sun. And she had helped him call down a storm.

"Is it too late?"

"Too late for who?"

"Can I catch up to him?"

"Do you have leave to go?"

Rose swallowed. "You said that only the fear of what prowls outside binds us."

He turned back to the fire and nodded. "Do you still have your gift from the storm?"

Rose touched the smooth wood in her pocket and nodded. "I'm older than Jack," she told the Red Man. "I'm not a little girl. And I carry a ball of lightning." Her heart was running so fast she was light-headed, almost giddy.

"Raff," she said, and her minder gave her a sharp look. "Jack's dog," she said, "Red Man's dog," and they each looked up. "Good-bye," she said to the dogs. "I have to hurry now."

"Wait," the Red Man said. Rose turned, but he had spoken without even looking up from the fire.

Rose's legs were shaking. "I have to go," she said. "I have to go."

The Red Man only nodded into the flames. His voice seemed to come from far away. "The Whisperers won't think much of you as long as they might catch the Beadle. So if you're going, go and find him quickly, and don't let him sleep— not if you ever want to come out of the Bound-lands again.

And guard your gift from the storm above all — until everything else is already lost."

Rose started to speak, to thank him, or to wish him well, but he held up a hand and spoke harshly now: "Go. Take the dogs until you find the Beadle, but go now, while my gates of gloom are still unmazed. Go!"

22

COMPLAINTS

———❖━❖◆❖━❖———

Rose ran into the black Tanglewood, urged on by the howling dogs. There was some path they knew almost clear of brush, and they roared on up slopes and down gullies, heedless of the muddy floor, careless of the thorns and twigs, and Rose went with them. Not thinking, only carried along by the rush of the dogs like a kite in a storm — with fear, her desperate hopes for Jack and Tam, and terrible excitement all mixed together.

She knew the dogs had come to a clearing when all at once they stopped their chase in a sudden knot of yelps and barks, and Rose tumbled on the ground with them. When she managed to scramble onto her knees among the snarling dogs, Rose saw the Beadle stood before her. He was panting, and leaned heavily on his musket. "Call them off," he said hoarsely.

"Raff! Jack's dog! Red Man's dog!" Rose called. "Down! Down, down, down! Quiet now, down. Your work is done. Quiet."

"Have you brought the dogs to help?" the Beadle asked.

"They have brought me, and will return to the Red Man's estate."

"No help from the Red Man or his big dogs—just little Rosie." He laughed wearily. "Have you become brave?"

"No," she whispered. "But there was no one else."

In the torchlight, Rose could see a kind of twisted smile. "D'you want me to tell you what you will see in the Tanglewood, or in Shadow-Town?"

Rose pressed her lips together and shook her head.

"Come if you want, then," said the Beadle. "But dun't fall behind."

Don't think about it, Rose told herself. *Don't think at all.* "Go back, now," she told the dogs. Raff sniffed at her and barked twice. Then, more quickly than she had supposed, the dogs were all gone. Now in all the reaching Tanglewood, she only had the Beadle.

The Beadle was already pushing his way out of the clearing. "Dun't fall behind," he said.

Rose already knew that in the Tanglewood it was easy to become lost in time as well as space. But it couldn't have been much after they left the clearing that she heard a sound like the rustle of dry leaves, like the sigh of sleep.

She looked at the Beadle doubtfully, but without turning to her, he shook his head. "I've heard worse. That's a liquor my head can hold."

In the torchlight, Rose could see webs stretching across their path—more and more of them as they went farther into the forest. When they came to a place where there were dozens and dozens of strands as thick as yarn closing the trail, she looked at the Beadle. But he was a strong man and simply tore them away in great handfuls.

After some long time the Whispers grew louder and more bold, and she looked at him once more.

"They say, 'Shadow-friend, you know what will happen,'" he told her. "They say, 'You know we rule the night and the shadows and the Tanglewood. Beadle, don't trouble Shadow-Town.'"

Rose was already trying to move closer to the big farmer when she heard the Words: —*klath.* —*t-ser rashk.*

"Nursery rhymes." The Beadle shook his head. "I willn't waste Words on that."

"Don't walk too far ahead," said Rose.

She was sweating, trying to keep up, and the night was warm and still. Now the gnats came, drawn to living blood.

There was no seeing them, not really, until they were on you, and for a while Rose slapped at her face, and the back of her hands, and the bare patches on her arms. Wherever she slapped, she killed gnats, and she could feel the wet bodies of the dead bugs, too small and too many to count.

But Tam's father did not slap himself, or pause, or speak. Only if she lagged behind, he would turn sometimes and she would see his angry face in the torchlight. "Why don't you even mind the bugs?" Rose asked.

The Beadle shrugged. "I can endure many little evils, and many big ones. I have suffered worse poisons to keep friends than this."

Rose stared at him. "But don't they even bite you? Don't they want the blood of a shadow-friend?"

Then the Beadle did slap his cheek, and held out his hand to show it smeared with dead gnats and the blood they had taken from him.

"I feel calmer after I've walked the woods on a night like this," he said. "I'm full of blood. I have more than I need.

And we'll endure worse before we bring Tam home and I can beat him for being foolish."

✳ ✳ ✳

Some time in the middle of the night, they came to another clearing, and the Beadle made her sit and drink watered wine from the skin he carried.

"Tamlin dun't complain either," the Beadle said.

"Not anymore."

"Not even when I beat him."

Rose couldn't keep from saying. "Why do you bother? You beat him and he still disobeys."

"If he dun't mind paying the price, I dun't mind beating him. He'll grow up to be a man who understands the world. A man of business."

"Like the Speculators."

The Beadle breathed heavily for a while. "The Speculators is good men of business at least. They follow rules. They pay the price they contract."

"But they try to cheat farmers," Rose said.

"Like wolves try to eat sheep. If sheep's stupid enough to let them. Smart sheep make friends of goats, or dogs."

"So you teach Tam to be friends with the Whisperers," Rose said.

The Beadle nodded. "But now the Whisperers have made friends with the Speculators too, so we's going to discuss—an amendment to the arrangements."

"Friends with Whick and Snap? But they sold whirligigs to keep the Whisperers away! Was that only some wicked combine for profit too?"

The Beadle shrugged. "All business." His mouth opened wide as he yawned, and Rose looked away.

"There are webs all around us," she said.

The Beadle nodded sleepily. "They've come while we talked. Din't you hear them?"

"The Whisperers make the webs?" Rose felt her stomach drop. "The Whisperers? Not just spiders in the woods?"

"I thought you were a timid girl, but you followed me into the Tanglewood. I thought you were a stupid girl, but maybe you can learn business." The Beadle talked on for a while, slowly, but Rose stopped listening to him. The webs around the reaching poplars had grown thicker already. She saw small shadows moving beyond the clearing. From all around them, fainter than the wind in the leaves, there was a kind of hissing, like fishers casting lines of silk.

The Whisperers made the webs. Not spiders. How many times had she brushed those webs from her hair and shuddered because she thought spiders had made them. But if she had known the Whisperers made them, how she would have shrieked instead.

Now she felt the weight of the Words beating in against them. "Don't listen!" she yelled at the Beadle. "They are calling you to sleep and you will never wake. And I will be alone. Don't listen!"

"Good girl," the Beadle said. "Let me rest a moment, and then I'll rise and smite them."

Rose pulled out the harrow blade Tam had given her and slashed at the webs closing off the path, shouting, "Get up now! Hurry! We must run!" But the strands were thick like ropes of wool, and sticky so they ripped her skin and tore the blade from her grasp.

She turned back to see the Beadle was closing his eyes. "No!" she yelled. She tore at his hair. "No! Get up!"

—*kecklath*, she heard, and—*t-thrak kerrech*. These Words were louder, hardly whispers at all, and she saw shadows standing on the webs between the trees. The rust—Rose clutched for her bag, but it was gone. Her bag was gone, and now one of the Whisperers wore a circlet of gold and it walked through the webs as if they were no more than a curtain of rain. And she had lost both her gifts of iron.

Now Rose looked a living Whisperer in the face. It would have been less horrible if it had looked eager or angry or afraid. But its mouth was hardly more than a slit, and its eyes glittered without feeling.

—kecklath, it said. *—sleep now, Beadle Smith—Rose Tender next.*

The Words gusted against her, and Rose staggered and fell on her knees beside the Beadle.

Without opening his eyes, he said, "Maybe Tam should marry you."

A wave of faintness came over her. Rose grabbed at the Beadle's musket and saw deep into its barrel.

—sleep and wake and to be Tam's bride, she heard.

Rose tugged the musket out of the Beadle's grasp and there was a flash and she was knocked down, and she thought, *lightning again.* Just for that instant, as she fell across the Beadle, she saw some kind of terror cross the face of the Whisperer, and then there was a kind of wet blackness coming out of it; and she heard hisses and someone shouting Words she hadn't heard before.

And there was a terrible smell, worse than the rot at the bottom of a silo, and blackness swallowed her.

✳ ✳ ✳

For a long time, Rose dreamed she was being carried to her wedding. Carried because at a country wedding the bride was supposed to pretend she didn't really want to go. And the guests slapped and scratched at her; and they whispered and murmured as Rose went by, but her ears ached and she couldn't understand them.

Then she heard the whistle of the coffin-train; not loud to her ears, but nearby, and then again more faintly. And now the train was leaving her behind, taking the properly dead west and west to the Blue Mountains, to rise like smoke towards the stars. The coffin-train at a wedding. But who was she to marry?

Then Rose's head hit against something hard. She opened her eyes to see she lay on the floor of the Tanglewood in the morning twilight.

"Wake up," she heard. "We's almost at the other side. It dun't do to cross the Bounds asleep." She put her hands to her head and looked up to see a ghost looming over her in the mist. No, not a ghost. An old man. He would be minister at her wedding to—

She blinked. Not a minister, but an old farmer crouching over her. No, not an old farmer. The Beadle.

"Wake up," he repeated.

"I thought I was to be a thrall," she said, and her words sounded strangely muffled. "That I was to be married to the king of the drowned and the dead."

The Beadle made a bitter laugh. "So you do want to be Tam's bride."

"No," Rose said. "I hate him. Everyone hates him. Even Jack, and he is Jack's only friend."

"But after you wed, you'll be the one that hates him most," said the Beadle. "A good match. You's pretty and he's ugly. He's cunning and you's a fool. Now get up. I have carried you like a sack of potatoes long enough. Get up and we'll walk into Shadow-Town like proud farmers, and then we will see what can be amended."

He pulled her onto her feet. "Your hair," she said.

The Beadle ran his hand over his head. "More grey?"

Rose nodded. "That was a long night in the Tanglewood. Every little Word costs a day and I called many Words, awful Words, the biggest Words. But I think I have some black hair yet to lose."

Rose said nothing. Really his hair was all grey now. Then she remembered. "The one in the golden circlet! And you were almost asleep—what happened?"

"What happened?" The Beadle stretched out his arms and with a kind of smile, he shouldered his musket. "You made the Whisperers afraid of gunpowder. Maybe my grandchildren'll be brave too."

Then the memory of the black wetness, of the smell, came back to her and Rose felt suddenly sick. "I'm not brave," she said. "I don't want to be brave."

But the Beadle only took her hand, and they walked out down the last slope of the Tanglewood and across the tracks. They were still hot from the train, and Rose could smell the blackened ties, the gravel dust.

Just as they entered dusty Shadow-Town they heard a rooster call. Then all the birds of Shadow-Town began to cry: crows and jays and magpies from where they sat on the wood-paved streets, on the false fronts of the old stores on the main street. On the thick webs that spanned the open streets, glimmering in the morning light.

And faintly Rose heard the creak and clatter of machinery from the Tall House at the end of the street. The Tall House that Jack had told her about in that night long ago. Where the thralls labored. Where they must go.

She began to tremble, and the Beadle shook off her hand. "Dun't become a baby now. Whisperers only walk in night and deepest shadow. With morning, Shadow-Town begins to sleep and dream its awful dreams."

"But my awful dreams are of Shadow-Town," said Rose.

23

THE BOY WITH
OLD EYES

The Beadle pounded the door of the Tall House. "Open in the name of the Beadle," he called, but his voice was old and weak.

From inside Rose could hear the slow beating of a hammer and anvil, the squeak and rattle of wooden machinery. She heard Tam's sharp voice—Tam's, not Jack's—and the slap of a lash. "They can't hear you," she said.

"Cover your ears." The Beadle lowered his musket and shot the hasp apart. He handed the smoking gun to Rose. "They heard that," he said, and swung the wide door open.

Inside, Rose saw the shapes of her dream made real. The dawn light poured through red-splashed windows and fell across the machines of torment, all stopped now, and the ragged figures of the thralls silently reaching out in supplication.

But only one thrall even dared raise his face to the open door. It was old Farmer Mathom, Rose saw, just as Jack had told her. Old Mathom who was dead, who had been put in his coffin and shipped on the train. And now he stood on the Endless Stair.

Mother Greene stood at the bellows before the fire-box. And the two rag-clad ones set up high at the loom and spinning wheel must be the Cutter children, Rose thought. The others she didn't know. And Jack—Jack was nowhere to be seen.

"Beadle, Rose," they whispered. "Help us. Help us leave. Help us die and leave."

Rose pressed closer to the Beadle. "More dead than you and me and better them than us," he said. "Don't mind them, unless you want to do their work."

Then she saw Tamlin stood beside them, pale and still. Not Jack here, but Tam—and he wore the crown of bone and iron, and carried his head to one side as if its weight had been too much to bear. Drawn and wrinkled, and ivory pale, like the bony points in his crown. The king. Tamlin-king. *What Words has he had to utter to wear that crown?* Rose wondered. *What orders has he had to fulfill?*

"Tamlin," croaked the Beadle.

A wordless moan rose around them, and Tam's eyes snapped opened, bright and fevered. He nearly straightened his head. "Quiet!" he hissed at the thralls. "Dun't trouble your dreams with speech! Work and make the time until your end pass faster!"

The noises of the workshop began again and Tam smiled thinly. Only then did he look at the visitors. "Father," he said. "How far you must have walked."

✳ ✳ ✳

Tamlin lifted a rough tray that held a wooden cup and a few mushrooms, pale and yellow and dry. "Accept the hospitality of your son the king," he said.

The Beadle knocked the tray from Tam's hand so that it broke, scattering the miserable food and drink. Then he struck his son with a harder blow than Rose had ever seen, and Tam fell across the floor and lay unmoving.

"Fool!" the Beadle said. "Even in your shadow-dreams, to offer your father the fruit of the dead! Wake up enough to speak to us like the living."

As he lay, Tamlin slowly passed his hand over his face; and he looked at the blood on his palm, and some terrible fear seemed to rouse him.

"What is it?" asked Rose. "What's happened?"

The Beadle closed his eyes. "I have shed my son's blood inside the workshop. Here, where the Whisperers insist thralls must never bleed. Or ever to suffer the bleeding to walk."

There was a little shriek from high up, from the balcony where the Cutter children worked, and the girl peered over the edge. *"Blood,"* she hissed and threw a wooden block close to Tamlin's face. *"Blood,"* her brother said, and his block hit Tam on the forehead. Not hard, but enough to make him bleed there as well.

Farmer Mathom stepped down from his Endless Stair and lifted a glass brick from the floor. Slowly the others began taking up tools, if they used them at their labors, or some stick or bar or brick if they didn't.

Rose looked at the red windows. Like a chicken coop — to keep chickens from noticing blood. Like a chicken coop, and now that the thralls had seen Tam's blood, they would kill him because he already bled. "But Tamlin is their king!" she cried.

It was horrible. She wanted to save Tam. She wanted to run.

"Wipe his face," the Beadle told Rose. "I'll cry them off."

"No!" Tam shrieked. "I am the king of bones and shadows, not you!" He got to his feet and turned to the thralls, fixing them with his gaze. *"Kerrech!"* he yelled. *"Kerrech!"*

"No, Tam," Rose said, setting down the musket. "The Words have made you older and thinner already. Let me wipe your face."

But Tam whipped his face from side to side like a baby, the blood flying from his forehead. The thralls had stopped moving, and Tam yelled it a third time— *"Kerrech!"*—and sank back down on the floor.

Then Rose did clean his face with her handkerchief and pressed it against the cut on his forehead. Tam's voice was weak and rasping. "I's the king, not you, old man," he said.

"You will die here as king," Rose whispered. "Let me take off the crown and we will go back to the Red Man." But when she tugged on it, Tam's whole head moved with the crown and his eyes rolled back. Rose shrieked.

"Living or dead it is fixed to my skull," Tam said. He put his hands to his crown and made a terrible smile. He looked at his father. "I remembered the Words you taught me. And I kept my pledge."

The Beadle nodded. Then he glared around at the thralls beginning to stir again about them. "Back to work! I amn't your king, but I am a shadow-friend, and I will curse yous by blood and iron. Go back to work. Climb the Endless Stair, Mathom. Spin at the wheel and rattle the loom, Cutter children. Pump and hammer, Miser Cooper. Work, Farmer Stout, Mother Vining—work!"

Rose watched as, slowly, the thralls obeyed and the workshop began to groan and rattle once more.

It was horrible—and then she stared at Tam. "But where is Jack?" she said again. "I dreamed of him in the workshop too.

Did he only get on the train and never come here at all?"

Tam's smile changed to one of pity. "I set him to work like every other thrall that arrives on the train."

"Where is he?" she demanded. Pity on Tam's face, yet there was something else as well, and she felt ready to begin shrieking once more. "*Where is he?* Jack wasn't nearly dead from the vapors! Jack hadn't fallen victim to the Words—not if he made it all the way to the train awake!"

Rose was panting now, and she grasped Tam by the collar, and she saw the Beadle watching, amused. Tam himself only moved his face away from the blood on her handkerchief. She said, "Jack—Jack shouldn't have been set to work like—" Rose stopped and looked at the Cutter children. At all the other lost and laboring thralls. "Not like these," she finished, more quietly.

Tam lifted her hand from his collar and shook his head. "I gave him a special task."

"Where? Where?"

Tam pointed at a loop of rope set in the floor. "In the earth closet. To gather mushrooms that grow in the earth closet."

"Mushrooms?"

"A worthy task, to gather the fruit of the dead," Tam said.

Still uncomprehending, Rose turned to the Beadle.

"It's an economy, to feed the thralls the fruit of the dead," he explained. "Of the dead, for the nearly dead. Rot-hood mushrooms grow on the earth over the dead."

Rose ran to the center of the workshop, and pulled on the rope with all her strength, calling, "Jack! Jack!" But the door wouldn't budge. Then the Beadle pulled too and the door flew open onto blackness and the smell of decay.

Rose was on her hands and knees peering in at once. "Jack!" she called again, less certainly. Gloom and glowing red spots and the smell of corruption. Heaped shapes where men or women might once have lain. "Jack?"

The Beadle bent down and looked in too. "Take a moment to look and smell," he said to Rose.

"Jack?" she said. The Beadle dropped the big trapdoor shut. "No one down there is still alive."

Rose started to sob, but the Beadle picked her up easily with one hand and slapped her across the face with the other. "You've come all the way through the Tanglewood to Shadow-Town. The nearly dead's all around you. And you'll see more dead than that before you ever get away."

He set her down beside Tamlin. "Stay here with your boy-friend," he said. "Dun't eat his food. If anyone comes, make no bargains."

Rose reached for him, but the Beadle shook her off. "Now I have to speak with the Mayor," he said.

III

THE TOWER OF GLASS

24

THE ANIMAL IN THE EARTH

The night before, when the candle-lantern had shone at last, Jack almost saw too much. Suddenly he could see the glinting specks of sand in the walls, the spiders and cobwebs. He could see the red jack-o'-lanterns properly. He could see the yellow rot-hoods growing where earth lay heaped over bodies.

Too much, and even as he fell back in relief, Jack had to cover his eyes. But when he took his hands away, he saw some hideous thing with shining eyes that looked right into his.

Like a snake caught in the middle of trying to become a squirrel, or an enormous worm with little crouching legs — something that was *wrong* somehow, and all at once Jack was up on his knees, shouting in alarm. The worm-thing began to run, in a hideous squatting way, and suddenly Jack's fright changed to revulsion.

He made a wild grab and caught it by its long tail. He whipped it away the way he once saw Tam treat a gopher that had been caught in one of his nooses but not quite killed. And like the gopher, the rest of the worm-thing snapped off from the tail and flew away to finish dying.

"They're vermin, and my father gives me a penny for each one," Jack remembered Tam explaining. Then Tam had smiled as he stuffed the tail in a pocket. *"It's the merciful way to do it."*

But this thing was a *skink*, Jack remembered; the wormy things were skinks, and everyone in the sandy hills hated them. But as the shiny body of the skink struck softly against the cellar's sandy wall, the tail in Jack's hand began to quicken and squirm, somehow became a living snake itself. Jack shouted and tossed that away too, but it didn't land far. For a long moment by the light of the candle-lantern he watched the tail go on thrashing and curling wildly—all the time expecting it to start worming towards him—until by slow degrees it grew still, and lay dead at last.

And the rest of the skink, the part with the arms and eyes, hadn't died at all. He saw the shiny body scurry off, bowlegged, up the wall and over a rough ledge. Now he was alone again in the earth closet with the mushrooms—the red ones that were poison, the yellow ones that fed on the mounded bones of the dead. Now he found himself sorry he had done it.

Jack held up the candle-lantern and looked into the shadows beyond the ledge. Not just shadows. A deeper blackness: a hole. A nearly man-size hole. And he remembered Tam had told him he had tried to leave the night before. Tamlin Badger-Boy, had.

He tucked the Smith's knife back in the sheath around his neck, beside Rose's bag of rust, and reached up to put the little candle-lantern on the edge of the hole. He scrambled and heaved himself up, and began to crawl blindly through the dirt, away from the unknowing things behind him.

* * *

Jack had been in Tam's tunnels before, and he had always hated being among the worms, hardly able to breathe. Hated feeling the earth closing around him, wondering if it would all collapse and bury him alive.

And those were short tunnels he had followed Tam through, tunnels that were just a way to get under a fence, into some old ring of trees standing in the middle of a field.

Now he was alone, with the lantern Tam had left him providing only the faintest memory of light somewhere behind him. Jack could raise himself on his elbows just enough to push forward a few inches before he had to sink back into the earth. Just a few inches, and he counted how many times he did it as a way to keep from going mad. Sometimes he forgot to count, and when he remembered again he would have to guess at how many he had missed. But at two hundred he found that he wanted to thrash and scream, and only the memory of Tam kept him from doing it. When he got to five hundred, he almost lost control again, but somehow it was the memory of the skink that saved him. When he got to eight hundred, he had been about to panic, but then found to his surprise that he was actually resigned to this endless squirming. When he got to nine hundred and forty-three, the tunnel ended and there was nowhere else to go.

Then Jack did panic, and thrash, and he tore like an animal, like Tamlin himself, at the earth. And it fell around him as he dug, and closed on him, and he would have screamed but dirt filled his mouth, and he would have breathed it in and died—but he felt the tips of his fingers break through to the surface, and he held his breath and pulled and squirmed and his hole crumbled around him even as he dug. And then his head was out and he felt the open air about his face and tasted it, damp but fresh, and breathed it in, saw bright day pour through cracks, and he crawled into the world above at last.

* * *

Jack finally emerged from a storm cellar attached to an abandoned house. For a moment, he stood blinking in the morning light, filthy and alone.

In the back was a yard with a ruined shed. The lawn and what had once been a garden were overgrown with weeds and long grasses, nearly wild again. And in front was a dusty street with the Tall House standing on the other side.

He could still faintly hear the labor of the thralls; the unceasing clanks and creaks and groaning. But there was nothing to be done. He had to leave the thralls and the workshop behind.

Jack turned and went through the yard, over a sagging fence, and south down along a rough lane. On either side other homes had once backed onto the lane. But they weren't homes now; just broken houses with spotty cracked windows.

Here and there crows perched on glinting lines running above him between the buildings. Webs again, like in the Tanglewood. Webs that were a shadow-boon.

He cut through yards and gardens overgrown with thistles and dandelions and guarded by their own broken-down sheds. Some of the yards even had laundry lines left, and odd scraps of clothing still hung on and flapped in the wind. Clothes that people had worn before this was Shadow-Town; clothes that had clad people who were dead long ago—dead, and the lucky ones had only died, and not first served out some long nightmare as thralls.

Somewhere Jack heard a screen door swing on a rusty spring; somewhere a dog made a thin, hungry bark; somewhere a cat screeched. Then from all around him and through the dismal streets, Jack realized there were faint whispers too: muttered shadow-rhymes and terrible Words.

He went onto the proper street, and even here, whispers, faint, but in the day: whispers, under the sun, in the open street. Rising and falling, the way Grandma muttered in her sleep. —*sleep and wake as thralls to sleep and work forever,* he heard. —*chotr, rashk.* They were here, nesting in the houses of Shadow-Town—he had always known that. But he hadn't thought to hear them mutter their vile Words and curses this way, aimlessly wicked even in their sleep.

Run, part of him thought. *No,* another part thought. I have been on the coffin-train. I have been in the Tall House with the sleeping thralls and the king with the crown of bone and iron. I have been cast in the earth with the dead and the things that feed on the dead and emerged alive. I won't run from whispers now.

Jack swallowed and looked around the empty and web-strewn streets. They had been trodden down. Thousands of little footprints covered them. Prints made by the boots of the Whisperers, pointed heel and toe. At every corner, the oily smoke rose from clay smudge pots. To the south, the bright part of the hazy sky, a road climbed towards a small hill crowned by a house larger than the rest, and then the town seemed to stop. South, where the desert was.

When Jack got as far as the big house on the hill, he saw that there were only a few shacks beyond it, then a wide field, and then a scrubby sort of open country.

Just a little farther and he would be out of Shadow-Town. Out of Shadow-Town, beyond the smoke, but on his way to the desert where no one went.

Now, go now, the old, frightened Jack thought. Instead, the new Jack went to examine the house. It wasn't just bigger than the other houses in Shadow-Town but grander. Shabby and long neglected like the rest, yet it had wide verandas, and three chimneys, and a turret. And it was made of biscuit-brown bricks, not wood.

It must have been the Mayor's house, Jack realized. The house Tamlin's grandfather, Founder Smith, had built. He thought of it full of the lost elegances that his grandma remembered. It would have had cut-glass bowls and china plates. Jack felt the whispers rising all around again and shook his head. Slip-covered footstools. Dozens of tiny porcelain animals. Smithton bricks sitting on crochet doilies.

Jack smiled. Maybe he could find some little elegances to take for his grandma. And seeing them would cheer her, and that would prove she wasn't ill, and the sleeping sickness wouldn't take her. He shook his head. That didn't make sense. She was either ill or she wasn't.

But he found he had already started going up the wooden sidewalk. His grandma would be better and then he would go home. He had an overwhelming desire to look inside before he left Shadow-Town to go into the desert.

He stopped. Shook his head again. —*suchoth neery,* he heard, and Jack thought they were the most pleasant Words he had heard. —*suchoth neery, Jack Tender.* —*come and see us.*

The Mayor's house. Yes, it had been the Founder Smith's house before the Accommodation, before this was ever Shadow-Town.

But what dark Mayor welcomed him now?

Jack didn't remember having coming this far. But he saw his hand was on the brass handle. —*suchoth neery, theery coth.* He was opening the door before he understood: these Words weren't the mutterings of a sleeping Whisperer. They were uttered just for him.

Too late, too late. *Run*, he told himself, but from the house he heard, —*klath-claw-crith.* Nothing pleasant now, only strong

Words meant to curse him into sleep. He thought to just walk in. It was day, and most of the Whisperers would be asleep at least. This time he could just walk in and pour Rose's rust on the Mayor's head, and it would smoke and melt. Then he could burn down the town. Then he would find Tam.

Now some stray breeze came and caught the sighed Words of the sleeping Whisperers and they drifted down on him like leaves. *—webs have trembled, farmers come.*

Jack blinked a few times. He would just walk in and pour rust on the Mayor's head.

—have them join us—make them rest. His knees went weak again. He began to fall down, to fall asleep, and he knew that he would wake to be a thrall, but some little part of him was happy that he had tried at least.

Just before his face struck the ground, something caught the back of his jacket and jerked him upright. Jack blinked, and he tried to get back on his own feet, but he began to fall over again.

Then he was turned around and someone slapped him across the face, hard—once, twice—and then Jack had his hands up. "Beadle Smith," he croaked.

25

THROUGH SLEEPING SHADOW-TOWN

———◆◦◆◦◆———

The Beadle's hair was all grey now—he had become old some-how, Jack thought—but he still held Jack up as though he were a puppy.

"Jack Tender," said the Beadle. "Is you awake now?" Jack nodded and the Beadle slapped him harder still so that tears started from his eyes. Jack tried to grab the Beadle's fingers, but the big farmer caught his arm and twisted it up behind his back until Jack squirmed in pain. "Is you awake enough to hate and be angry?"

"Yes!" The Beadle suddenly dropped him and now Jack did fall onto the ground. "I hate you," Jack said.

The Beadle smiled. "A good start. Now what's you doing, matted with dirt, here outside my father's house?"

Just for a moment Jack wondered whether the Beadle

meant something quite terrible. No; the Beadle's father had been Founder Smith, the Mayor before it was Shadow-Town.

"I can't go back to the Tall House. But I can't just leave and go back through the Tanglewood. I can't just leave."

The Beadle looked at him curiously. "Do you and the girl like Tamlin so much?"

"Rose?" Jack said. "No, Rose doesn't like Tam at all."

"But she came with me all through the Tanglewood."

"*Rose*—is she here?"

"In the Tall House, watching after Tamlin," the Beadle said. "Safe enough, for now, for Shadow-Town."

"Rose walked through the Tanglewood at night for Tam?"

The Beadle nodded. "For Tamlin and for you, I think. Is she his little girlfriend?"

Jack shook his head slowly. "I told you, Rose doesn't like him at all." He tried to work out why Rose would do such a thing. Or why he had. "It's just that we all entered the Tanglewood together. And there was no one else."

"So," said the Beadle. "So. And how did you plan to help Tamlin here at his grandfather's house?"

"I planned to walk in and empty my bag of rust on the Mayor's head." The Beadle stared at him for a moment, and Jack added, "It's day. Most of the Whisperers sleep."

"You and your cousin both," the Beadle said.

"What do you mean?"

"I knew your fathers," said the Beadle. "But perhaps they married women weak in the head."

Jack began to bristle at that, but the Beadle cuffed him. "Here's Jack Tender so tired he nearly falls asleep on the sidewalk outside the Mayor's house. Feel the Words beat down! Sleep, sleep! How heavy they'd fall over you inside, with the Mayor of all the Whisperers and his aldermen right here, muttering Words in their dreams."

And Jack could feel that the Words were still coming, and felt himself almost begin to sway again. "Then what?" he said. "What can we do? Should we just burn the town?"

The Beadle smiled. "I wanted to be sure they still nested here, that Whick and Snap hadn't moved in instead. Now I'll show you how to worry their dreams—until they wake and want to parley."

From behind a curtain in the parlor of the Mayor's house, just for an instant, Jack thought he saw a flash of gold. "But I don't think the Mayor sleeps, not really," he said.

The Beadle grabbed him by the arm. "So you and I will go all through the town today, to worry him so much he will have no rest at all—and come back to this house before evening falls."

* * *

As they walked the main street of Shadow-Town, past the false fronts and faded signs, crows and jays and magpies greeted them—"thief birds," the Beadle called them. A smoky north wind blew down the street, tossing leaves that had fallen early, old scraps of paper, and some dirty, gauzy things: tumbled-up balls of old whisper-web, Jack realized. Grit and dust flew through the air.

"A fine day to grow old," the Beadle said. "Grow old and die, maybe."

He took Jack by the chin and looked down into his face. He wants to see the bruises he gave me, Jack thought. Maybe he will regret them, or maybe he will think they weren't big enough.

"You have said shadow-Words," the Beadle said, and his hand was firm around Jack's jaw. "Not many, not often. But you dun't have young eyes anymore."

"Tam taught me," Jack said.

"Is that why you hate him?" The Beadle's hand tightened. "No lying, not now."

"I hate him because he boasts and he sneers and he is too mean to my cousin. We fight and he always wins. And he threw me in the Clay Pool."

"In the Clay Pool?" the Beadle said, with a kind of satisfaction. "Well then of course you'd hate him. Those is all the reasons Tam hates me." He gestured at the nearest shop. "Can you hear the whispers from this place?"

The shop's glass windows had been broken out long ago. Above one of them was a faded sign:

⚜ D.Q. TAPPER, GENERAL MERCHANT ⚜
Complete stock of goods
always on hand at lowest prices.
Highest prices paid for furs.
We are always up to the times!

And whispers came in and out of the building as if it were breathing: —*klah, t-ketch.*

"Your shadow-friends are in there," Jack said.

The Beadle smiled. "You see, I hate my friends too." Then he took out a bag of rust and poured a line of it across the windowsill and another over the threshold. "Go on in now. Dun't worry about knocking. Mr. D.Q. Tapper willn't mind."

The lock had been snapped long before, and when Jack pushed the door it made a terrible creak, but it opened easily enough. Jack took an uneasy step inside. He could see that once, Tapper must really have sold almost everything: Skins and furs. Bolts of cloth. Tin toys. Nails. Peppermints. Raspberry-drop candies. Now it was all broken up and lay scattered across the floor.

"Why did they do it?" Jack asked. "Whisperers don't need any of these things."

"Maybe D.Q. Tapper did it himself because he cudn't stand to leave his store to them. Or maybe once some farmer-lads came in on a dare and broke things just for fun."

"Maybe when you were young, you came and did this with some friends."

The Beadle looked around. "That wud've been a dangerous thing to do."

"Maybe you do hate all your friends," said Jack. He grasped the hard edge of the shop counter. "Where are they? Cast iron on them and let's go."

Tam's father used the end of his musket to lift up the edge of a wolfskin. Under it lay a small grey figure, and Jack stepped back. The Whisperer would have been less frightening if it had looked more like a person—or more like a wooden stock. It was the *in-betweenness* that was horrible. It moved as it breathed too, with terrible regularity, like some clockwork thing at a carnival.

Now the whispers in the air sounded almost awake—frantic and desperate: —*kleth, t-ser*—*no, no*—*he is no shadow-friend.*

The rest of the pile of furs began to quiver. The Beadle took out an iron chain—and all in one motion he stepped forward and wrapped it around the Whisperer, like a farmer tying a steer.

The Words stopped at once. The stock-shape opened its eyes and met Jack's gaze, and for the first time Jack thought one of the Whisperers looked like a real living thing, and it began a high, horrible scream. A long scream that didn't pause for any breath.

Now something beneath the pile of furs was writhing, and the Whisperer's blank face changed to a mask of pain, and then changed again to look like some twisting shape of thorns, and then like a human baby in torment, and the room seemed to spin. Jack closed his eyes and smelled something like burning flesh and acid. "No!" he shouted. "No! Stop it!"

The Beadle grabbed his arm and Jack heard him begin to roar: "Down, down, you others! *Kerrech! Korch, t-thrak!* Dun't think you can leave! I have poured rust on the sills and rust on the threshold! Stay asleep in your covered nest or I'll cast more rust and bind yous to a turning wheel of iron! Down!"

To Jack he snarled, "Your little cousin stared a greater Whisperer than this in the face and shot it with a musket. Open your eyes!"

Jack saw a charred and twisted shape where the Whisperer had lain. Whatever else lay beneath the rest of the heap of furs was quiet and unmoving.

"How many of them are there?" he asked.

"Enough to trouble your dreams," said the Beadle. Then he took Jack outside and gave him a little push down the street. "Do you hear the voices differently now?"

A gust of wind rose up and cast grit into Jack's face. Tears welled up and he blinked and tried to brush his eyes clear. There were a few whispers coming from D.Q. Tapper's store again, others drifting from down the street. "They sound less certain," he said. "They sound distressed."

The Beadle smiled broadly. "You can do the next one," he said. "Then they'll hate you too."

26

THE MANTLES OF GOLD

<hr />

Through the morning, Jack and the Beadle had searched out
places where the Whisperers might be resting. And in each,
they *troubled* them, as Tam's father put it.

They had fought off the sleep and dreams that rose
above the woken things, and even as the whispers had risen
to screams, they had imprisoned the shadow-things in lines
of iron dust, and bound them with threats and curses, and
terrible Words.

Slowly the whispers that drifted like smoke through the
streets had begun to change. The lulling mutterings and calls
to sleep became anxious and disturbed. Even the shadows in
the open streets seemed sharp and rough.

And Jack had taken his turn in the troubling, and now
in their hisses and curses, the Whisperers called him by

name. They had learned to hate and fear him, just as they did the Beadle.

When he had sealed the sixth house with lines of iron powder, Jack sank onto the dusty sidewalk as the Beadle closed the door behind them. He felt himself begin to shake and tremble as though a fever had come over him. "This is terrible work," Jack said. "They are monsters, but hear them scream. This is terrible to do even to them."

"Get up, boy," the Beadle said. "It in't done."

"I have been crawling through the Tanglewood and the earth closet below the Tall House and Shadow-Town since the day before yesterday," Jack said. "I have no more strength, and the whispers are growing worse."

"It's less trouble to stay awake now," the Beadle said. "Who would want to join them in these bad dreams?"

Jack shook his head. "The dreams seem only bitter now. But before they were so sweet they turned your stomach."

The Beadle stood over him for a long moment, and Jack felt the sun grow warm and heavy. He hadn't smelled the vapors, not rising in the daytime streets, but it felt as if the sleeping sickness was stealing over him anyway. The Whispers scratched loudly in his ears, in his head:

—*Jack Tender, farmers' son, we will come in the night.*

—*we will bind sleep over you.*

—*you will sleep like the dead, and your family will ship you alive onto the coffin-train.*

—*Jack Tender, we will come in the night for you.*

"You's dizzy," the Beadle said.

Jack looked up. The sky behind the big farmer seemed to spin. "Can't you hear them?"

"I hear them, but I dun't listen. Do your business." The Beadle kicked him hard in the side. "Tamlin and your cousin wait in the workshop for us."

Jack turned over and was sick onto the dirt, and then sick again. He rolled away from it and onto his back. Like a beaten dog he looked up at the Beadle.

The Beadle smiled thinly. "You should have room for more bile now."

—Jack Tender, we will visit your grandmother tonight.

* * *

As the warmth of the day began to settle over the dusty streets at last, the Beadle stopped at a corner to pick up a burning clay pot. Jack wrinkled his nose.

"A smudge pot," the Beadle said. "A kind of little elegance to the Whisperers—makes a foul light to cast shadows in the nighttime; makes filthy smoke to shade the sunlight in the day."

"Leave it," Jack said. "It stinks."

The Beadle laughed. "I spent the night in the Tanglewood. You escaped the Tall House crawling through the earth like a worm. Nothing stinks compared to us. And we may need a light."

They turned south once more for the broken street that led to the Mayor's house. When they stopped before the big house on the hill, their shadows were hardly long enough to cross the wooden walk.

"Just noon," the Beadle said with some satisfaction. "Listen to the town."

"Quiet," said Jack hoarsely. "Quiet and miserable. I can even hear the wheels in the Tall House creaking from here. But this place will be the worst. Do you know what you will say to the Mayor?"

Tam's father was old and bent now, Jack thought, but he stretched out his big arms and made a hungry grin as he cracked his knuckles. "I'll tell him the sun is risen and he is weak," the Beadle said. "I'll tell him I still have time to burn Shadow-Town and sow rust across the streets, and bind him to a turning wheel forever and ever. I'll tell him we must amend our arrangement."

Jack shuddered. "Think how he will scream."

"Think what they will do now that they hate Jack Tender. Is my curse more horrible than the sleeping sickness? Than seeing your family shipped in coffins, alive, to Shadow-Town?"

"Don't speak of it," said Jack.

But the words — *sleeping sickness* — had been let loose in the air already, and above the faint creaking of the machinery at the Tall House, through the steady buzz of the grasshoppers and the flies, almost as loud as the bark of a hungry dog, the Words came again: — *kleth, t-ketch, kleth — sleep farmers, sleep and ail, and wake to be our thralls.*

"They will catch us after all," said Jack. "They will infect us with their own sleep because we are too tired ourselves already. You are too old."

For a moment, Jack thought the Beadle meant to strike him again, but the big farmer only pulled his hand through his thin white hair. "Am I an old man now?" he asked. "Am I very old already?"

"*Old*," whispered Jack. "You were old when you came into Shadow-Town from the Tanglewood, and your Words here have cost you years since."

The Beadle twisted his face in a smile that reminded Jack of Tam in one of his most horrible moods. "You have grey hairs now too," he said.

He went through the gate and strode up the long walk as though he were young again. He poured a line of rust before the threshold and then hammered at the brass knocker. "A courtesy," he said to Jack. "It was my father's house once."

After a moment, the door opened, and they stepped inside, but no one came to greet them.

Ahead of them was a long and dusty hall. Tall old windows let in broad shafts of daylight. The wooden floor was bare, but Jack saw an umbrella stand. A table with elaborately carved legs. There was a staircase curving up to the left, and an oak door with a cut-glass knob to the right. No Whisperers waited. They heard no sleeping Words. Only a kind of living silence. And the door that opened onto the parlor swung in and out, just a little, and in time with the smallest rattling breaths of whatever stood inside.

Jack tried to think of Words that might help him, but none came; he tried to think of anything to say at all, but his mind had become as quiet as the hall.

When the hiss from behind the door came at last, Jack screamed.

"Quiet!" the Beadle bellowed over him, and over the chorus of hisses that ran into the hall. "Quiet! I bear iron! I know Words to bind yous! I am Beadle Smith, the shadow-friend, and I know all your most feared curses and torments! I have wandered your mazy woods! I have kept your secrets — and now I say *quiet!*"

For a moment the hall was quiet again, and Tam's father took Jack's wrist and pulled him into the parlor.

The Beadle set down the smudge pot, and one by one, he tore the curtains from the windows. Jack blinked from the smoke, and from the midday light suddenly pouring through it. This was a parlor out of his grandma's dreams, Jack thought, the parlor as it must have been when Founder Smith lived here, master and Mayor of the town he had made. The silverware was tarnished, but it shone in the sun; the crystal glasses were dusty, but they sparkled in the noon light. There were lamps with stained-glass shades. Fringed coverings over the backs and arms of chairs. Little porcelain animals in glass cabinets.

Around the room a half-dozen small figures stood stock-still. *Whisperers.* And not just Whisperers, for they all wore golden circlets too: these were the aldermen, the Whisperers who were next to the Mayor in authority. Half even had mantles of gold cloth over their shoulders as well. And one of these stood before the fireplace, undistressed by the bright light of day.

The others in golden mantles opened their eyes, and then one by one, the three who wore only circlets too.

—it begins, Jack heard. *—it begins.*

Awake. How was that even possible, when the sun was the first of the shadow-banes? Awake—and the ones with the most gold were most awake—

Before Jack could follow that thought, the Beadle had plucked the golden circlet from the alderman nearest him so that it stood bare-headed in the sunlight. Its pupils flicked from long flat slits to wide circles. The hole it used for a mouth opened to begin making the awful thin scream Jack remembered. The Beadle reached into the bag around his neck and cast iron at the Whisperer's face, and it began to smoke, and it was no longer as still as stone.

The next instant it was a step farther away, then three steps, as if it moved during the blinking of Jack's eyes, and then the Whisperer began to spin in quick circles around the edges of the parlor.

It went on screaming as it moved. As it spun around them it smoked like firewood just before the flames begin. Then quicker yet, it darted towards the long front hall.

"You can't!" cried Jack. "It has been sealed with iron!"

The Whisperer made the loudest scream of all, and it began to spin in place—like a top. Faster and faster, and somehow it ripped up the floor as it twisted and screamed, and floorboards and nails and woodchips and sawdust flew out. As if a cyclone had appeared in the big parlor, as if some huge drill turned fast and hot inside the room, digging down, down. The screaming mixed with noise of the shattering floor, and Jack had to shield his eyes from the flying bits of wood.

When he looked again there was only a dark, rough hole in the floor. The Whisperer had vanished someplace below, and there was only quiet again in the parlor.

For a moment, a cloud dimmed the bright windows. Then Jack heard one in a golden mantle whisper again as if nothing happened, or as if didn't matter—*it begins.*

"Which is the Mayor?" the Beadle demanded. "We have a bargain to discuss! Is you the Mayor?"

—*too late*, the Whisperers hissed. All of them, for they were all awake now. —*too late—he was gone before you arrived—he has taken his long cloak of gold and walked through the sunlight to the Tall House to see the king.*

"He will find Tam and Rose!" Jack cried.

—*too late*, they hissed again, and each of the Whisperers began to turn. Not so quickly as the first, but as they turned, they cast out thick strands of silk. They spat webs from their mouths, and soon the room began to fill.

* * *

"Get out my father's knife," the Beadle rasped.

Jack pulled the blade free and held it in both hands.

—*the Smith's knife!* called the Whisperers, and that made Jack smile as he cut down across the spinning silk. They remembered this blade. He would cut his way out with the Smith's knife then.

—*the Smith's knife has come to trouble us again—bind them!— tie them with webs!—drown them in sleep!* The webs were thick and gluey, but not enough to stop the heavy blade. He struck at them again and again, parting them easily—but not as quickly as the Whisperers could cast them.

Webs were being cast around his feet, were winding up his arms, and he shouted Words that Tam had taught him, Words to slow and bind. As he shouted, one or two of the Whisperers would falter, but the others would only turn faster and make the thin breath that cast more silk. How often had he heard that hiss in the Tanglewood without understanding what it really was? He would have struck them, but they were too far from his blade, and now he felt webs falling over his eyes.

Then there was a spray of rust, and the sound of Whisperers screaming, and more rust, and the acid smell. "My father's house!" he heard the Beadle roar. "Leave! Leave or perish!"

But the rust slid off the golden mantles, and one of those stood in front of him and spat webs into his face. He heard the Beadle roar on, but Jack was blind now. And he swung his blade blindly all around him and roared like Tam, and felt the Smith's knife strike deep into something that screamed— like a pig in a slaughterhouse, he thought. He tore the webs from his eyes to see all the other Whisperers were spinning around the Beadle, winding a cocoon around him.

Jack cast iron all around, and the Beadle tore webs from his mouth and spat and roared out a stream of horrible Words that made the Whisperers stagger. Before they could recover, Jack cut webs right and left, and with two swift strokes, he parted the cords that bound the Beadle.

The Beadle gave Jack a look of amazement and then tore himself free of the rest of the silk. Before the webs could begin again, he shouted a Word Jack had never heard; a Word so terrible that Jack could never even bear to remember it. Only three Whisperers remained, and they staggered back and then toppled over, and then the Beadle began struggling to pile them on top of one another, like logs for a bonfire. "Quickly," he said in a ruined voice. "Help me, Jack, quickly."

"No, run, let's run," Jack said.

But the Whisperers, still unmoving, were opening their eyes again. One of them made a laugh like dry leaves rustling and then a soft hiss.

—*suchoth neery, Jack Tender.* —*neery, suchoth neery, the Beadle Smith.*

It was too much. The Beadle was too old. Jack was too young. They were both at the end of their strength.

Jack reached for the smudge pot and put it on top of the alderman that was speaking.

He raised up Founder Smith's heavy blade in one shaking hand. The Beadle closed his fingers around Jack's. Together, just as everything was going black, they smashed it down across the clay pot, and it spilled, and the oil caught fire as it poured down across the Whisperers stacked like firewood, and then there was only smoke and screaming, and then, without knowing how, Jack and the Beadle were outside.

Screams and smoke spread through the air as the Mayor's house and the aldermen they had found in it began to burn. Much sooner than Jack would have imagined, the whole house was flaming like a giant torch. Eventually the screaming stopped.

But Shadow-Town's Mayor himself had escaped them. And he would be protected by a long cloak of gold.

27

THE PENDULUM

———◆━◆━◆━◆———

Jack held up the Beadle and tried to hurry him though the streets.

Now they heard not whispers in the air but hungry howls and angry shrieks, and the crows and ravens and magpies and even the blue jays screamed down from webs that ran gable to gable along the houses, lining the streets of broken Shadow-Town. Shadow-webs, Jack understood now.

"The mill-wheel is quiet," said the Beadle. His voice was weak and quavery. An old man's voice. "The whole engineery is silent. The workshop has stopped."

Outside the Tall House, the Beadle raised himself up to kick at the wide wagon door. The old man leaned on Jack and kicked again and again, until it opened and the afternoon sun spread across the silent workshop.

Inside, Jack saw the dim shapes of the thralls again. Farmers like his parents; farmers' children like him and Rose, and they reached out to the open door and the afternoon light. Like they are dying of thirst, and we hold water, Jack thought.

He couldn't bring himself to go back inside until the Beadle went first, and then Jack saw gold glint here and there in the gloom. More of the gold-crowned aldermen, awake in the day, untroubled by the open door, the strong southern light.

"Rose?" Jack whispered. "Tam?"

The flames in the open furnace seemed to breathe and twist, but everything else was still. On the ledge above, the Cutters' loom and wheel were quiet. Farmer Mathom's Everlasting Stair was at rest. The thralls stood at their machines, but the huge wooden gears had stopped turning.

One new thing moved: a great pendulum mounted high in the attic where the crows roosted swung above the other machinery. It passed low over their heads, crossed the whole workshop in a long, silent arc. Jack counted four heartbeats as it swung from one side of the workshop to the other, four as it swung back again.

The weight was some dark and heavy lump. A weighted barrel perhaps, wrapped in a clump of the whisper-web. It seemed to be slowing, whatever it was, and Jack counted again. *One — two — three — four* and then back. Still four heartbeats to a swing. For a moment Jack had a terrible thought, that the pendulum didn't mark how quickly time passed, but how it slowed — how it didn't move at all. That there were only these few heartbeats, four one way, four the other, over and over for eternity.

Then one Whisperer began to chant, in time with the pendulum. *— klah, rok — kleth, klah.* It kept the same time as a lullaby, Jack realized. Some horrible lullaby.

But he shook his head. "Too late for your whispers. We won't sleep now."

"*Tamlin,*" said the Beadle, but his voice was creaking and weak, and Jack wondered if he had been wrong, if the old farmer might sleep yet.

"Tam!" Jack called, but there was no answer except for the ripple of whispers. Still four heartbeats to a swing, but the arc of the swing was shorter now. It wasn't time but the pendulum that was slowing.

—time for sleep, tired shadow-friend—you have done your work.

—t'ketch, kecklath—through the Tanglewood your years were passing—now take your long-earned rest.

Tam's father shook his head, passed his hand over his eyes.

—chotr, klah—sleep, sleep, and let your work and worry end.

"Tamlin," the Beadle said softly.

The great weight began to twist and wobble as it swung.

Tamlin. Jack's eyes were used to the dim now. It was Tam wound up in a cocoon, and only his crown and ugly face sticking out. Tam swinging upside-down at the end of a long line of whisper-web.

"Tamlin!" the Beadle moaned. He stepped forward and reached up to cut the swinging line with his big knife, and old man or no, he caught the heavy bundle as it fell.

"Tamlin, tell me is you alive or dead? Tamlin! Answer me or I will beat you! Tam!"

"And Rose—," Jack said. "Rose!" he called. "Rose, are you here?"

Jack didn't hear the Words the Whisperers made then, but he felt them beating down hard, very hard. Tam's face was grey, and he was bundled in grey webs, and the workshop was grey—grey like his own father's face had been when they put him in the coffin; grey like his dream of the crown of bone and iron.

This is what the world must always be to a thrall, Jack thought. All thin and grey and quiet, and Jack thought how easily he could slip into it, even now. Only he saw one bright patch of gold. No crown or mantle, but a great draping of golden cloth. "Look!" he said to the Beadle. "Look! This is the Mayor—all in gold! Look!"

But the Beadle only looked to Tam and slapped him hard, and he tore at the ball of web-stuff and slapped his son again.

The gold-clad Mayor stepped forward, stepped unafraid into the daylight that came through the open wagon door, and his face was as terrible and blank as all the others, but his figure wasn't twisted and dim. He stood brighter than any living creature Jack had ever seen, bright like something that had been born in the heart of the sun. The Mayor glittered and shone like living gold.

"Cloth of gold," Jack said quietly, understanding the business at last. "That's why the Whisperers want the Speculators' gold. To weave cloth of gold and outface the sunlight, to escape the first of the shadow-banes."

Jack spoke, but maybe these were things the Beadle already knew, or maybe he no longer cared. "Is Tamlin dead?" the Beadle asked the Mayor.

—kleth, techlath, the Whisperer said. *—not dead. not yet—the boy is the king of the drowned and the dead—not dead, not yet.*

"Why would you string up your king?" Jack asked.

—you have the shadow-bane of rust; you have the Words we taught to Founder Smith as the price of Accommodation—we have the Beadle's son—and his suffering tells our time.

Now Tamlin lay curled at the Beadle's feet, pale and still. Dead, thought Jack, he is dead after all. But then he saw his friend's arms and legs twitch, as if rehearsing some agony he had suffered before he was fixed to the line. "A deal," croaked the Beadle. "We will amend the bargain. Let him come back to me. We will make some better deal."

The Mayor made a rattling hiss. *—we have a contract already, shadow-friend, with all the farmers and with you especially—you have*

the Words we taught your Founder Smith as a private Accommodation —
you drew your son out of the warm Clay Pool to make him fit for us —
your son pledged himself to us.

"He din't know," the Beadle said. "I never knew this was what you might do."

—we never knew farmers would cast rust on our hidden hollows,
close our paths with turning wheels.

—who stepped into the shadow-march even in daylight? —who
entered the Bound-lands at night? —who twisted terms and broke faith
first?

"We will stop. I will never trouble the shadows with iron again. Only dun't redeem the pledge with my son," the Beadle whispered.

—whose son or daughter, then, oath-breaker, shadow-speaker,
farmer-traitor?

Faintness and fever had crawled over Jack's flesh as the Mayor whispered. The sleeping sickness was surely closing over him after all, like the water from the warm Clay Pool, and he would never really wake again.

—this one? said the gold-clad Mayor. *—he was drawn from the*
pool and breathed again—and he is still young yet, like your son.

Jack's eyes flickered and then the Mayor was standing right before him. *—will you redeem your friend?* the Whisperer asked, and Jack felt himself falling, falling far into the water.

He gasped before sleep swallowed him completely, and as Jack clutched at his throat, he felt the little bag of rust he had taken from Rose.

It was almost empty now, but there would be enough for this. The Mayor would scream, and he would be properly awake again. Jack even thought he saw Tamlin at the Beadle's feet make some pale smile. Yes, he thought, this was how the nightmare should end. He would do this one thing and then he would wake; they all would wake.

Jack cast the last of the rust into the Mayor's slate face. The Whisperer only made a long and quiet laugh.

—a circle of gold is enough to protect my aldermen against the shadow-bane of sunlight, from the bane of wheels that turn—my cloak of gold is proof enough against any farmer's cold and lifeless iron.

As the Mayor spoke, Jack felt fate winding about him like a great brass chain. *Locked and wound and locked again,* he thought—ever since they stepped off the long-road. Ever since he had taunted Rose at night. Ever since he had begun to roam the hills with Tam. Ever since his mother had first told him about his father's sickness. Jack sank his head onto his chest. His fate, and he had thought he would escape it with the Beadle's help, but now he would have to bear it after all.

Only two days ago and he would not have believed it, not really. Or he would have screamed and wept, like a baby. Now Jack saw the Mayor turn towards the white-haired Beadle. *—old man, do you like these new terms?*

Jack's ears filled with the slow sound of his beating blood. He wouldn't die and be borne on the coffin-train like his father. He would end as king of the drowned and the dead. He was glad after all that they hadn't found Rose. Wherever she was would be better than here.

His fate. He looked at the Beadle and nodded.

"Bring me a pen," the Beadle said.

28

THE PROJECTORS

That morning, after the Beadle had left Rose to despair in the Tall House, for a long time she had only watched the thralls labor in their misery.

And Rose had watched over Tam too, but she tried not to think about anything. About what the Beadle had gone to do. About what would happen to her and Tam. About what had happened to Jack. Above all she had to keep from thinking about what had happened to Jack in the earth closet below the floor.

To hold all those thoughts at bay, to keep the waiting panic at bay, Rose fixed her mind on imagining the workshop as a kind of painting.

A tall canvas. Only the unused engineery at the top of the canvas would emerge from the gloom, with small grey panels for the windows, and ocher, perhaps, or rust red for the shafts of ruddy light that came down through the dusty air. And in the middle, two fine lines of glittering gold for the work the Cutter children did on their high ledge. Then at its base she would add rough charcoal lines and thin washes of black ink for the bent figures of the thralls, and foul-smelling sticks of yellow sulphur for the brass machines. And the door to the earth closet — but she made herself stop.

"It is like a chicken coop," she said aloud. "All the thralls stupidly moving around, the dust and the red windows. It even has its own stink."

Tam smiled thinly. "And even my subjects ready to peck me to death for bleeding."

Rose wet the end of her skirt and wiped first at her tears and then at one of his cuts. "Why do they hate blood so?"

"Because they's ordered to."

"But you are their king."

"I wear the crown, but I amn't the one who makes the rules."

"Then why do the Whisperers hate blood?"

"Go ask them. Or wait until they come to visit."

Rose shook her head. "Your father has gone to parley with the Mayor. So they won't come to visit. He will make some arrangement and we will be able to leave." She heard Mother Greene's dry cough and saw the old woman working the bellows before the fire. Rose turned away and saw Tam's bitter smile. "Not these, I know. They are caught in this nightmare forever."

"What bargain could my dad make?" said Tam. "The Whisperers need a king to drive the thralls, despite day and iron and turning wheels. No, I'll never leave. And tonight the Whisperers will come and make you learn to spin and you will never leave either."

"Jack wouldn't have let you stay here," Rose said.

Tam turned and spat so that a bloody bubble lay on the dirt floor. "Better clean that up," he said.

Rose took out her handkerchief and wiped at the mess. "But why do they hate our blood?" she asked again.

"And you a painter." Tam made his ugliest smile, but before she could ask him what he meant, there was a sound at the great wagon door, and first a crack, and then a flood of proper light poured into the dusty workshop.

Two figures stood against the light and made long shadows that stretched right across the floor.

Men, not Whisperers, Rose thought. Tall men who could help. One of them waved a stick, and its shadow flickered rapidly over Tamlin and Rose.

"You are right again," the man with the stick said. "Look what we have found."

The shadows grew shorter as the men came closer and bent down over Rose and Tam. Rose's stomach dropped. Whick and Snap.

"Not one but *two* children, Master Snap. Farmers' children—*rational* children."

Snap smiled. "Rational children." He looked around at the labors going on around them, at the machines of torment working. "Not like these thralls, I think, not at all."

"No, no. Thralls wouldn't do, Master Snap. But according to all the rules and regulations of the Dominion, even a child would serve—as long as it's rational."

Snap twirled his stick. "Then we must hurry and choose one, Master Whick. For I think something in the air is changing. We must call the tower done, and get our witness and write up the best claim we can."

The tower. The Tower of Glass the Red Man had shown her. The tower he had said was for weeding. The tower in the desert where no one went. Of course, somehow it had something to do with the Speculators.

"Yes, quickly," said Whick. He gave Rose and Tam a smile that was sweet like licorice. "Who wants to come for a ride on the sand?" He spun his finger in front of Tamlin's face. "Little king!" he said and touched Tam's nose. Then, "Little girl-thing!" he said, doing the same to Rose.

"My name is Rose Tender," she told Snap. "We've already met. You said I was ugly but clever."

"Not at all, not at all," said Whick. "We would never have said that about you, not you, my dearie. It must have been some other girl."

"That doesn't even make sense," said Rose. "If you said that to some other girl, why would I remember it?"

"A logical fork, Master Whick," Snap said in an undertone. "Whatever this girl's name is, she has you there."

"My name is Rose Tender," Rose repeated carefully. "We have met before. We talked about the Lakeland Development. We talked about Crattle, Snope, and Windburn."

Whick blinked and then smiled broadly. "Crattle, Snope, and Windburn," he said to Rose. "If you remembered them, then I certainly don't understand why you couldn't remember us."

"But—" Rose gave it up. "I do remember and I still don't want to come with you. Not to the desert, not anywhere."

"Yes, she does," Tam said. "She wants to see the tower."

Rose gasped. "I came here to help you—like Jack did!" she cried. "Are you really so wicked?"

Tam cocked his head as if he were listening to some quiet thing beyond the workshop and made a dreamy smile. "And Jack is gone. It dun't matter," he said.

Whick took Rose by the wrist. "Say farewell to your little friend. We have to go bye-bye and ride the fast-fast cart. Before Shadow-Town closes."

Snap nodded and slashed his switch across Rose's face. She made a little shriek and touched her hand to her cheek. Her fingers were wet with blood.

She heard a moan from up high, and she saw the Cutter girl had let her wheel stop spinning again. Rose put her handkerchief up to her cheek and felt it rough against the open skin. It was a small cut, but her handkerchief was already wet. Soon the other thralls would notice too. She stared at Snap. "You just wanted me to bleed," she said.

"I wanted you to want to come with us on the fast-fast cart," he said.

Tam pushed himself up against the wall. He shouted some shadow-Words. Then he turned to Rose.

"Farewell," he said, as if he was satisfied with how it had all turned out, as if she would want to have his good wishes. "We willn't see each other again, I think. Farewell."

Rose would have made some horrible reply, but as she saw the reddened light play over his features, she suddenly understood something. "Rust makes paint red," she whispered. "Iron makes blood red. The Whisperers fear blood because it is a living shadow-bane."

Tam bowed his awful crown. "Farewell," he said again, and for once Rose thought he sounded sad.

Just at the door, Rose strained in Whick's grasp to look back. Tam sat still in his broken-back throne, glancing here and there at the terrible machinery but not moving. For a moment their eyes met, until Tam looked down and the crown cast his face in shadow again.

"Clever ugly girl," said Whick, and then he pulled her arm very hard. Then Snap swung the wagon door behind them, and Tam was shut in with the half-dead thralls inside the dim workshop. And Rose was alone in the open street with the Speculators.

"Yes," Whick said. He bent down to look her in the face, then smeared his thumb over her bleeding cheek so that she felt the sting of his sweat. "And now she must — stop — being — " He paused and smiled widely, showing his two silver teeth. " — clever."

Rose pulled away. She felt her heart racing. But it wasn't just the Speculators.

There was a change in the air. The sky was greyer somehow. Clouds were closing in from the north. There was smoke in the air from the smudge pots that lined the street and from fires burning here where no one lived. Rose saw what she hadn't noticed before, the webs spanning the building limply, or lying in old tangles in the corners.

And she heard a kind of hum. Unpleasant music or words she couldn't make out, as if the air itself was anxious.

* * *

Just at the edge of town, in a wide rough field ringed about by pines, the Speculators brought the piebald horse to a stop so they could change the carriage's wheels for wide metal runners.

Whick and Snap might have been Speculators, Projectors, Inventors, and whatnot, but they were slow at this sort of work. As they struggled on, Rose looked about. Once, this must have been a field for footraces or ballgames, or the Smithton fair — if Smithton had ever had its own fair before the quiet ones came. In the center of the field a crow watched from an old iron pole that flew a tattered flag, just faintly yellow still.

A plague flag. Rose thought of that moment when the Accommodation had been made at last. All through Smithton men and women and children who had grown fevery amid the growing whispers and the deepening shadows, who had raved and babbled and finally only whispered to themselves before they had slipped away forever, would have been left behind, because it was too late—because it was Shadow-Town now.

But a few of those last town dwellers had still come here at the end to raise the plague flag. This was the final thing they could do for Smithton: to warn others never to trouble its sleep.

From the top of the pole, the crow made a cry as rusty as the ringing chain. The pole hardly cast a shadow. Noon had come to Shadow-Town.

As the Speculators went on cursing, Rose walked out from the ring of pines and found herself on a little path among old fence-rows of red cedar. She moved slowly now, thinking about the strictures that Grandma had given them: Against the Clay Pool, where all their troubles had begun. Against the Red Man, where they had fled to escape the Whisperers, only to find themselves bound in service after all. Against Shadow-Town, where Tam and Jack had been lost forever. And against the empty desert where no one went. It was like they had been pulled on some string ever since they left the long-road, drawn from one bad choice to another.

And now to the tower the Red Man had shown her. In the desert where no one went at all. What had he said—that it was for weeding? How much had he known or foreseen?

Before her in the path was a little depression, deep with old leaves and cedar droppings. She wondered if she could just walk off down this lane, if they would even notice. Of course, she would still have no idea of how to return, not to her home, or her ailing grandma—not even to the Red Man's if he had once more locked his gates of gloom.

But really what she wanted most of all just at that moment was to sleep. Real sleep. Not from vapors or whispers. Just sleep here against the cedar in these unhaunted shadows.

Or maybe—and Rose was nearly drifting off to sleep already when she saw the leaves begin to rustle and quiver. Before Rose had left Grandma's farm—a long time ago, she thought—that would have horrified her. She was too tired to feel horror now.

But when Rose got to her feet and brushed at the leaves with the toe of her high-laced boot, they began to writhe like a hundred grabbing arms. No, not arms—a ball of snakes, dozens and dozens of long green snakes all twisting together, and Rose shouted in horror after all. Then she began to run, back towards the Speculators.

"If it isn't Ugly the farmers' girl, Master Whick!" she heard. "Did you even notice that she was gone?"

Rose stopped and panted for a while. The work on the wagon seemed to be finished at last. The piebald horse looked worse than ever, she thought: all skin and bones and mangy hair. But it gave her a look that might have been sympathy. Then Snap climbed up to the front, and on the seat behind, Whick wedged Rose in between him and an old case of patent medicines. Snap turned around and the Speculators gave each other a nod. "Time for some legal business," Master Snap said.

Whick bounced on the sprung cushion of the bench seat, but the horse had taken no notice of the switch. "Time is money!" he yelled at the horse.

"And glue!" yelled Snap as he cracked his whip. "Glue from old horses is money too!" The carriage bumped forward and Snap whipped at the horse's hindquarters again, and they began to make their way down the sandy road.

Slowly first, then slowly faster as Snap plied his whip. Down the lane and into the scraggly hills, and through the hills sickly with witch's broom, and over the grasping tangles of juniper—some alive, some dead but for a still green and living crown. Webs on them—proper spiderwebs, she thought—that shimmered vaguely in the midday light.

"Why did you build in the desert?" Rose asked Whick, somehow bold now that all hope was lost. "It is worse than the Tanglewood. More forbidden even than Shadow-Town. No one lives there. It is the worst place of all."

Whick leaned forward. "The ugly girl says the desert is the worst place of all, Master Snap!"

The Speculators laughed together for some time. "By all the seven spirits of discomfort! The worst place of all!" Snap wheezed as he wiped at his eyes with his gingham handkerchief. "Still," he said, "to be fair, Master Whick—"

"Late in the day to begin that policy," Whick put in, smartly.

"To be fair, it is the worst place she is likely to ever go."

"Certainly at this point, Master Snap. The worst place she's ever going to go now."

Nothing but the barren waves of sand, catching the heat of the sun and shining it back on to her, and a long track made by the little boots of the Whisperers. It went west, straight west, and somewhere west behind the hills Rose saw a tall spear of light burning under the midday haze.

The Tower of Glass. Where the journey that had begun when she had lied about going to Shadow-Town would come to an end.

Just her. Not Jack, not now. Not with the Red Man, like the high place she had been before. Not with Raff. Not even with Tam.

Her hand went to the smooth storm's egg she carried. Somehow it was a comfort.

29

LEGAL MATTERS

Under the wide, dull sky, the Speculators' carriage—now their sleigh—went on. Not quickly, as if it were speeding over snow, but steadily, monotonously, following the trail packed down by uncountable numbers of tiny pointed boots. *A slow ride to an unpleasant end*, Rose thought.

How would she paint the sky? On a bright day in the hills, you just used blank paper and a jagged line for the spruce, rising and falling. But this kind of hot overcast was different. How would she make the air seem this itchy? Grey and blue and heavier towards the horizon—so heavy the paper would warp. And make the sand look dark, but not dark like sand in the rain. There would be no rain today, not in the desert.

Rose felt as if her cheeks were drawing in, like a withering apple. She squirmed in her seat beside Whick. "Is there water?"

she asked at last. "Is there water I can have?"

"The child wants water, Master Snap," Whick called ahead.

"Note that, if you would, Master Whick," Snap replied. "Let the record show that the witness Rose Tender asked for water."

Whick paused to write something in his memorandum book. "'In progress to overlook the area in question, the witness, one Rose Tender—a rational child—asked for water,'" he read out.

"Is there water I can have?" Rose asked again.

"We need a proper, legal witness, Master Whick," Snap said.

Whick nodded. "And a paid witness is not witness."

"But I need some water," Rose said. "I will die of thirst, and then I will be no witness at all."

Whick tapped his mechanical pencil on the end of her nose. "Careful, Rose Tender. That sounds as though it might be clever."

Rose looked from Whick to Snap, and then to the old nag that pulled them. "Doesn't your horse need to water?"

"Clever again, Master Whick," Snap said.

Whick tapped her on the nose once more. "There is a little oasis," he said. "With a muddy slough. You can drink some of that."

Rose stared at him. "No, thank you."

Whick nodded and wrote in his memorandum book again. "'Let the record show that witness Rose Tender was offered water—*and declined it.*'"

"As we near the end of our time here, I fear I become sentimental," said Snap. "I shall venture to offer her some of my own water."

"Remember, 'Fools are always begot by sentiment,'" quoted Whick. "But I suppose your flask is no business of mine."

"I shall trust you to warn me when I approach the foolish," said Snap.

He turned in his seat to face Rose and pulled a large flask from his coat. "As a warrant of its quality, I shall drink first," he said. He took a long pull, wiped his lips with a cloth, and passed the water back to Rose.

She could feel the flask still warm from his body, see his spittle still wet and sticky around its mouth. She handed it back.

"No, thank you," she said.

Snap stared, then he dampened his handkerchief with water from the flask and held it out for Whick. "Let Master Whick wipe your cut clean at least," he said.

Rose shuddered and turned away. "Don't touch my face," she said.

"You see," said Whick. "As the saying goes, 'The muck of mercy only engenders ingratitude.'"

Snap screwed his flask shut and turned to the front again. "Compassion shall be my ruin yet," he said.

"'Dreams, trust, and charity point the way to perdition,'" Whick quoted.

"True. How sadly true."

Whick turned a page of his little book. "But let's the pass the time pleasantly at least, my dear," he said to Rose. He licked the end of his pencil. "Tell us more about Crattle, Snope, and Windburn. Tell us about what happened to your old farm by the water. Tell us about...Lakeland."

"Lakeland?" Rose rubbed her eyes and looked out the window. The horizon seemed to be twisting like a snake. The trail ahead, and even the hills of sand, swam under the bright, hazy sky.

The hazy sky. Whick and Snap were talking to her about Lakeland again, and she was even answering back, but she hardly knew what anyone was saying. She closed her eyes, and opened them to see the hazy sky again. There was still more talking, but after a long while something like sleep fell over her.

Rose woke coughing. The carriage had stopped, and Whick was pouring water from his flask onto her face, and now she was happy to swallow whatever dripped between her lips.

She was hot. It was the middle of the afternoon. And before her rose a spire of burning light: a pillar that reached to the sky, filled with the stuff of the sun. At the bottom she could see it was made of round upon round of glass bricks—Smithton bricks in countless thousands—and then they rose taller than anything she had known, brighter than anything she could imagine—rising too high. And every part of it streamed with the hot dull light, too bright for her eyes to follow.

The Tower of Glass at last, and for a moment Rose thought of legends from long ago across the sea—tales of towers built too high, until the heavens themselves grew jealous and cast them back to earth. She turned away.

The Speculators slid stiffly down from the carriage. Whick struggled to get out some clumsy apparatus of tubes and poles and clockwork gears, and then they dragged Rose onto the hot sand.

Whick gave her a push with his free hand. "We must climb the stairs."

"How high does it go?" Rose croaked.

Now Snap pushed her. "All the way to the top."

"There are three hundred and fifty-six steps," Whick added.

Rose felt nausea coming over her. "I can't climb so many."

Whick rubbed along her cheek with his thumb so that her cut stung with his salt sweat. "Yes you can."

✳ ✳ ✳

As Rose was pulled and prodded up the stairs of the glass tower, she found that she had stopped thinking about what the Speculators meant for her, about what her role as a witness was to be.

The worst place she is likely to ever go. The worst place she's ever going to go now. There wasn't any point in thinking, not if this was going to be the end of it.

"How many steps are there?" Rose asked when it felt like she had been climbing almost forever.

Snap was wheezing from the effort of climbing. "Master Whick will tell you," he said, then he pulled on Rose's arm to make her follow more closely.

Whick wasn't wheezing, but he was carrying his tubes-and-clockwork-and-poles apparatus, and his face was slick with an oily sweat. "Three hundred and fifty-six, Master Snap," he said. "As I have told you twice today." He gave Rose a clumsy push from the back.

Rose stumbled, but a tug from Snap kept her upright. "How many *more* steps?" she asked.

"If you had been counting, you would know," Snap said.

"If *you* had been counting, you would know," Rose said.

Behind her, Whick said, "One hundred and ninety-three."

"One hundred and ninety-three," Rose said. The number made her dizzy.

"One hundred and eighty-nine now," Whick said.

Snap gave her arm another yank. "You would know that if you had been counting," he said.

30

THE VIEW FROM
THE TOWER

At the top of the tower, while Snap wheezed and Whick fiddled with his poles and gears, Rose looked out across the desert. The sand stretched a long way, the color of damp biscuits, before the darker line of spruce and scrub oak began. Past that, she could see the shadow of the Tanglewood, and then even farther, because she was so high, the open spaces of farmers' fields.

And because other Speculators had driven them off their farm by the Inland Sea, somewhere off to the east, beyond the horizon, and far beyond the sandy hills, her mom and dad and her new baby brother worked to break the land on their new farm. Worked without her, because she would only get in the way.

Even so far up, the heavy clouds were some vast distance higher. But up here, the wind could toss her hair. A damp wind from the north, where all things cold were born. It wasn't water,

but she put her head down across the glass bricks along the top
of the wall and breathed it in.

She looked down. All the way down, and everything
swam again.

Whick straightened at last. He had turned his apparatus
into some sort of telescope-glass on a tripod—a survey-glass
with gears and dials to measure just which way it pointed.

"Here, Farmer-girl," he called.

There was just one good thing about being so near the end,
Rose found. You didn't have to care whether anyone thought
you were brave or smart or polite. "Use my name, Master
Whick," she said.

Whick sighed. "All right, then. Little Ugly, come here."

"My own name," said Rose.

Snap exposed his teeth. "Fair's fair, Master Whick," he
said. "Let's keep it all proper and legal-like, according to all
the formalities of the Dominion."

Whick wiped his oily brow. "Legal-like," he said. "Miss
Rose Tender, then, do us the favor of looking through this
glass."

"Why?" Rose said. "Will you give me water?"

"*Why?*" said Whick.

"Why, so we won't dash your brains against the base of the
tower, my dear, that's why," Snap finished.

"That's fair, isn't it?" said Whick. "That's laid out simply
enough for even a farmer girl to understand, Miss Rose."

Snap tried a kinder voice. "Just a look, missy," he said.
"What's the harm in that?"

Whick made a small clicking adjustment to the dial on the
tripod gears. He tried a kinder voice too. "Have a look, Miss
Rose Tender," he said. "Have a look before the weather turns
bad."

"What for? What do you want me to see?"

"Why, all of it," Snap said.

"See anything you want!" said Whick.

Rose looked at them in turn. Rose still didn't know how her story would play out, but she knew it was coming to a close. See anything she wanted. "All right."

The survey glass was more powerful than she had dreamed; she felt like some kind of magician, like a giant. She could see a hawk nesting on a lodgepole pine, miles away, miles out of the desert and into the Tanglewood. Whick clicked the dial and her view stretched out farther, to a creek, and farther to farmers working in the fields. Squares of yellow sunflower and gold-pale wheat. Steely blue flax. And beyond those, stretches of bright green meadow. It was something to have seen this, at least. The whole world spread before her like a painting, the wind blowing. How a storm-eagle might see the world, as it flew high to take tidings to the King of the Winds. A storm-eagle. And she felt the wooden ball she carried, the gift from the storm. To be kept until everything else was lost.

"Do you see it all, Miss Rose?" Snap asked, but she ignored him.

"Where is my grandma's farm?" she asked

Whick gave Snap a look and he said, "Your grandmother's farm?"

Rose took a moment to feel the wind in her hair. All things neared the end. She had surveyed the world like a storm-eagle. "The Tender farm," she said sharply now. Snap rustled the large map he had shown Rose before and called out some numbers, and Whick clicked his dials and spun the survey glass.

Far, far away, and tiny—tiny—Rose saw a little white house.

"Well," Whick asked, "is that correct? Is that the Tender property?"

And by the white house, Rose thought she saw a little lumpy figure moving. Grandma—was it Grandma?
Was Grandma better? "Yes," Rose said, feeling suddenly
lighter, easier. "Yes it is!"

"Excellent," said Snap, and he made a note among
his papers.

"And the Red Man's estate now?" Rose asked.

The Speculators exchanged another glance. "It's not a holiday, Miss Rose," Whick said.

"You wouldn't even be able to find it, would you?" said
Rose. "Not unless he unmazed his gates of gloom again."

Snap laughed nervously. Whick only fiddled with his dials.
"Now south, look south. Here, do you see?"

Rose felt the ball of wood warm in her pocket. Not until
everything was lost, the Red Man had said. She wanted to
know, at least, what all this was about, before the end. Rose
hardly bothered with what she saw; she only bent to the lens
and nodded. Even if she had only these last moments left, it
was good to feel the wind in her hair.

"And now east," Whick said, and Rose did it again.
To the east she saw the Tall House and all the grey buildings
of Shadow-Town, the scrubby meadows beyond. She saw the
rickety railway bridge leading over the wide river where the
water rolled slowly east. In time, it would roll even to where
her parents were breaking land on the new farm. How high a
tower would she have to climb to see that far?

Now Snap pulled her away from the glass. He had spread
out his chart across the platform at the top of the tower, and
weighted it down with stray glass bricks against the rising wind.
"Do you agree that this map is a fair, complete, and accurate
representation of what you have seen?" he asked.

Rose stared at the map—the same one they had shown
her a long time ago, when she met them on the long-road,

when she still thought she was going to see Great-Aunt Constance. "I don't know," she said. "How would I know— I don't even know what this is for."

Whick grabbed her ear. "Master Snap didn't ask if you knew," he said. "He asked if you agreed." He twisted her ear until she thought it would tear off.

"Then yes!" Rose said, pulling away to look at the map again. "Let go! Yes, I agree!"

Snap smiled and spread out a smaller paper and took out a pen and a little bottle of ink. "Master Whick," he said. "It's time for us to make a Preliminary Claim to Change of Possession."

"What do you mean, a Change of Possession?" Rose said. She almost understood. She was almost at the end.

Snap only bent to scribble a few words on the page. Then Whick scribbled some words. Then they took turns signing their names with great flourishes.

"Here," Whick said to Rose, holding out his pen. "Read this. Quickly. Then sign it."

Snap sighed in happy satisfaction as Rose knelt down by the paper. "Almost. We are almost in possession, Master Whick."

Whick sighed. "One could say, 'The deed is done.'"

"One could almost say that," said Snap. "It is almost a deed, and it is almost done." He bent low over Rose. "Promptly now, Miss Tender," he said. "The Dominion Authorities do not hold with unreasonable delay."

Despite the glass bricks, the wind was curling at the edges of the papers. The map spread before Rose showed a big round dot surrounded by marks for hills and trees and rivers and fields. At the bottom it read: "The Whick-Snap Claim."

Attached to it was a sheet written in the most formal kind of letters:

CLAIM TO LAND AS SURVEYED IN ATTACHED MAP*

(the Whick-Snap Claim)
SURVEYED BY: *Gluttony C. Whick, Esquire*
CLAIMED BY: *Avarice C. Snap, Esquire*
WITNESSED BY: *Miss Rose Tender*
(a farmers' girl of sufficient reputation and adequate intelligence)

Witnessed by Miss Rose Tender. Now it was all laid out for her. Of course, it was all part of their scheme to steal land — just as Crattle, Snope, and Windburn had driven her family off before. Whick and Snap had surveyed almost the whole of the sandy hills from this tower, and now somehow they were making a claim to it. And her signature would make it all complete.

And then what would they do with her? She had already begun to doubt she would ever leave the tower alive, but now she understood. All she had to do was sign. Only she didn't have to care anymore.

Snap looked at the sheet with satisfaction, smiling at the large signatures he and Whick had put beside their names. Suddenly he stood straighter and said, a little uncertainly, "You do know your letters, my dear?"

"Of course I know my letters."

"*All* of them?" Snap asked.

"Reading *and* writing?" Whick asked.

"I know all my letters and numbers," Rose said. "I helped my father with the accounts."

"Not really a testimony of skill, there, Master Whick," Snap muttered, but Rose only picked up the pen. In his anxiety to peer at her work, Whick was leaning forward on his toes. Rose moved the pen closer to the little inkwell.

Snap wrung his hands together. Rose gave him a sideways glance. He held his breath.

Now everything was very nearly lost. And she carried a gift from the storm. Rose pulled the pen back and tapped it against her teeth. "How far is it to the ground?" she asked.

Whick suddenly dashed his hat against the glass floor. "How far to the ground?" he shouted. "How far to the ground!"

Rose watched as Whick purpled and made a little dance of speechless rage. "*Breathe*, Master Whick," Snap said quietly. "More Speculators have died of apoplexy than were ever lost to the hands of justice."

Whick made a sudden gasp and began again: "In the name all the Seven Arbiters of Discomfort! It doesn't signify! By the Imp of Malfunction! By the Inevitable End of Quiesence! How far to the ground? Surely you can sign your name whether it's ten feet down or three furlongs!"

Somehow the more annoyed the Speculators became, the calmer Rose felt. She smiled gently at Snap. "To be clear, to be—legal-like—this is a claim to all the unworked land you have surveyed?"

"Yes!" he snarled. "Unworked, unused, or soon-to-be-abandoned."

"That last is a slightly complicated codicil I devised with the aid of some other legal minds of my acquaintance," Whick put in modestly.

"And you would own it all?" Rose said.

"Own it, rule it. Do as we liked," said Snap.

Whick, still breathing hard, mopped his brow and made something like a smile. He tapped the page. "Right here, my sweet child," he said. "You sign it right here. Along the blank line. By your name." He tapped again. "This. Your name. Here."

"But if I am to be able to attest that it was possible to see so far—," Rose began.

"That's, that's—" Whick recovered himself just in time. "That's only theoretical, my dear," he said. "It will not be necessary if you are in a position where you would be unable to provide any testimonial at all."

No, no they would not want her to leave the tower alive then. They would rather dash her brains against the ground. Rose smiled as sweetly and reasonably as she could. "But I would have to be *able* to, at least theoretically. Even in that unlikely circumstance. Or the Authorities wouldn't hold that my signature *could* count. So I need to know, to make it legal. I can't," she added, "sign something if I am in doubt it would satisfy the Dominion Authorities."

Snap sighed. "It's true, she can't, Master Snap," he murmured. "You know it wouldn't withstand the briefest scrutiny."

Whick looked up at the clouds and made a hissing sigh. "This is what comes of choosing the ugly, clever one," he said.

Suddenly Rose realized she did care about how it turned out. All this time the farmers had been so concerned about the Whisperers, but somehow, for good or ill, the Whisperers at least belonged to the hills too. Not like Whick and Snap.

She never stopped smiling, but the rest of her began to tremble and shake.

31

BEING CLEVER

On the tower, Snap looked up at the darkening clouds. "Tell the ugly girl how high the tower is, Master Whick, if she must know," he said, and his voice was quivering. "Quickly now. I believe it will rain soon. Even in the desert, it will rain. The drops will spoil the deed. And the map. Hurry."

"The platform of this tower is currently one hundred and six and three-quarters paces high," Whick told Rose.

"Does that include how tall I am?" Rose asked.

"Master Whick, *don't* forget the height of the viewer," Snap said.

Whick turned from his survey glass to look at Rose. He held his hand up level with her head and considered, "Call it one hundred and eight — and four-fifths. More or less."

Rose put her hand to the top of her head and nodded.

"And what is the total viewing area from such a height?"

Whick sighed. "If I explain it to you, will you remember? I have spent much of my life explaining this very thing to Master Snap."

Snap squinted up at the sky again. "Yes, either I only poorly comprehend or you only poorly explain."

"You will only have to explain it once to me," Rose said.

"We have already advised you not to be clever," Snap said shortly.

As Whick explained first the formula, and then the results in square feet, yards, rods, and furlongs, Rose nodded as if she were really paying attention. She walked to the edge of the platform and looked down. Down one hundred and six and three-quarter paces, more or less, to the desert floor. Her stomach lurched and she clutched at the glass bricks on the top of the half-finished wall. Her heart was racing, but she closed her eyes and took a long breath in. She put her hand around the strange wooden ball the Red Man had given her. What a fine thing the storm's egg was — smooth and warm and beautiful. And the wind in her hair; she would never know anything as fine as that again either, she knew.

And Jack was lost in Shadow-Town, and Tam was lost in Shadow-Town, and her grandma was failing. And as soon as she signed, Whick and Snap meant to do away with her and then file a claim for the whole of the sandy hills...

Suddenly Snap gasped. "Oh no, my dear, you mustn't fall!" he cried. "You would break your head!"

"Indeed," said Whick. "Or jump. No, don't jump. You would break your head and everything else. Approach her cautiously, Master Snap! She might think she could jump."

"Missy Rosie Tender," Snap wheedled, "sand isn't really as soft as it might seem when you are playing in the sandbox with your dollies. The farther away it is, the harder it gets."

Now Rose stood with her back to the short wall. "But how quickly would I hit the ground? Perhaps I wouldn't break my head."

Whick blinked. "You would strike the ground in four and one-quarter seconds," he said. "And in the last half-second alone you would fall twenty-six paces—more or less. That's, that's six and a half stories! Your head would certainly crack open."

Her head would crack. Yes, that would be high enough. Snap was reaching for her gently now. "Smooshed," he said soothingly. "Cracked and burst like a ripe tomato. Careful, my dear, or you will never have the chance to sign this historical document. The ants and the spiders will dine on your mixed-up brains."

"And the skinks," Whick put in.

"No, Master Whick," said Snap, crossly. "The skinks do not eat flesh. Or brains."

But before the conversation could turn back to Rose, the wind began to gust harder. The chart on the floor of the platform curled, then flapped, then almost pulled free of the glass bricks that held it down.

Whick fell to his knees and spread his hands over the map. "It will blow away, Master Snap! It will tear!"

"Hurry, girl!" shouted Snap. "Be our witness and sign. If you jump, you will be smooshed and die!"

Rose felt herself shaking from head to toe. She could hardly stand, or keep her grip on the glass wall at her back. But she nodded to Snap and held up the pen he had given her.

Until everything else is already lost. Whick was sprawled on his belly across the papers now, and Snap held his arms open wide to Rose and nodded at her encouragingly.

With her other hand, Rose pulled out the wooden egg the Red Man had given her. She tossed it behind her, over the wall, and now that she no longer had hold of anything, the wind staggered her and she stumbled forward.

Snap grabbed her around the waist as quick as he could, but he already knew something was wrong. *One...two...* Rose smiled at Snap as she counted in her head. How strange that these were the last moments of her summer. *Three...* For the first time since she had left for the sandy hills, she felt tears begin for her mother and father and little baby brother and the home she would never see on the farm along the river.

Now a terrible gust came, and sand whipped in her eyes, and Rose saw a ragged piece of paper flying across the open tower, and she heard Whick begin to scream. *Four...*

Snap wrapped his fingers in Rose's hair to keep her tight. But Rose felt as though her hair was crawling already, and her skin itched in a way she had only felt once before —

The sky tore open, and from bottom to top, the Tower of Glass blazed with a blue and burning light, and the glass bricks beneath Rose's feet gave way.

IV

THE ACCOMMODATION

32

THE CROWN OF
BONE AND IRON

❖✦❖

"Bring me a pen," the Beadle had told the Mayor of Shadow-Town. "And take off his crown."

From somewhere off in the west, Jack heard a roll of thunder. Now he would become the king in Tamlin's place—because he, too, had been put in the warm Clay Pool and drawn out again alive.

A kind of blackness swelled over him. There was no escaping this, no lever to pull, no magic word to cry. This was his fate, just as his dream had warned him.

Tam was still half-wrapped in the bundle of shadow-web, but he began to writhe and scream. "No! The crown is mine!" He screamed again without words, and Jack tried to console the Beadle.

"He doesn't realize that this was all meant to happen,"

Jack explained. "He doesn't understand that this will set him free. He's only afraid of being a thrall like these."

The Beadle kicked Tam. "Quiet. The crown was only yours for a time. Someone else will have it now. And you'll never be a thrall."

Tam screamed and thrashed again. "You will never be a thrall," the Beadle said. He looked down at his paper and pen. "Quiet, my son, quiet."

At those words—"*my son*"—Tam did fall quiet. Now everything was quiet. Then the Mayor reached for Tam's crown and began to whisper some long and terrible spell.

Jack looked at Tam's fevered face. He tried to look at Tam's father, but the Beadle had turned to his paper again. Jack looked at the Whisperers, but for the moment, they only watched the crown of bone and iron. And Jack looked at the crowding thralls.

"The dream of Tamlin-king is ending," the Cutter girl whispered. "Long sleep Tamlin-king," murmured her brother.

About this at least, the thralls seemed able to speak. "Does our dream end too? Can we wake now?" they asked. "Will we lie in our coffins again?"

"Farmer Mathom, who will tell us when to turn and when to spin?"

Who would tell them? Jack thought. But the fate that stretched before him and all the thralls was too bitter to explain. He would wear the crown and sit enthroned and drive the thralls to do the Speculators' work. He would make the Whisperers rich enough to all wear gold, to walk the day, and make the vapors rise and spread across the hills. But he would live only in that grey world and never really wake, except to walk to the Clay Pool and drown again at last. And then he would rest in the water, unshipped, until someday the world might be made again.

And Farmer Mathom said nothing in answer to the other thralls, but he came and stood by Jack. And as they watched the Mayor work, muttering, at Tamlin's crown, the old farmer reached up so gently that he had drawn the big knife from its wooden sheath before Jack realized what Mathom was doing. He went completely still.

"The Smith's blade," the old man said wonderingly. Then he held the bright edge close to Jack's face, as Tamlin had once before. "Only a little moment before the sleep comes strong again," Mathom said.

What did he mean? Only a little moment. A little moment between the end of Tam's nightmare and the beginning of his own long rule. Jack looked at the knife, at the old farmer in his ragged coffin-suit.

Then Mathom bared his chest, and Jack suddenly understood. "My blood will be your shadow-bane," Mathom said. "It holds living iron, not cold rust."

Jack heard his own blood thump in his ears. Living iron. Of course. That was why the Whisperers had taught the thralls not to suffer the bleeding to live, on pain of being burned alive.

Living iron. Mathom's heart's blood. Jack shook his head. "I can't."

"Only a little moment," Mathom said. "Use the knife, or you will bear the crown and I will labor under you till the end, and children will sneak into Shadow-Town to watch me climb the Everlasting Stair, watch us all turn wheels or rattle looms, watch us suffer and work for no real end."

"I can't," said Jack.

Now the Mayor was beginning to tug at the crown on Tam's head.

"I watched after your father when he was a boy," Farmer Mathom said. "I was your father's friend when he was a man. Give me the gift your father received, and save yourself as well."

"I can't," Jack said again.

Then he saw the rag-clad Cutters, and their hollow eyes, silently beseeching. "Do it now," said Mathom.

Jack heard Tam scream. The Mayor turned away at last, some kind of triumph on his dull features. The crown was made of bone and iron, but this time, all clad in gold, the Mayor could bear to hold it high. The Mayor would bring the crown to him now, Jack knew.

Jack looked down at the blade in his hand. "Founder Smith's knife," Farmer Mathom whispered. "I have seen it do worse things than this, Jack. Make it atone for all the wrongs Smith left behind."

The Beadle wasn't able to bear the sight of Tam anymore. Now he scratched at the paper, writing out the new contract that would make Jack king. The Mayor stepped closer. Jack could see the thorns along the ring of the crown already writhing, as if they couldn't wait to dig into his skull. The contract. The crown. Then there would only be the grey world for him, forever and ever.

"Please," Mathom whispered. "Kill me."

The pen paused just before the Beadle finished with his signature. The Mayor held the crown over Jack's head, but his wide eyes grew round as he saw the knife and Mathom's bare chest.

Then Jack found himself slipping the knife into Mathom's flesh, pushing it into his heart, and then before he fell, the old farmer turned himself. And Mathom's life pulsed out in jets of blood that splashed across the gold-clad Mayor.

There were horrible noises: the screams of soulless things, and smoke, and the smell of acid on stone.

* * *

And Mathom was dead, and the Mayor was gone. The light from outside was obscured by the dark cloud of the storm.

And for a long time only the crows made noise within the Tall House.

33

WHAT WILL HAPPEN NOW?

———◆◦◆◦◆———

Jack's clothes were still wet with Farmer Mathom's blood as
the thralls gathered around him. The Cutter children. Mother
Vining. Farmer Sawyer. Miser Cooper. Mother Greene. Others
Jack had never known.

"Is the blood-commandment broken?" Cooper asked.

"Are you our king now?" Mother Vining asked.

"Will we live again, or will we be dead?" Mother Greene
asked. "Properly dead?"

"What will happen to us?" asked the Cutters.

"I don't know," Jack said. "Take care of Mathom first."
He wiped the Beadle's knife clean on the Mayor's cloth
of gold. "Lay this cloak under his head for a pillow. Then,
I don't know."

The storm-damp air began to blow through the stale

workshop. Carefully, the thralls cleaned Mathom of his blood. Thunder rolled and the floor shook, and slowly they wound him in rags, and scraps of cloth, and endless strands of shadow-silk, to serve in place of a coffin. Mathom's stairs began to quiver. The unworked looms rattled.

Jack looked for Tam. He sat with his palms pressed against a dirty bandage tied around his skull.

Beside him crouched the Beadle. He had let his paper fall unsigned. He said foul things. Not shadow-Words, not spells or invocations, but bitter things.

Beyond them, away from Mathom's blood, and still and quiet in the dim light, a dozen Whisperers in golden circlets stood. *Aldermen*, the Mayor had called them. Their eyes were open, blankly wicked; and they muttered slowly among themselves — not Words, but still in their own secret shadow-talk. Dull and confused, Jack thought, like ants who have lost their queen. Dull for now, but soon enough another queen was always born.

There was Rose to worry about yet, Jack thought — Tam told him that she had been taken by the Speculators. And Tam himself. And somehow now Miser Cooper and Mother Greene, and the Cutter children were his to worry about as well. All the thralls. Even the Beadle.

And his grandma, dozing at her farm. And all of the sandy hills, really. The Red Man might tend the hills, but he didn't rule the creatures within it. Somehow, for this day, it was Jack who had to worry.

They could destroy the aldermen here easily enough now; could make more iron powder in the workshop and sow it through Shadow-Town. Even now the Beadle could help with that cruel work. They could take the sleeping Whisperers and bind them to turning wheels and hear them scream. They could burn down every house and building where shadow-things might nest.

That could be the start of a new Accommodation, a better

Accommodation for the farmers. They could build anew on the ruins and it would be Tender's Town.

If they could find all the Whisperers before night fell. If he could bear hearing their screams as they returned to the shadowed earth. If he were stronger and wiser than the farmers who had made the first Accommodation so long ago.

High up, crows flew into the Tall House. More and more, hiding from the storm.

"Beadle," Jack asked, "what should I do?"

The Beadle's old face was so bleak and frank that Jack couldn't suspect him. "Ring the pole," he said, and when Jack looked at him uncomprehending, he said, "The pole that flies the plague flag, in the field where my father made the first Accommodation. I'll show you. Then you can ring the pole and summon them all."

Tamlin jerked, and seemed to return to the waking world. "Father," he said, and passed his hand over his eyes as though he had awoken from some bad dream. "Father, your hair is white," he said, wonderingly. "You's old at last."

The Beadle nodded. "So you have cost me," he said.

"Will you whip me, beat me?" Tam said.

"Later," the Beadle said. "Too much has happened today." The storm passed into the south and faded to rumbles, and finally grew quiet.

* * *

Late in the afternoon, after Mathom's body had been cared for and laid on a bier made from a broken loom, Jack took the Smith's knife in hand and led them out into the streets, Tam and the Beadle and those who had been thralls.

Last of all, in a wavering line, the twisted figures of the Whisperers with golden circlets, and the rustle of their shadow-talk followed with them: uncertain whispers, some hopeless,

some defiant, some suggesting sleep, some demanding gold.
Confused whispers, above all, Jack thought as he led the
strange parade. Too confused to have any power:

    —they have defied our plans of gold.

    —we walk like beggars through our streets of Shadow-Town.

    —they have struck with living iron.

    —the Speculators have betrayed us.

    —what new Accommodation can be made?

  So they all walked and stumbled through web-strewn
Shadow-Town. The Mayor's house still burned, but from its
foot crawled two of the aldermen in golden circlets, smolder-
ing like logs rescued from a fire, hissing:

    —this shadow-friend has betrayed us.

    —this boy has burned us.

  Jack grasped the knife tight and looked at Tam's father,
but the Beadle said, "Let them join your parade. They only say
what's true."

At last they came to a wide field with a tattered yellow
flag on a great iron pole. The Beadle gave Jack a nod, and he
climbed the platform set against it and struck the pole with the
butt of Founder Smith's knife, and the sound rang out across
the field—out over Shadow-Town, out to the hills beyond, into
the Tanglewood, into the desert, down the lonely steel tracks
of the Clatterfolk.

"So they'll know," the Beadle had told him quietly.
"So they'll wake already knowing, and they will come."

"Are there others left?"

The Beadle looked at the ones in gold circlets and nodded.
"Others. Many others."

Tam and his father and the stumbling thralls set themselves in a small circle with their backs to the great iron pole.
But Jack stood outside their ring with the Whisperers and
waited for those who would come with the dusk.

34

ROSE IN THE DESERT

Rose woke surrounded by a pearly light. Bits of glass were all over her, and when she pushed herself up, pebbles and rainbows from the broken Smithton bricks scattered silently across the floor.

She was still high up in the broken Tower of Glass. Off to the south the last of the storm clouds were sliding away through the late-day sky—dark clouds, bright around the edges, gold towards the west.

Rose was waking up properly now. She was surprised to be there, alive, but her ears ached, and she snapped her fingers and heard nothing.

She looked at the cracked glass above and around her, trying to understand. The lightning stroke must have broken the top of the tower and she had fallen through onto the floor below.

A great heap of broken bricks lay beside her on the open floor; the glass was cloudier the deeper it lay: pearly, milky, grey. Dark shapes at the bottom, and just at the edge, something pale: an outstretched hand.

Rose nearly shrieked—Whick or Snap. They must have fallen too—but hadn't been so lucky. Now they were buried under the glass, and now one of them reached out to her with a white still hand.

She scrabbled across the floor to the cracked and winding stair. She was tired, hungry; so thirsty she felt she might go mad. She had a hundred tiny cuts from the glass. She couldn't hear anything. Her head rang. But she had to get away from that still hand. She had to get out of the tower. She had to get out of the desert before night fell.

✳ ✳ ✳

A long time later, when Rose finally emerged from the bottom of the tower, the sand was still hot, the air warm and heavy. And the glass tower above her still burned in the sun. But the shadows had grown long, and where they faced the sun, the biscuit-colored hills might have been spread with butter.

The Speculators' carriage was gone, of course. Rose could see a confusion in the sand where it had been, with a jumble of old sample boxes and clothing. And beyond that the runners had left a ragged, wavering trail, back the way they had come. The piebald horse must have bolted—or at least done whatever hurrying it was still capable of—and half-overturned the carriage before managing to drag it on again, trailing odds and ends behind it.

Rose staggered and fell on the sand. Countless little flies appeared and flew soundlessly about her and lit on her face. Once the Speculators' seedy horse had seemed sinister to her, but now somehow seeing that it was gone was the worse part of all. Not even the old nag for company.

* * *

Rose lay on the sand for a long time and then she realized she was still thirsty, impossibly thirsty. She found herself laughing, then weeping. Maybe she would climb the tower again and look for Snap's flask — all twelve-million and sixty-seven steps. Or whatever Whick had said. Less the last flight to the top floor ... Or maybe she could dig down through the sand until she found water. Or maybe if she lay back and opened her mouth the Red Man would wave his staff and then the King of the Winds would blow a rain cloud to pour over her.

Or maybe — *No*, she thought. *I am only mad with thirst. I will fly like eagles myself until I see the gleam of water below — No*, she thought, *the lightning has disarranged my thoughts. Only I am thirsty. And I am mad.*

Slowly she began crawling over the sand towards the scattered things the wagon had left behind. Two spare black hats. A cracked mirror. A shaving kit that had broken apart leaving an open straight razor.

She knew better, but she tried the edge with her thumb and cut herself and saw drops of blood darken the sand like rain. She put her thumb in her mouth and rummaged through the broken sample case with her other hand.

Dozens of little patent medicine bottles, each a viler and more unusual color than the last. Emetics. Cathartics. Internal Binding Agents. Antipyretics — for *Reduction of Fever*. Pyretics — for *Induction of Fever*. The labels began to swim in front of her eyes. Then she saw a bright pink bottle with green spots and an elaborate label:

DR. BRIMMER'S **HIGHLY-WARRANTED** STOMACH REMEDY
Loosens *or* Tightens **Internals** as Required
Safe! Soothing! Efficacious for All!
⊰ *With the* **GW & AS** SEAL *of Quality Assurance!* ⊱

Since it was something the Speculators had sold, the label was almost certainly a lie, but if it might relieve her thirst without killing her, Rose was prepared to drink it. She sat up, unscrewed the cap and sniffed, and then—desperately thirsty—drank it all. Whatever it might mean for her internals, it did at least soothe her throat.

In only a moment or two, Rose felt the Remedy beginning to have some effect on her internals—an unpleasant feeling of being loosened and tightened at once—and she fell on her back again. She lifted the bottle and read the small lines printed on the back:

> *Dr. Brimmer is not just a name on a label!*
> *Dr. Brimmer—also known as the **Amazing Explodo!** —*
> *has **personally** assured us that in the **unlikely** event of*
> *fatality, any who contact him with **proof of purchase** will be*
> ***cheerfully** provided with a **full refund!***

Promise of a full refund. The mark of an honest business, her father had said.

No, there was something wrong with the warranty on the bottle. The lightning, she thought again slowly, has disarranged my thoughts. For a while she wondered if she would be sick, and once again she lost track of time and place.

✳ ✳ ✳

She lay, unmoving, unthinking, alone in some place deeper than dreams.

For a long time, for hours, for nights, for years, for unknown worlds—and then suddenly, even as she slept, she knew herself to be Rose once more and her own little world began again. Rose knew herself—and she knew that she was not alone. Even before she was awake she understood that somewhere outside of her something was watching. Some wild dog, some spirit of the desert, some Whisperer, or—worst of all—Whick or Snap, somehow preserved. *Whick, Snap.*

All at once Rose woke properly with a great gasp. And out of the corner of her eye, she saw something slip away—a great worm, or a snake. No, it had hands—and then the last of its tail had disappeared into some crack in the sand.

Rose got up on her hands and knees and saw that all around her on the sand were little marks. No wild dog or Whisperer or Whick or Snap, but something that walked on tiny spread fingers had come and watched her in her sleep.

What was the thing the Speculators named, the thing that did not eat brains? A *skink*. A skink had watched over her. Had woken her.

As Rose's thoughts arranged themselves again, she realized night had not yet come. The sun was already below the line of the hills, in the west, but the Tower of Glass was high enough to catch it still. In the last light, the whole of it shone like a glass filled with sunset, and the broken crest burned like a crown of flames.

Rose forgot about her aching stomach and stared, while the glass shone redder and redder as the light of the sinking sun crept up, up to the very top. Then the tower went dark.

As the cool night breeze began to rise, she thought she saw something moving out of the corner of her eye again—but this time she couldn't catch sight of so much as a tail. No, this time,

Rose was just alone in the desert at night and she clutched her arms around herself. The desert where no one went.

Run, she thought, but there was nowhere to run, except into the tower where the pale hand still lay reaching.

Then a wide, thin booming sound. She rubbed her ears, not sure how much she could really hear anymore. It might have been the biggest sound in the world; it might have been half the world sliding off into the darkness, leaving her alone in the unsheltered void.

But just then, faintly, from somewhere behind her, Rose heard a long, high peal—a little howl, or an enormous howl she could hardly hear, or the blowing of some strange great whistle. Almost beautiful, she thought, but hardly real. There was another from somewhere in the south: a long, lonely howl that rose and sank. Then another and another; little howls from all around the horizon. Wild dogs, she thought, remembering the creature that had frightened them on the road.

Wild dogs, but she had seen more horrible things than wild dogs now. She found herself fascinated by the weird harmonies that changed and went on and on, like the music of the Red Man's clock.

And when the dogs were done and the sands were silent once again, the desert seemed an emptier place. The dusk was getting deeper. The tower's light was gone, and soon everything would be dark. *Go, run, now*, she told herself. Anywhere.

Instead, Rose lay and waited for whatever horrors might come under a night sky that was clear at last.

First the evening star, and then slowly all the others began to shine. And then it was like she was held gently and slowly turning under the whole Hall of the Stars.

She shivered from the cold, but she was not afraid after all. The desert was wide and empty and quiet. There was no place for anything to hide.

Above her a quick star flashed north across the sky and disappeared in some hidden place behind the hills. Rose smiled. The stars themselves might disappear, but there was nothing to be scared of. She lay cradled by the desert and only watched the turning sky.

Somehow small pieces of paper were floating around her. Rose almost laughed as one landed on her face. They were only pages from Whick's memorandum book, drifting over the sand here below while above the moon and stars and planets went wheeling across the sky.

Rose looked at the paper that had fallen on her. At the top Whick had scratched today's date and then the word "Lakeland."

There was more beneath, written small: "Lakeland Development — Legal Errors Committed and Profitable Means of Extortion at the paper . . . " Whick had filled the whole page with observations on the legal errors committed by Crattle, Snope, and Windburn in the Lakeland Development scheme.

It hardly mattered, though. That farm was already gone. She had no way to get home. Jack and Tam might still be lost in Shadow-Town.

For a long time she only looked up at the gibbous moon. Not quite full, but bright, bright.

35

THE NEW KING

As Rose lay on the sand, Jack waited in the meeting ground under the yellow flag, as gnats flew and bit in the still, damp air.

Dusk, and still Jack waited, his head bowed, thinking of all he had seen. Then there was the small sound he had been waiting for, and he turned to see red lanterns shining among the pines, and little shadows all around the field.

More Whisperers. Dozens and dozens of Whisperers hissing and muttering in the trees, some of the aldermen in gold circlets coming into the field to join those he had led from the Tall House, closing in on him. But Jack strode through them, and into the little group of people that he had led from the Tall House too; and he climbed onto the platform by the pole once more and took the knife he had used to sacrifice Mathom in both hands and raised it high.

Jack looked at the Beadle, and when the old man gave him a nod, he struck the pole once more with the butt of the blade, the way he had done to summon the Whisperers. The way he had struck at the thorn-gate of the Red Man when the Whisperers had gathered close once before. But this time he didn't loose his grip, and the iron pole rang like an anvil.

"Shadow-things!" he cried, and somehow, from some book Jack had read long ago, from some forgotten story of his father's, from some obscure corner of the *Encyclopaedia*, or by some ancient, unnamed birthright, he knew what to say, knew to name them in three ways, to utter the shadow-banes to bind them:

"Whisper-speakers!" he shouted. "Shadow-lurkers! Stone-faced spitters of webs! By the sun, by turning wheels, by blood and iron, I call you! Gather here to parley as you did long ago."

Jack struck the pole again and again, as if he found some kind of relief in the simple toil. Over and over until he paused for breath and realized at last that all other sounds had stopped. He lowered his blade and looked out at the dark shapes all around the clearing.

Dozens and dozens of Whisperers that had hidden in shut-up homes and in ditches and caves and under the roots of trees. All the shadows that had ever lurked in closets or troubled his nights. By instinct, he clutched for Rose's bag of rust, but it was empty of course; and there were too many of them. Then Jack almost did let the knife slip from his fingers. Far more of them than he had ever imagined: a wide wall of shadows, red lanterns and red eyes shining among them. The Whisperers might just close over his little band he had led from the Tall House, he thought. The darkness might swallow them whole.

The thought came not from the whispers all about him but Jack's own heart: Rose was gone away somewhere already. Why should he keep struggling, on and on, when he could just slip into the blackness?

Rose had never wanted to hear about Shadow-Town. Neither of them had even wanted to be sent to the sandy hills. Only a long chain of instructions from their families, and mistakes and accidents, and vows and promises they had made together with Tam had led them to this moment.

Maybe some other time some other farmers' children would try this thing, but now he would just close his eyes and drift into the grey world of the thralls. He would half-sleep through their long labors and pains, until at last he would pass away and be left, unshipped, to rest in the earth closet, food for mushrooms until the changing of the world.

Then he heard the Cutter boy say, "There are so many of them." And the Cutter girl said, "They are all the bad dreams together."

But now Tamlin stood beside Jack, wearing his bloody cloth like a crown. He spat on the ground. "Now you is the king of the drowned and the dead, if you want to be. Act like a king. Rule the thralls. Make me your subject after all. Pronounce some laws and see if you can walk away."

Tam's father wouldn't even meet Jack's eyes. "I have nothing else," the old man said. "No strength, no life, no hate. You must do what you can and live with it."

Jack closed his eyes and felt the weariness wash over him. He had nothing left either.

Then he heard the sound of scraping sand somewhere in the southwest, and he grasped his blade and stood tall. The scraping grew louder and he heard the jingle of tackle as well. A ringing bell. It was Whick and Snap's carriage coming.

"You see," the Beadle said placidly. "I knew she'd come back to help her little boyfriend."

Closer. And now they could see the nag dragging the broken carriage.

"But where is Rose?" Tam asked.

✳ ✳ ✳

Slowly the horse pulled the empty carriage right across the field. No Whick, no Snap, no Rose. The carriage was as empty as Shadow-Town.

Rose. All that he had done, and Jack had forgotten to go on worrying about Rose—Rose, whom he was supposed to watch after, Rose who had left the Red Man to come through the hills at night to try to find him.

The nag went on pulling, until the carriage was gone out the other side of the field and back on some hidden lane. Jack looked at the nearly dead thralls, at the exhausted Beadle, at Tamlin—bandaged and with only a little meanness left for spirit. The Badger-Boy shrugged. "In't nothing to do about it now," he whispered.

The boughs around the field had begun to toss, and the heavy clouds above swelled and flowed and gathered again as they crossed the darkened sky. Night was nearly there, when the Whisperers would rule, and the red lanterns shone brighter, but for Jack the words were gathering as they used to when he had poured them out to trouble Rose's sleep. He looked at the last ruddy light in the west and raised the Smith's knife again.

"Long ago, oaths were sworn here!" he shouted. "Who in the shadows was witness to that Accommodation?"

—I was, one of the aldermen with a golden circlet hissed.

—I was, whispered another.

—I was—I was, Jack heard from all around. *—we all were— we are all one—we all were.*

He held out the knife and waved it in a wide circle. *—the Smith's knife,* he heard, and then they all went quiet.

"And you have all broken faith. You have made an arrangement with the Speculators to unmake the Accommodation.

You have cast walls of webs in the Tanglewood once more.
You have woven cloths of gold and tried to walk in the day.
You have made the vapors of sleep rise from the deepest hol-
lows once more!"

—*the night is ours*, they whispered. —*that is the Accommodation.*

—*the shadows in the Tanglewood are ours, the dark copse and the
hidden hollows.*

—*who burns those to make more meadows?*

—*who closes our paths with turning wheels?*

—*who claims our darkness to graze more cows and sheep?*

The whispers came faster and louder, until they gathered
into a kind of chorus that filled the dusk:

—*WHO TROUBLES OUR DARK AND QUIET WORLD?*

The great rush of shadow-Words almost staggered Jack.
He looked at Tam and his father.

The Beadle nodded. "Farmers do," Tam croaked.

"Farmers do," Jack repeated. He spoke quietly, but the
words soaked the heavy air. "I am Jack Tender, the child of
the child of one of the farmers who made the Accommodation.
And the son and grandson of Founder Smith are here. This is
his iron blade!"

Silence now, and Jack spoke as if he were in a dream,
when you never stammered, where your thoughts shone
out in clear, just words: "We acknowledge that we have forgotten. We have forgotten the letter and the spirit of the
Accommodation."

—*oath-breakers*, they heard.

"We have forgotten to fear you enough!" Jack called, and
this time no words but a long and rattling hiss—a horrible
whispered laughter of satisfaction.

But it was Tamlin who stepped forward then. "We's your
enemies, but it in't you we hate. We hate the Speculators."

Tam spoke the words softly, but the Whisperers seemed to hear him well enough.

— *Whick and Snap,* Jack and the thralls gathered under the flagpole heard. — *Snap and Whick — build the tower, get gold from Whick and Snap.*

"Gold to help you rule the day!" Tam answered back. "But how do Whick and Snap mean to use the tower?"

— *farmer business — we pay no heed — farmer business.*

"Whick and Snap," Tam said, very quietly. "Projectors and Speculators. They have you spread the vapors of sleep, to make more thralls, to make more bricks, to make the tower. They have roused you, so the Beadle and Jack Tender, and soon other farmers, will come back to Shadow-Town to bind you with blood and iron dust."

Jack called, still with the assurance of a dream, "And where have these Speculators gone? Why aren't they here for this parley? Where will your gold come from now?"

— *Whick and Snap! — bind them with webs of sleep! — make them thralls to do our work!*

"Other farmers will come," said Jack. "You will haunt their every night. They will hunt you every day. You will make the vapors rise and cast Words from the shadows to make them fall ill and sleep. They will burn you in your homes in Shadow-Town."

"And you will trouble one another's dreams," Tam whispered.

— *no,* they heard. — *no — the Accommodation — honor the Accommodation!*

Jack held Founder Smith's knife out towards the deepest shadows. "The plague must end!" he cried in a voice so masterly he might have been a child of the wind.

— *only those that burn our homes and haunts.*

The Whisperers were saying the right words, Jack thought,

but the night had almost come. Soon the whole of the field except the iron pole would belong to the Whisperers again no matter what was said or done.

"Beadle Smith and Tamlin his son and I will travel the sandy hills and tell the others of the terms," Jack called. "Hold us to account if it isn't done."

—but leave Shadow-Town—leave it to the shadows and whispers—swear, now; we swear, we all swear by the Founder's blade—you swear, farmers swear now too.

"Then I declare the old bounds renewed!" Jack cried. "The farmers to stay out of the shadow-march always, and never dare to visit the Bound-lands except by the day's strong light. The Whisperers to leave the farmlands untroubled, and only think to enter the Bound-lands in the shelter of the dark of the night!

"And then," Jack cried again, "then, in the name of the farmers, by the blade of Founder Smith, by the living iron I have shed; and by the vapors in the hollows, by all the shadow-Words, by the labors of the waking dead who rot in the earth—then, according to all these things, I declare the Accommodation renewed!"

Jack felt an uncontrollable trembling run through him, as though the ritual words he had been speaking had carried a power too great for him to bear. The deed was almost done. He had come to Shadow-Town and rescued Tam, and made a new Accommodation, and now his grandma would be safe. He gripped the big knife tighter. The old Beadle gave him a nod.

Jack had almost raised Founder Smith's blade one last time when Tam whispered, "A codicil, Jack—for the sake of those I used to rule."

Jack turned from the dark shapes to see the Cutter children peering out from behind Tamlin. He had almost finished, almost escaped from Shadow-Town. But a codicil. *This agreement yet needs a codicil.*

Jack could hear the tired hopeless sounds of the rag-clad thralls, sense the eager whispers emerging from the Tanglewood. His shuddering was so strong now that he could hardly keep hold of the knife. Now he would have to struggle to find the words, and struggle to hold the knife too. What would happen if he dropped it? He tried to speak, but his teeth began to chatter. He didn't feel like a child of the wind anymore. *Swear to anything*, he thought, *but don't let the shadows close*. Founder Smith's blade felt too hot, too heavy, began to jump in his grasp. He heard the horrible hiss of silk again.

He had tried to do too much. Everything was too late now, and when he opened his mouth he heard himself make a kind of rattling noise and he tried to lift the knife and felt it begin to slip from his numb grasp.

36

IN THE RING
OF BLACK PINES

———◈———

The Beadle wrapped his own gnarled and shaking fingers around Jack's. "Dun't drop the knife, boy," he said.

It was just enough, and Jack nearly sobbed with relief. He took a shaky breath and called out to the crowding shadows: "But we will leave with the thralls you have now."

—they are dead already—their funerals have been made.

Beside the Cutter children, Mother Greene raised herself to stand nearly straight, as if some pride roused her from her long thrall's dream. "Then let us be properly dead. Let us go on the coffin-train, and let our ashes rise to the heavens."

—who would grind our barley?

—who would spin our rags?

Jack looked at the hopeless Cutter children. "Let us go," he heard them say.

—a king must decide that.

—a king of the drowned and the dead.

—a king was pledged long ago and to renew the Accommodation we need a king again.

Jack was shaking so hard he didn't think the Beadle would be able to support him, and now he had no authority left in his voice, but he said, "You can't have Tam."

He felt Mother Greene clutching at his clothes. "They will do what they want when the parley finishes, when the night is full," she whispered. "Listen to me, Jack Tender boy, I played hoops with your grandma here when we were both girls. One way or another, the Whisperers must have a king."

"They can't have Tam," Jack said more quietly, and then the whispers beat down on them:

—that king was broken when he lost his crown.

—but we will have a king who was cast in the Clay Pool and drawn out again alive.

The Clay Pool. Jack remembered the dark warmth of it. Remembered how strange and cool it had felt to be pulled out. How, just for a moment, he had wanted to squeal like a newborn calf, the kind they used to sacrifice to stones and statues, long ago across the sea.

He had thought he had escaped this when he had opened Mathom's heart. But now he had said it wouldn't be Tam. So his words and deeds had only brought him back to the same fate. Now only the old Beadle's arms kept him from falling. He was one small step from the very end.

The Cutter girl bowed and drew the crown of bone and iron out of her rags. The crown—she had carried the crown from the workshop, as if she had known this would be Jack's fate all along. She held it out.

This would be the final price of a new Accommodation, Jack realized. The price to be paid to drive away the shadows that had fallen over the sandy hills: he would take up the crown of bone and iron. The Whisperers would have their king.

This was what he had earned by being so cruel to Rose a long time ago. How he would be paid for rescuing Tam. This was the revenge he was due for letting Mathom's life blood spill over the gold-clad Mayor.

To be the king alone forever.

✳ ✳ ✳

"Stupid boy," the Beadle whispered in his ear. "Why din't you offer them me?"

Jack said, "Because this is what I dreamed."

"Stupid child," the Beadle said. "To think dreams and fate is the same."

Then he took the crown from Jack and pulled it down onto his own head, and by light of the red lanterns, they saw the iron thorns curl and grow and fasten into the Beadle's scalp.

—*a king!*

—*a king!*

—*long rest the king!* the Whisperers hissed.

The Beadle extended his arm and pointed at all the thralls. "Call me king!" he croaked. "Now I rule the drowned and the dead forever!" His eyes were sunken, were red in the lantern-light.

"But I was going to free them," Jack said.

The thralls made a kind of moan. "Honor the king!" said Mother Greene.

"Beadle-king!" said Miser Cooper. "Long rest the king! Serve him till your unknown end!"

"Beadle-king! Long rest the king!" whispered the Cutter children. "Long rest the king!" whispered the other thralls.

—*king, give them orders.*

—set them to grind and spin again.

"If I am king, I shall celebrate my new throne," the old man said.

—long rest the king! called the Whisperers.

The Beadle turned to Jack and made his most thin and horrible smile. "Take my son. Leave Shadow-Town. Keep out of the Tanglewood. Live in daylight, if you can."

Tam stared at his father, uncomprehending. "Learn to treat with strange and wicked things," the Beadle told him. "But stay out of the night and the shadows."

—shadow-friend, thrall-king!

—orders, orders, set them working!

"I amn't your servant yet, blockheads, stock-things!" the Beadle rasped. And Jack thought these would be the last words he would ever speak loudly again. "I am the king!"

The Beadle turned to the thralls. "So we begin our reign in mercy: We release yous from bondage. We set yous free to seek a proper rest."

Now Jack saw the thralls begin to straighten and stagger, confused and stupid like the newly woken. Plump Mother Vining, who was closest to him, shook out her arms and legs. Farmer Sawyer plucked at his trousers and made an awkward jump, as if he was remembering a dance he had done when he was young and strong.

At the same time a kind of shiver ran through the crowding shadows; a wind came up that made the needles on the trees begin to quiver and hiss.

The shapes came closer, silhouetted in the light of their red lanterns, and their blank faces seemed more hungry and awful than ever.

The Beadle stretched his shaking hand out to them. *"Tharkle, crith,"* he began, but his voice was uncertain as he said the Words that Tam had told Jack never to utter.

The pledge to serve. His hand fell.

—*Now is later*, hissed the Whisperers. —*and now only you are left to do our work.*

The Beadle had been cruel to Jack and his cousin, more cruel to his own son. But Jack couldn't bear to watch as the Beadle bowed his head to accept the Words of the Whisperers, and turned away.

Only Tam saw that his father took a long, slow step into the crowding shapes. "Dad," he whispered, but there was no answer, and soon the shadows had disappeared from the clearing, and only small red lights spread out beyond the ring of black pines.

"Dad," Tam said again. Jack felt his friend clutch his arm in trembling hands. "This is the end," he said. "Help me, Jack, I'm going to scream."

"Scream then," Jack said. "After all this, who wouldn't scream?"

Tam had fallen to his knees, his bloody head bowed. Above them the north wind had blown the sky clear at last, and the stars began to appear. Tam squeezed Jack's arm harder. Two nights before Jack would have cried out at that much pain, but now he only looked down and saw what he had never seen before: Tamlin in tears.

Tam brushed his forearm across his eyes and looked up. The moon was just above the trees now, and in its light, Tam's ugly face looked suddenly wild and ghostly, and then it twisted into an expression Jack did not recognize.

Tam shook his head. "No one ever heard my father scream," he said. "And they wun't hear me."

"But he left us one more thing to do," Jack said.

"What we have been waiting for," said Mother Greene.

Jack turned to look at her, and the others, still walking about awkwardly—like puppets released from their strings.

As he watched, Jack let the Beadle's knife drop at last. He would not need iron again. "Tam," he whispered, but his friend had gone.

"Gone into the night," the Cutter boy said.

"Like his father before him," said Mother Greene. "Poor boy. Poor old king."

After some unknown time, Jack felt a small hand slip into his. The Cutter girl. And beyond her, hand in hand, all the others who had served as thralls, their faces palely shining in the light of the risen moon, ready to lead him away.

* * *

The north wind cast sand and grit and scraps of filth down the streets of dark Shadow-Town. The houses they passed were grey and leaned on one another wearily, and smudge pots lit the black corners with greasy orange flames.

If the burning pots smelled foul, Jack didn't notice, for the memory of the white fire in the engine of the coffin-train drew him forward. And if the Whisperers who had lit the pots had already come back to hide and mutter Words for their own ends, he didn't hear them. And if bats rose up on the heat of those flames to fly between Shadow-Town and the fanning stars above, he didn't see them. For everyone from the waking world had left him, and his eyes were cast down in sorrow.

Then they lifted Farmer Mathom on his bier and carried him up the long wide steps of the station, to wait for the train, and Jack sat coffin-watch with them, as he had for his father. And sometimes those who had been thralls spoke softly to one another out of their shared dreams, but mostly they were silent.

Once, Miser Cooper whispered, "I want my mommy to hold me," and Mother Greene said, "Soon," and she took the old farmer and rocked him back and forth. "You will go to see her soon."

Only the Cutter boy and girl seemed to be properly awake, seemed to be frightened, and Jack said, "It's not so bad. The Clatterfolk are little fellows, you know, not as big as you. The one who works the engine is soot black and the one who works the post and the funeral trade is ash white. And they'll take care of you now. They'll help you pass into the sky."

"We know," the boy said. "But it's hard to board it a second time."

37

THE TRAIN

In the desert, Rose lay back and watched the sky.

Some hours passed, and Rose must have nodded off, because when she blinked again, the moon was in the south, and the sand was grown cold, and she felt herself begin to shake. And a long, long moon-shadow stretched over her. And she saw a slender figure standing in silhouette against the sky. Rose wasn't quite sure she was awake yet, and she blinked.

Now it was right beside her. A man; a boy. Tam. His voice was thin, as if he was speaking from some faraway place. "I amn't here because I like you," he said.

Rose blinked again, saw Tam with the carriage on the hill behind him. She shook her head. "I don't like you either."

"I amn't the king anymore," he said, and when Tam put his arms around her and tried to make her warm, Rose shuddered. "Jack in't either," he said, and she had to put her ear close to his mouth to hear him. "Because he pushed my dad's knife into Mathom's heart and sprayed the blood all over the Mayor."

"Where is Jack now?" she whispered.

"He'll be keeping coffin-watch. For all the thralls."

"Even the Cutters?" Rose asked.

Tam shrugged. "My father wears the crown of bone and iron now. Better to ride the train than to serve under him."

After Rose had recovered a little, she said, "Why are you here?"

"It in't 'cause I like you," he said.

"Why are you here?" she said.

"Where else would I be?" A quick star flashed across the sky and was gone.

Rose laughed. "Why are you here?" she said.

"Once you came with my father through the Tanglewood to rescue me," Tam said. "Why'd you do that?"

"Not because I like you. Only there was no one else. Why were you always mean to me?"

Tam shrugged, and for a long time they watched the night turn above them, and, trembling, each held the other to stay warm.

Faintly, as if from somewhere far, far away, Rose heard one of the wild dogs howling again. Tam scrambled to his feet. "Time to go," he said.

"Don't be scared of the dogs," she said.

He shook his head. "The coffin-train arrives just before dawn."

"So? Are you expecting mail?"

Tam raised an open hand out of habit, and then he looked at it and let it fall. "I amn't expecting anything, not ever," he said.

"Only I dun't think Jack should meet the train alone. Not after all night in Shadow-Town. Not if he misses his father so. Not if he in't afraid of dying anymore."

Then the carriage again, this time with Tam for company. After some long miles they began to hear the train making its way to Shadow-Town.

✳ ✳ ✳

From the coffin-hall in the station house, Jack could look over the platform. Beyond that was a drop into the river, and from the darkness the rattle of the approaching train echoed loudly.

"That's the sound of the end," said the Cutter boy. "That's the train come for us at last," said his sister. And they clung together and shivered in the warm night air.

Once again, Jack saw the train come scraping to a stop, its bell ringing. It waited for them on the rails, low and black; and it hissed and panted, and smoke and cinders rose up from its chimney to mix with the stars and sky. Mother Vining and Mother Greene looked up and nodded quietly at each other, and then the others lifted Farmer Mathom's bier and Jack led them out the coffin doors and onto the platform.

From the cab of the train he saw the Engineer peer out; black like he remembered. All black, coal black. And far down the tracks he saw the pale figure of the Conductor standing stiff and white by the caboose.

"All aboard," the Conductor called ahead in a strange flat voice. "All dead aboard for west and west to the great Blue Mountains. All dead aboard to rise to the stars."

The thralls bore Farmer Mathom's body into the first car, and then Mother Greene repeated, "All aboard. All aboard to rest and rest." Jack saw a fire-man, a human fire-man, but not the one he had known that night long ago.

"What train is this?" he asked. "Is this the *Iron Stellification?*"

"That old thing! Bless me, no! She is farther west tonight. This is the great *Terrible Star of Morning* — the *Morningstar* for short, if you want to be short about a thing of such significance —"

The fire-man held out his hand to Mother Greene. "Welcome to the *Terrible Star of Morning*, old mother," he said, helping her into her coffin. "Let her carry you in thunder and glory to your rest."

She took a deep breath, and shut her eyes, and closed the lid upon herself and joined the peaceful dead at last.

"The *Morningstar*," said Farmer Sawyer. "A different, longer rest," and he stepped up and closed the lid upon himself in turn. So did the others — four to each car. "Rise to the stars!" they said, and "West beyond the mountains!" they said, and "Burn it hot, and let our ashes rise!" And they climbed into their coffins more willingly than Jack had ever gone to his bed.

But only three went into the last car before the caboose, and there were still the two Cutter children waiting on the platform.

"Jack!" he heard someone call. Rose's voice. "Jack!" he heard Tamlin call. Rose and Tam — living voices, from his waking world. He felt his heart lift, and then, *Too late*, he thought. *I don't want to hear them now.*

But they were already on the platform, running towards him. "No!" Rose called. "Not these. Not when they're so young."

Jack blinked, as though he were half asleep too. "Everyone dies," he said. "It will free them from their weary bodies and let them rise like stars into the sky."

Tam nodded, panting, exhausted. "It in't something bad — not when you's dead already," he told Rose. "It's a gift my dad willn't have." Tam turned to look out at the Tall House, looming over everything in the weak light before morning. "My dad will suffer and die unshipped."

"Children younger than these board the train," Jack said.

To Rose's ears, their words seemed to come from far away. She shook her head. "No. It's not fair."

"It's not fair. But it is too late," said Jack. "Their funerals were made. Their time was marked as done, just like the others. Just like Mother Greene. Just like Miser Cooper. Just like old Mathom."

"Look at their clothes," Rose said. "They didn't have proper funerals. They had no family left to speak over them or sit the coffin-watch. They were dressed in flour sacks."

"The sleeping sickness came to our mother first," said the Cutter girl. "We sat watch for her when she died," said the boy.

"But she passed for real," the girl added. "She was shipped into the west and never came to Shadow-Town."

"It wun't have mattered," Tam said. "She wun't have been their mother in Shadow-Town. She would only have been another dreaming thrall."

"She was lucky," said the Cutter boy.

"It wasn't a proper funeral," Rose said again.

"They were already shipped in their coffins," said Jack.

"Our time was marked as done," repeated the Cutters, as if they were reciting a lesson in their sleep.

Rose took each of the Cutter children by the hand and looked into the car lit by its small funeral lights. "But there's only one coffin left," she said.

Tam said, "They were laid in it together, the poor ragged, beggarly things. And I laughed because that was all the money they'd left between them—two pennies for the coffin, and two pennies for the train. But my dad hit me, and said they'd have worse soon enough."

The Cutter girl nodded. "We were only poor, ragged, beggarly things," she explained to Rose. "All our family already gone."

"We were laid in it together," the boy remembered, "and pennies over our right eyes, and we kept our left eyes squinted shut, and slept all still in the dark, but we weren't dead. Not properly dead."

"Now we will be properly dead," said the girl. And she and her brother let go of Rose and joined hands, and, trembling, they took a step towards the grimy, reaching hand of the fire-man.

"This is the very end," Jack whispered. "After we've sent them off, then we can go where we like—each of us."

Rose couldn't hear him, but she shook her head. "No," she said. "Shut up."

They heard the clacking voice of the Conductor, come up from the caboose. The Conductor stood in front of the children: ash white, pale as some long-dead thing. After a moment they heard it speak a human word: "No."

The Cutters fell back to the platform, uncomprehending.

"Not these," the Conductor told the fire-man, and then there was a rattle of Clatter-talk no one could understand.

"What?" Rose said. "What?"

The fire-man leaned forward and spoke very loudly: "Pennies pay for bodies, not for coffins," he said. "Even in one coffin two pennies only paid their way to Shadow-Town. Not west, and to the sky. Not these, not yet. If they don't stay in Shadow-Town they are still farmers' business." He laughed. "You can keep 'em!"

The Cutter boy was weeping and he struck at Rose with his fists. "No!" she said, "No, you won't take the train. No!"

He struck at her with his fists, over and over until Tam yelled, "Din't you hear? You won't get on the train."

The two children were weeping harder. "And go where?" said the boy. "And do what?"

The Conductor's flat voice interrupted them. "Rose Tender," it said. Rose shook her head, not hearing. "Mail for Rose Tender," the Conductor repeated, giving her a thick envelope.

Before she could look at it, Jack asked, "What's going to happen now?"

The Conductor shook its head and clattered some, made a whistling noise. In human words again, it said, "Nothing. The end. The very end. Unless you want to come aboard and learn the fire-man's trade."

It swung the door to the shut. There was a huff from the fire-engine. A bell rang.

Jack began to run along the platform towards the front of the train. Tam and Rose followed him, pulling the Cutters by the hand.

"No," Rose called. "No, Jack, don't board the train. Not now."

Tam said, "Jack, you'd only be the Engineer's boy, and do his fire-chores forever."

Only when he had got to the cab of the engine did Jack turn back to them. "I would go west with the train," he said. "A little farther each year. I wouldn't have to climb into a coffin. Not like the thralls, not like my father, not ever."

The door to the engine swung open. "Look, then," rattled the Engineer. "Watch the work!" And he threw open the fire-box, showing the burning world inside. Charred wood glowing red, roaring orange and yellow flames, and at its heart white bones glowing in the shape of a man.

Behind him the fire-man appeared again, grimy with soot and sweat, and he drew a coffin from the tender and by himself he heaved it forward and into the open fire-box.

For a moment they stood and watched, and first the Cutter children, then Rose, and finally Tam turned away. Only Jack looked as the flames rose over the coffin.

Then there was an iron ring as the door to the fire-box slammed shut. The whistle blew again and again, and Rose heard the fire-man call the words in his rough voice, "All aboard! All aboard for west of west and rest of rest! All aboard for beyond the Blue Mountains! All aboard to rise in bright ashes to join the stars in the sky!"

There was a horrible rusty noise as iron wheels began to turn and pull on the steel rails. But Rose couldn't bear to open her eyes until she heard the whistle and knew it had left the station.

Jack still stood beside Tam, with her and the Cutter children on the platform. They watched the train move off, spitting sparks and embers. The whistle sounded lower as the train moved faster, and made some turn, and was lost behind a hill somewhere in the night.

"You didn't go," Rose said to Jack, and she started weeping.

"If he'd wanted to work forever he cud've stayed in Shadow-Town and been king instead of my father," Tam said.

Jack shook his head. Above them, Rose saw a star fall through the wide night.

"It would have been good work, on the train," Jack said. "But I will ride it someday without working. And my coffin will be fired, and I will rise and follow my father into the sky."

Tamlin bent down before the Cutter children and smiled a bad Tam-smile. "Like yous two—like all of us, someday," he said.

The Cutters blinked at him, like small children still waking. "But first yous have a long, long walk in the Tanglewood

with us. And then we will come to a farm with three great
howling dogs."

"Tamlin, be quiet," Rose said.

Tam shook his head. "It's true," he told the children.
"Someday we all die, and the lucky ones get shipped on the
coffin-train, while the unlucky dream in Shadow-Town or
wait until the world is broken and remade. But now we will
go and find the three great howling dogs.

"Oh, they frightened me terribly when I was little like yous.
But they will be your friends."

Jack had to say "Rose" two or three times before she heard
him. "Rose, who wrote you a letter?"

Rose hadn't even looked at the letter, but now she smiled
through tears and clutched it to her chest. "My mom and dad."

38

THE SETTLING DARK

When they came to the Red Man's estate late that evening, foot-sore and hobbling, his three great dogs seemed as wild as Tam had warned the Cutters. But when Rose called the names she had given them, the dogs barked with pleasure and led the way through the ordered woods to the House of Woven Trees.

"Rose Tender, you left to find a way into your nightmare," the Red Man said, "and look what you have brought back. Jack Tender, you meant to run away, but here you are again, with new grey hairs. Tamlin Badger-Boy, I thought I was done with you, and you return like a little old man."

"You is done with my father," said Tamlin. "But I will be Beadle in his place."

"Beadle and shadow-friend?"

"Maybe."

"And Daisy Cutter and Giles Cutter, farmers' children," said the Red Man. "Stay and rest with the others, and wake and eat and sleep again. When the night comes, you will hear the train, but don't mind its whistle; it isn't meant for you."

"We know," Giles said. "Not for our bodies, not for our souls."

"Not tonight," Daisy added. "We know."

So they slept, and the next morning, the children came down to see the Red Man had set out a breakfast for all of them, bigger even than the one he had shared with Rose.

He ate as much as all the rest of them together, and after his second plate he set down his fork and said, "The air in the sandy hills has changed. I think you have done good work."

Rose and Tamlin shared a glance. "But what is good work to you, who only cultivate the hills?" Rose said.

Jack watched the Red Man's face as he almost smiled and almost scowled.

"I tend the hills," the Red Man said. "And if a gardener has too much fern he digs it up and plants goutweed. The Whisperers needed cutting back, I think."

"And if the farmers spread too much, will you want us cut back too?" asked Jack.

The Red Man looked at Rose for a long time. "If they do not act like reasonable beings."

"You only cultivate the hills," Rose said. "You summon rain and storm and drive back the desert."

The Red Man nodded. "Inch by inch, each year."

"Then don't let the green land grow unchecked either," Rose said, and she was surprised that she didn't care if this angered the Red Man. "Don't drive all the sand away."

"Is this your business?" the Red Man asked. "Is this farmers' business?"

"It is our business now," Jack said. "There is a little lizard that comes out of the sand. Rose and I both saw it. It watched over us. Leave some desert."

The Red Man stood and grabbed his staff from the door. "A reasonable amount," he said. "Now go, Rose and Jack and Tam. This is not an inn, not a playground for farmers' children. Go, and I think you will find your grandmother's fever has lifted."

"What about us?" asked the Cutter children.

"Yes, what about Giles and Daisy?" said Rose.

"They hardly belong with the living yet," said the Red Man. "They can stay until they are no longer weak and pale, and need no tending."

"They are only children," Rose said. "You mustn't frighten them or work them hard."

"Dun't be stupid," Tam said. "As if the Red Man would whip them or frighten them as much as I did in Shadow-Town."

✳ ✳ ✳

When they got back to the Tender farm at last, Jack and Rose's grandma was quite herself again. After Rose and Jack told her everything, she huffed and nodded, and huffed again. "Well, I suppose that's the end of your story," she said. "The story of what happened when you didn't do as you were told. And stories are good, but it's best not to be in them.

"And your story ended before you ever got to your Great-Aunt Constance. And you will only go back to see your parents soon enough, and I will be left by myself, and I am old and tired, and my bones ache."

The children were quiet for a moment. "I'm going to have to go sooner than that," Jack said. "Tamlin and I have to leave and travel the hills to talk about the new Accommodation."

Tam shook his head. "Stay here with your grandma a while, Jack, and leave me to tell the farmers about the new Accommodation. They're used to hearing hard things from the Smiths—and know it's best to do what we say."

So the next day Tam left by himself, while Rose and Jack stayed on at their grandmother's farm. And for the rest of the summer, they only bickered lightly, and never counted themselves unlucky to have their grandma's chores to do.

Then one evening when the summer was nearly over, their grandma huffed awhile over the supper table, and then told them the next day it would be time to pack their things to go back to their own homes. "And don't mind that you'll be leaving an old woman alone," she said. "Best to get out of the way now, anyway, so I can get things ready for the proper harvest hands."

Rose and Jack nodded, and sat quietly, each trying to understand if they were glad to be going or not.

Then through the evening air they heard the slow clop of an old horse nearing, and the familiar voice of its rider singing:

"And Roses are scorned, because they have thorns—
So ugly that they fright us!"

It was Tamlin, of course—wobbling astride Whick and Snap's old nag—and Rose felt herself begin to blush. But Jack only smiled as he pulled open the screen door and cried, "Why, here's a harvest hand!"

But as Tam came in, Grandma screwed up her face. "Tamlin Smith-son," she said. She shook her head. "Badger-Boy. Too wild and dirty."

Rose said, "But you can't put him out. Where would he go?"

"This one? He could go many places. Why would I want him here?"

But Tam only smiled and pulled out a glass brick. He set it beside the one Grandma kept on the mantel. "As a remembrance of lost elegance," he said softly.

Grandma huffed again. "You remind me of your grandfather." She looked Tamlin in the eye a long time. "But if you learn to wash, you can stay here."

Tam didn't thank her, but he made a quiet nod.

✳ ✳ ✳

On that last night before Rose and Jack set out, the three children lay in the little attic — Rose and Jack on their bunks and Tamlin on the floor — and listened to the settling dark, and talked long and quietly of what they had seen and done, long enough that they heard the whistle of the coffin-train, the faint rumble of the tracks.

Rose's hearing would never be very sharp again, but even after the last echo of the fading whistle was gone, Jack heard the wind bring some other small noise of iron wheels that rose and fell in a familiar rhythm.

"What is that?" he asked.

"A handcar," said Tam. "Someone's driving a handcar along the coffin-line."

"Who would travel in such a way?" Rose asked. "On the coffin-track, at night?" But really she knew the answer better than anyone, and in time that rusty tune ended too. Slowly the dreams of the night came over the children; good and bad, but none of them were haunted dreams. None of them were dreams of whips and chains and labor and despair.

Just dreams, so they would rise looking forward to the waking world.

✳ ✳ ✳

"Look, Master Snap," said Master Whick as he pumped his side of the little handcar that night. "I believe that is the remains of our tower, gleaming in the moonlight."

"*Please*, Master Whick," said Snap. "A good Projector does not dwell on unsuccessful enterprises but only looks forward."

"But I *do* count it as a success, Master Snap. Think how nearly we died under the broken glass. Only those as both hard-headed and hard-hearted as ourselves could have survived such a thing."

They were quiet for a while, for they had to save their breath to pump their way up a hill.

"Perhaps," Snap said at last, "perhaps." For a while he whistled in time to their work. "But now that we have another warrant from the Dominion, my thoughts are entirely given over to our new project."

"Yes. Yes. And I believe I have the essential process in hand. But where will we get enough material?"

"Kittens and puppies are like weeds, Master Whick. Providence has so organized the world that they will increase on their own."

"Look, Master Snap! Shadow-Town station is approaching. And the Tall House where we had our workshop."

"No nostalgia, Master Whick. For a time, that project seemed a beautiful rose, but let it fade, let it fade."

* * *

So that night the children all slept in the attic on the Tender farm. And Whick and Snap schemed and labored along the tracks of the coffin-train. And in their paths among the Tanglewood, and in the smudge-lit streets of Shadow-Town, the Whisperers walked or spun webs in patterns that delighted them — or hissed to one another about their hopes for a darkness yet to come. And in the deepest hollows of the sandy hills, vapors waited still.

But that night Tam's father sat alone in the Tall House, enthroned in silence, and neither truly slept nor truly woke. And his head bore a crown of iron and bone, and his face was creased with pain.

ACKNOWLEDGMENTS

Five years ago my computer still seemed to belong to another book, so I took out a small notebook to begin writing this bad dream born from holidays in Manitoba's Carberry Hills.

Financial assistance from the Canada Council for the Arts gave me time to make those scratchings into something like a book. Large parts of it were finished while I had the chance to serve as writer-in-residence for the Winnipeg Public Library.

My writer-wife, Brenda Hasiuk, waited for me while I spent the night alone in the desert, and helped me with everything else, every day—all while bringing her own first novel and our two children into the world.

Since the bad dream of *Shadow-Town* kept getting darker, and in case it's not obvious: those holidays in the Carberry Hills with my grandparents and all the aunts and uncles who helped watch after us were the best part of my childhood. That place will always be my heart's home.

When my children are older I will take them with me, even into the desert, to look for signs of snakes and skinks, and listen to the coyotes chiming in the darkness after dusk and before the dawn.

ABOUT THE AUTHOR

Duncan Thornton was born in God's Lake Narrows, a Cree community in northern Manitoba, where he played ancient games with toys made of hollow bones and deer-hide and traveled by toboggan across frozen lakes to visit neighbors.

As a boy he spent holidays at the farms of his mother's family in Manitoba's Carberry Hills (the model for the geography of *Shadow-Town*). Although he was too bookish to be interested in farm chores, Thornton dropped out of school at thirteen to stay with his father's family in Northern Ireland. At twenty, largely self-educated, he entered university and worked his way to graduate studies.

The father of two children, Thornton now writes from a small, well-insulated shed in Winnipeg—the center of Canada, and the coldest big city in the world. He has written three fantasy novels for young adults, including the award-winning *Kalifax*.